teach

yourself

the israeli–palestinian
conflict

teach yourself ®

the israeli–palestinian conflict
stewart ross

For over 60 years, more than 50 million people have learnt over 750 subjects the **teach yourself** way, with impressive results.

be where you want to be with **teach yourself**

For UK order enquiries: please contact Bookpoint Ltd, 130 Milton Park, Abingdon, Oxon, OX14 4SB. Telephone: +44 (0) 1235 827720. Fax: +44 (0) 1235 400454. Lines are open 09.00–17.00, Monday to Saturday, with a 24-hour message answering service. Details about our titles and how to order are available at www.teachyourself.co.uk

For USA order enquiries: please contact McGraw-Hill Customer Services, PO Box 545, Blacklick, OH 43004-0545, USA. Telephone: 1-800-722-4726. Fax: 1-614-755-5645.

For Canada order enquiries: please contact McGraw-Hill Ryerson Ltd, 300 Water St, Whitby, Ontario, L1N 9B6, Canada. Telephone: 905 430 5000. Fax: 905 430 5020.

Long renowned as the authoritative source for self-guided learning – with more than 50 million copies sold worldwide – the **teach yourself** series includes over 500 titles in the fields of languages, crafts, hobbies, business, computing and education.

British Library Cataloguing in Publication Data: a catalogue record for this title is available from the British Library.

Library of Congress Catalog Card Number: on file.

First published in UK 2007 by Hodder Education, 338 Euston Road, London, NW1 3BH.

First published in US 2007 by The McGraw-Hill Companies, Inc.

This edition published 2007.

The **teach yourself** name is a registered trade mark of Hodder Headline.

Typeset by Transet Limited, Coventry, England.
Printed in Great Britain for Hodder Education, a division of Hodder Headline, an Hachette Livre UK Company, 338 Euston Road, London, NW1 3BH, by Cox & Wyman Ltd, Reading, Berkshire.

The publisher has used its best endeavours to ensure that the URLs for external websites referred to in this book are correct and active at the time of going to press. However, the publisher and the author have no responsibility for the websites and can make no guarantee that a site will remain live or that the content will remain relevant, decent or appropriate.

Hodder Headline's policy is to use papers that are natural, renewable and recyclable products and made from wood grown in sustainable forests. The logging and manufacturing processes are expected to conform to the environmental regulations of the country of origin.

Impression number   10 9 8 7 6 5 4 3 2 1
Year   2010 2009 2008 2007

contents

figure 1 the Middle East – a political map

note from the author

The subject of this book raises the fiercest of passions. Although, as a neutral observer, I have made every effort to be objective and even-handed, I am all too aware that it is impossible to produce an account that pleases all sides. Therefore, if my reading of events is not yours, I crave your indulgence.

SR

Asked by an anxious worshipper when there would be peace between the Israelis and Palestinians, Allah paused for a moment before replying, 'Never... at least, not in my time.'

[Joke current in the Middle East, 2006]

'I beseech you, in the bowels of Christ, think it possible you may be mistaken.'

Oliver Cromwell

01

biblical beginnings

This chapter will cover:
- the origins of the terms 'Palestine' and 'Israel'
- Palestine in classical times
- Crusader and Ottoman Palestine
- the religions of Judaism and Islam.

This is a story of two peoples and one land. Throughout the twentieth century and beyond, the Palestinians and the Israelis have fought bitterly over a small strip of territory, about 192 kilometres long, that lies between the shore of the eastern Mediterranean and a line, about 64 kilometres further east, marked by the River Jordan, Lake Galilee (Tiberias) and the Dead Sea. The conflict has caused countless deaths and brought immeasurable suffering and hardship. Moreover, for more than 60 years, it has destabilized the entire Middle East.

The historical origins of this tragic impasse lie in the nineteenth century. Its complexity, ferocity and longevity, however, cannot really be understood without some knowledge of migrations and struggles as ancient as human civilization itself.

Philistines and Jews

The Fertile Crescent

The land with which we are concerned was once part of what scholars term the 'Fertile Crescent'. Around 10,000 years ago, in this broad arc stretching from the Rivers Tigris and Euphrates to the Nile Valley, some of the earliest human civilizations emerged. Considering the region's low rainfall, made worse by its underlying porous limestone and hot, harsh summer weather, the decision of our distant ancestors to build their first permanent habitations here might appear almost perverse. However, at the time, closer by some ten millennia to the end of the last Ice Age, the Earth was cooler than today and the fruitful crescent was greener and its climate more clement.

Under these favourable circumstances farming flourished, allowing settled rather than nomadic communities to develop. One of the first permanently inhabited sites was on a small hill, just north of the Dead Sea and less than 16 kilometres west of the River Jordan, which received a plentiful supply of fresh water from a lively spring. By *circa* 8,000 BC, it had become one of the world's first towns. Enclosed within a massive stone defensive wall, some 2,500 people lived there. The site, abandoned and re-settled many times over the millennia, approximates to the modern town of Jericho.

The natives of the earliest Jericho have long since disappeared and their city and the land around it has served as home to many other peoples. Some called it a 'promised land', a 'land of

figure 2 the Middle East – a physical map

milk and honey', although it was not just fertility that over the years made this scrap of coastal plain and inland hills so attractive. It was, and still is, of considerable strategic importance from both a military and commercial point of view. Its main roads link Egypt to Syria, and the Mediterranean to Jordan and Iraq. Whoever controlled this vital thoroughfare had great power.

Palestine

The people who gave this land the name by which it has been known for most of its history, were the Philistines. Nobody is certain where these vigorous people came from, or where they went. They emerged, it seems, from the Aegean, perhaps Crete, in the twelfth century BC, and attempted to settle in Egypt. Rebuffed, they landed on the coastal strip between modern-day Tel Aviv and Gaza. Here, empowered by their monopoly of iron-making technology, they established themselves and built five rich cities. Originally called 'Philistia', the territory they inhabited has come down to us through the Greek version of its name – Palestine.

Palestinian hegemony initially lasted about 300 years. After conflict with their immediate neighbours, they later fell under the domination of Egypt, Babylon, Persia, Greece and Rome. By the first millennium they had all but vanished as a distinct people: their religion, political organization and even their language remain a mystery to us. Little but a name and a few semi-historical stories are left to remind us of their existence.

Nevertheless, names and stories are potent cultural symbols. In the Christian West, a cruel linguistic development has linked 'philistine' to barbarity, and this in turn has subconsciously coloured some people's thinking about those who today call themselves Palestinians. Stories, too, have played their part in creating awkward modern imagery. The most powerful of these stories were told and written down by the Philistines' great enemies, the Israelites. Over time these stories passed into the Old Testament of the Christian Bible, from where they continue to influence the thinking of millions of people. Two cultural icons of the Western tradition, David, the shepherd boy who slew the bullying giant Goliath, and the heroic strong-man Sampson, both fought the same enemy – the wicked Philistines. Although today's Palestinians share only a name with the Biblical Philistines, it's a name that bears a dark and heavy legacy.

Israel

If the Palestinian name presents difficulties, they are nothing compared with that surrounding the second group that here concerns us, the Israelis. We begin with a Semitic people who called themselves 'Hebrews'. Interestingly, 'Hebrew' seems to be related to the word 'Habiru', meaning an 'outsider' or bandit. These may have been part of the band of warriors whom the Egyptians beat off – the future Philistines. In other words, the Hebrews and the Philistines may have shared the same ancestry. Other scholars claim that DNA testing shows the Hebrews to be more closely related to the peoples of the northern part of the Fertile Crescent, such as Kurds, Turks and Armenians.

'Hebrew' is the same as 'Yehudi', which the Romans wrote in Latin as 'Judaeus' and from which derives the French 'Juif', the German 'Jude' and the English 'Jew'. The Hebrews, divided into 12 tribes, were said to be descended from Jacob, who was also known as 'Israel', meaning 'standing with God'. In about 1,200 BC these 12 Hebrew or Jewish Tribes of Israel settled the land between the Mediterranean and the River Jordan. To cut short a long and extremely complicated story, they fought the Philistines, with varying degrees of success, and also fell out among themselves, splitting into northern and southern kingdoms. The north was conquered and its scattered citizens largely absorbed into other peoples of the region, although some survived as a distinct group in Persia. The southern Hebrews remained a separate entity in an area that others knew as the Kingdom of Judah (of the Jews) but which the Jews themselves came to refer to as the Land of Israel.

Bound together by their powerful and distinctive religion, which taught that they were the people chosen by the one god, Yahweh, the Jews of the Land of Israel maintained their identity despite periodic repression and deportation by Assyrians, Babylonians, Persians and the Hellenistic (Greek-style) Seleucids. Their state was based around the city of Jerusalem, at the heart of which lay the great temple. Despite this focus, however, by the second century BC, the Jews were already known as a scattered people found in most countries of the Middle East and beyond. The diffusion of the Jews is known by the Greek word 'diaspora', meaning 'dispersal' (see p. 13).

Conquest, Christianity and Islam

Rome

During the first century BC, Rome extended its power across the Mediterranean world and beyond. To begin with, its control over Judea was tactful and light-handed. This changed following serious revolts against Roman rule in 66–73 AD and 132–135 AD. Legions sent to restore imperial control razed Jerusalem to the ground and utterly destroyed its new Temple, slew or exiled thousands of Jews, and established Roman colonies in their former homeland. Even the name 'Judea' went, replaced by the Roman province of 'Palaestina'. Jerusalem was rebuilt as Aelia Capitolina, a city which no Jew was allowed to enter. Those remaining in the region lived further north, in and around Galilee. Hebrew all but disappeared as a spoken language.

By 150 AD, therefore, the Jewish state, like the Philistine one before it, was nothing but a fading memory. Yet the Judean land – Palaestina, or Palestine as it will henceforth be called – continued to flourish because of its strategic, commercial and religious importance. The latter was much helped when the Roman Empire formally adopted Christianity in the fourth century. Almost overnight, from being a troublesome outpost of empire, Palestine became its religious heartland. Pilgrims and others seeking spiritual solace flooded into the 'Holy Land'. Many new churches were built, including the Church of the Holy Sepulchre in Jerusalem. Towns grew and agriculture expanded as Palestine enjoyed what has become known as a 'golden age'. Some say that not until the twentieth century would the land again enjoy such prosperity.

Byzantium

The Roman Empire was by now divided in two, the Western part remaining under the rule of Rome and the Eastern owing allegiance to an emperor based in the ancient city of Byzantium (soon re-named Constantinople; nowadays Istanbul). Palestine came under Byzantine control and for administrative purposes was also divided in two.

With one eye on the twentieth century, when two peoples would claim that Palestine belonged to them by right, we may wonder who lived in Palestine at this time. Precise ethnic or racial definitions are impossible to ascertain, even if they were, they would be largely irrelevant to a society that did not think in our terms of nation or race. Instead, there were three principal cohesive bonds: the empire and its local manifestation in the form of the governor or prince; family and tribe; and religion.

By these criteria, the Palestine of the early seventh century AD bore little relation to the modern region. The overarching allegiance was to Constantinople. As the land had been peopled by a variety of conquerors and settlers for thousands of years, its family and tribal pattern was extremely complex. There was a handful of Arabs – Arabic-speaking desert peoples who worshipped a variety of gods – and there were probably a few dozen Jewish communities. The great majority of those living in Palestine (the modern term 'Palestinian' would be anachronistic) were Christians who spoke Aramaic, although Latin, Greek and other languages were also used. A few pockets of paganism remained in which ancient deities such as the fish-god Dagon were worshipped. It was all a very long way from the explosive mixture that would detonate so forcefully 1,300 years later.

Islam

A major ingredient of the twentieth-century conflict was added in the 630s. Byzantine power was already under threat. Early in the century, a Persian army had overrun Palestine and destroyed its churches. Understandably, but perhaps unwisely, the Jews had sided with the invaders, so the recapture of the province by the Byzantines was accompanied by a retaliatory slaughter of the Jews. Seven years later, the Byzantines were driven out again, this time for good.

The latest wave of invaders were Arabs inspired by a new religion, Islam. The conquest was launched by Abu Bakar, the first caliph (successor to the Prophet Mohammed), who united Arabia and announced a Holy War – *Jihad* – to spread Islam further afield. His successor, Caliph Umar, executed the policy with dramatic success. Under his leadership the Muslim Empire expanded east into Persia, north into Armenia and west into Libya. Palestine was taken in 636, although Jerusalem held out for two more years. Umar's successors of the Umayyad Dynasty made Damascus the capital of their empire and maintained Palestine (*Filastin*), with a capital at Ramlah, as an administrative district of the province of Syria.

Muslim Palestine

The new conquest did not immediately alter the face of Palestine all that much. There were two reasons for this. First, the conquering Arabs were very few in number and had to rely on native peoples to maintain their empire's administration and agricultural and commercial life. Second, the Umayyad Muslims, whose dynasty lasted until 750, showed considerable tolerance towards other 'people of the book' – Christians and Jews who shared Islam's monotheistic heritage.

Over time, however, the situation changed. The Umayyads were succeeded by the Abbasids (750–1258), whose capital was Baghdad. Needing a power base to the west, they paid special attention to Palestine and encouraged large-scale conversion to Islam. As Arabic was (and still is) the language of Islam, it gradually spread as the province's common language. Simultaneously, there was a steady influx of Arab people from the more arid lands to the east and south. Jerusalem was adorned with remarkable new Islamic architecture (see p. 14). At the same time, a small Jewish community re-established itself in the city – Muslims did not share Christian antipathy towards those supposedly responsible for the death of Jesus Christ.

The Palestinian battlefield

Crusaders

Palestine was rarely at peace during the Abbasid Caliphate. Invasion, oppression and massacre were frequent, lending the land more the aspect of a battlefield than a place of habitation. The population, which in the heyday of Byzantine peace and prosperity may have reached one million, fell to perhaps a quarter of that.

In the tenth and eleventh centuries, Palestine was conquered first by the Fatimid Dynasty from Egypt, then by the Seljuqs (Turks from South-West Asia) and finally by Christian crusaders from Western Europe. The latter, who took Jerusalem in 1099 and the following year established the Christian Kingdom of Jerusalem, were a rag-bag coalition led by kings and princes on the make. No doubt some of their number were fired by a genuine wish to see the Holy Places of the Bible in Christian hands, but the motives of many were a great deal less idealistic. Conquest is rarely an altruistic undertaking.

Palestine was in Christian hands until the emergence of Salah al-Din Yusuf ibn Ayyub, a formidable warrior and administrator of Kurdish extraction. Better known in the West as Saladin, he smashed the crusaders in battle and took Jerusalem. Although the Europeans fought back and managed to re-capture the city, by 1244 it was back under Islamic governance and remained so for the next 700 years.

Sadly for Palestine, the end of the crusader kingdom did not bring peace. The next power to take control were the Mamluks – a dynasty descended from the slave warriors, mostly of Turkish origin, who had played a key role in Islamic armies. In the later thirteenth century, having defeated a force of invading Mongols, the ex-slaves killed the sultan and established themselves as a ruling dynasty in Cairo.

Ottomans

The last power to seize and hold Palestine before modern times was the Ottoman Turk. Named after their first notable leader, Osman, the Ottomans were a nomadic Turkman people whose military prowess was honed by their being sandwiched between two much larger powers, the Mongols in the east and the Byzantine Empire in the west. Finding the Byzantines the weaker of the two, the Ottomans began a series of conquests that took them into Arabia and Egypt and even to gates of Vienna. In the process, they swallowed up Palestine (1516).

For most of the next 400 years, Palestine remained more or less under Ottoman rule. For administrative purposes it was divided into three: the districts of Nabulus and Acre (modern-day Akko or Akka), which were subordinated to Damascus, and Jerusalem, which was under the direct control of Istanbul, the Ottoman capital. Under these arrangements, which gave leading local families (the 'notables') a great deal of power, the various inhabitants of Palestine lived for some three centuries.

The majority of the population were Arabic-speaking Muslims, and therefore came under the loose definition of 'Arab'. Christians made up perhaps a fifth of the population, depending on the degree of toleration being shown at the time, and there were always several thousand Jews. Relations between the communities flared periodically into violence, and the history of the period is punctuated by bouts of civil turmoil and war.

Signs of change

Ottoman rule was not without its advantages. In the sixteenth century, Jerusalem benefited from major public works which included a new water system and massive surrounding walls. During the eighteenth century, trade and urban life picked up after a century of decline. Nevertheless, early modern Palestine was an isolated, backward and surprisingly unvisited land. Few pilgrims went there and the handful of European visitors who made the journey were shocked at the dilapidated state of its buildings and historic monuments. When the Frenchman Constantin Volney travelled to Palestine five years before the French Revolution, he declared that Jerusalem was in such a sorry state that he had difficulty recognizing it.

The first catalyst for change came when the Emperor Napoleon invaded Egypt and marched into Palestine with the intention of establishing a French empire in the Middle East. Disease, the British fleet, and Ottoman arms put an end to these unrealistic dreams. Nevertheless, a legacy survived. In a vain effort to rally local support, Napoleon had said he would restore Jerusalem to the Jews if they helped him in his conquest of Palestine. The offer was rejected. Even so, the French not only opened Palestine to the outside world, but also sowed an imperial idea that would take root and grow in other minds. The French might not have settled, but in the next century others would. Their arrival had consequences few could have foreseen.

The land of faith

Judaism

Judaism was the only one of the three major Middle Eastern religions linked to a specific people – the Jews (Islam was espoused to a language, Arabic, but not to a race). At Judaism's heart lay the belief that the one God – creator of the universe and the embodiment of divine love and divine justice – had chosen the Jews to be the vehicle of His way: 'For you are a people consecrated to the Lord your God: of all the peoples on earth the Lord your God chose you to be His treasured people' (*Book of Deuteronomy*).

The Jews' very personal God had made a pact or covenant with them: in return for being His chosen people they were to obey

His pattern and structure of life set out in His teaching, in the Biblical Torah and the post-Biblical Mishna. This led to a division between Orthodox Jews, who took the Torah literally and interpreted it strictly, and Reformed Jews who adopted a more liberal, individualistic approach. Nevertheless, both believed that one day their efforts would be crowned by the arrival of the Redeemer, the Messiah, whose brilliance would allow all other people to recognize God's ways and adopt them. Then the whole earth would bear witness to the love, peace and justice of God.

Another part of God's covenant involved giving His people a specific 'Promised Land' – 'Judah' or 'Israel' – with its sacred capital of Jerusalem. However, after the Diaspora (see p. 13) very few Jews actually lived in their former kingdom and only a few went back there on pilgrimage. Until the nineteenth century, most Jews understood 'returning to the Promised Land' in a non-literal way, meaning the establishment of perfect peace and harmony on earth.

Islam

Islam, which means literally 'surrender' (to God or 'Allah'), was the historical successor to Judaism and Christianity. Inheriting aspects of both, it accepted the Biblical figures of Noah, Moses and Jesus as true prophets. It reserved the position of last and greatest prophet for Mohammed, a seventh-century inhabitant of the Arabian town of Medina who, Muslims believe, received God's word via the Angel Gabriel. Mohammed had it written down in the Koran. Hence the basic Muslim profession of faith: 'There is no god but God; Mohammed is the prophet of God.'

The Koran, backed up by early traditions set out in the Hadith, forms the basis of the Muslim faith. This incorporates a set of specified religious practices and, more widely, an entire way of life. These linked Islam to politics so that, before the twentieth century, the idea of an Islamic country with a non-sectarian government was an anathema.

Islam's blunt simplicity gave believers certainty and self-confidence: they had accepted the right way and so were destined for a heaven redolent with physical as well as spiritual delights. The unwavering rituals of prayer five times a day, the annual fast and the once-in-a-lifetime pilgrimage to Mecca, settled the lives of believers within a secure and reassuring framework. The faith's emphasis on community – the essential equality of all believers and the need for the wealthy and fortunate to support those less well-positioned than themselves – helped give the faith a mass following.

From the beginning, Islam displayed undertones of violence that distressed adherents of more pacific beliefs and philosophies. Much of the faith's early expansion was carried out by a Holy War (*Jihad*), and from time to time since then, more extreme Muslim groups have resurrected the concept of *Jihad* to justify armed resistance to perceived oppression.

Despite the precise nature of many of its teachings, Islam has had its fair share of schism and split. The largest and most enduring of these began with a dispute over the leadership of the movement and the two sides went on to acquire distinctly separate theological positions. The majority, comprising mostly Arab Muslims, were the Sunni. The minority, based originally in Iran (Persia), were the Shia.

Toleration and conflict

For centuries Jews and Muslims were generally much more tolerant of each other than Christians were towards either. From the point of view of the Palestinian Arabs, from the mid-nineteenth to mid-twentieth centuries their conflict with immigrant Jews was not primarily a matter of religion but of land. The same was not true of all Jews, however. As we shall see (p. 19), the movement to return to the Promised Land had the powerful backing of Orthodox religious leaders.

It is important to note at this stage that the Palestinian community has always contained a fair number of Christians, some of whom have been highly influential. Ibrahim Sus, for example, one of the Palestine Liberation Organization's (PLO) representatives in Paris, was a Christian. It is no great surprise, therefore, that it took so long for Palestinian anger towards the Israelis to acquire a religious hue. When it did though, it raised the conflict to new levels of bitterness, intolerance and violence.

In depth: the Jewish Diaspora

The Jewish people, identified by their distinguishing faith, originally appeared on the historical records in the region of Palestine. Between the eighth century BC and the second century AD, huge numbers of Jews were either driven from Palestine or voluntarily migrated elsewhere. As a result, for almost 2,000 years the Jews remained physically dispersed yet managed to retain an extraordinary religio-cultural cohesion. This paradox – unity despite disunity – is what has generally become known as the Jewish Diaspora.

Historically, the Diaspora began with the destruction of the northern Jewish kingdom in the eighth century BC and the dispersal of many of its citizens (see p. 5). Then came the 'Babylonian Captivity' when the southern kingdom of Judah was conquered, the Jewish Temple in Jerusalem destroyed, and many Jews taken to 'exile' in Babylon (Mesopotamia).

By the first century AD, there were more Jews living outside Palestine than within. The contrast was even sharper following the brutal suppression of the anti-Roman revolts of 66–73 AD and 123–135 AD that involved the total destruction of the rebuilt Temple. Henceforward, the Jewish faith and way of life were maintained not by a central authority but by rabbis and law codified in the Mishna and Talmud (see p. 11).

Over the following centuries, Jewish communities were established around the Mediterranean and Middle East, then in Western and Eastern Europe and, eventually, in the United States. Even after years of immigration to Palestine and Israel in the twentieth and twenty first centuries, the Jews of the Diaspora – those living outside the 'Promised Land' – remained a majority. In 2005, for example, Israel's Jewish population was outnumbered by the 5 million Jews living in the US. A further 1 million lived in the former USSR and another 500,000 in France.

In Jewish teaching, the term 'Diaspora' has had a variety of religious and philosophical connotations. The very idea of 'scattering', for instance, emphasized the place from which the dispersal took place – i.e. Judea/Israel. Thus Orthodox Jews supported the return of Jews to the modern land of Israel in preparation for the arrival of God's Messiah (see p. 11). Reform Jews, on the other hand, held that the scattering of the Jews around the world was part of a divine mission to spread knowledge of the One God.

In depth: Jerusalem, holy city

Jerusalem, a city uniquely holy to three faiths, lies at the very heart of the Israeli–Palestinian conflict. As well as being dear to Christian hearts as the place of Jesus' death and resurrection, for Jews it is both holy and historically precious, while it is also the third holiest site in Islam.

The Jews did not found Jerusalem. However, at the end of the eleventh century BC, King David conquered the city and made it the political and religious capital of his kingdom. His successor, Solomon, built the first Temple on a platform known as Temple Mount. Strict Jews believe that the divine presence has never left this sacred spot. Although the first and second Temples have long since been destroyed, part of the Mount's ancient western retaining wall remains intact. Known as the Wailing Wall, it is paramount as the physical focal point for Jewish worship and prayer.

The Prophet Mohammed, who openly acknowledged the Jewish and Christian roots of his teaching, knew the spiritual importance of Jerusalem in the monotheistic world. Indeed, he bade his followers face Mecca when praying only after he had failed to attract Jews to his faith by ordaining that the direction should be towards Jerusalem. There is also a tradition that one night a winged horse named Lightning had carried Mohammed from Mecca to Jerusalem. Here, from the Sacred Rock that once marked the centre of Solomon's Temple, the Prophet had climbed a ladder of light to heaven. He noted the delights there, met Allah, then returned to Mecca the way he had come.

True or not, this story was sufficient to make Jerusalem a site worthy of Islamic pilgrimage. At the end of the seventh century, a magnificent, gold-capped shrine, known as the Dome of the Rock, was built over the place from which Mohammed was said to have made his ascent. A few years later, the impressive Al Aqsa Mosque was erected nearby.

For over 400 years, Ottoman and British control over Jerusalem saved it from excessive sectarian nationalist feuding. This changed in 1948. After Israel had declared itself an independent state, its forces seized West Jerusalem (see pp. 56, 100, 102) and the city was made the capital of the new state. Nineteen years later Israeli troops occupied the entire city. The action presented would-be peacemakers with a conundrum that none of them has yet managed to solve.

whose land?

This chapter will cover:
- the development of nineteenth-century Palestine
- the emergence of Zionism
- Arab nationalism and the roots of Palestinian national awareness
- diplomatic wranglings over Palestine during World War I.

During the century or so that elapsed between the withdrawal of Napoleon and the ending of World War I, Palestine changed more swiftly and dramatically than at any other period in its previous history. Slowly at first but with gathering momentum, a thinly-populated Middle Eastern backwater was transformed into a burgeoning, bustling and cosmopolitan land rarely off the front pages of the world's newspapers. Sadly, the news was not all good.

Although by 1918 the Ottoman Empire had collapsed, the people of Palestine were not in control of their own destiny. New masters, the British, were imposing their distinctive style of paternalistic colonial rule on the territory. More depressing in the long run, the swelling population of Jews and Arabs was becoming more divided almost by the day. Two forces had been at work, imperialism and nationalism, creating an inflammatory mix that would soon catch fire and burn for decades.

Nineteenth-century Palestine

Reform and rebellion

It is estimated that the population of Palestine at the time of Napoleon's visit was probably no more than 250,000. Jerusalem, a shabby shadow of former glory, housed around 8,750 souls, of whom some 4,000 were Muslim, 2,750 Christian and 2,000 Jewish. The other principal towns – Nablus, Hebron and Ramallah – were little more than large villages, and the Mediterranean ports, with the exception of Acre, were tired and inward-looking.

As we have seen (p. 10), the brief French occupation introduced Palestine to the wider world. More important was the occupation 40 years later by the forces of the independent viceroy of Egypt, Mehemet Ali, who was carving out an empire of his own within that of the Ottomans. Led by the viceroy's adopted son, Ibrahim Pasha, the Egyptian force not only took over Palestine but also set about introducing a series of administrative and economic reforms intended to make the province more efficient and profitable. Change was not welcome and the demands for taxation and conscripts provoked a fierce uprising, based in Nablus, that was crushed with blood-curdling ferocity.

The Egyptians' attempt to take over the entire Ottoman Empire was halted when a coalition of European powers intervened and the rule of the Sultan in Istanbul was restored. A lesson had been learned, however, and over the years that followed, the Ottomans pursued a number of policies similar to those introduced by the Egyptians. Town councils helped with local administration and an attempt was made at more efficient tax collection. Land ownership had to be registered, making purchase easier. From 1867, to encourage inward investment, for the first time foreigners were allowed to buy land within the Ottoman Empire. In an effort to boost the standing of Russian Orthodoxy in the city, no less a person than the Tsar of Russia bought several Jerusalem properties.

Economic expansion

Comparatively speaking, the economy boomed as measures to encourage cash crops rather than subsistence farming were introduced. Boosted by taking over unregistered land, large estates did well, especially those with enough capital to move from cereal crops into orange growing. By the end of the century, Palestinian oranges, soap and olive oil were being exported in large quantities to Europe. This in turn helped the ports. The population of Haifa, for example, rose from around 3,000 in 1830, to double that by 1850 and 20,000 by the outbreak of World War I. Communications slowly improved to cope with demand. By 1914, railways linked the coastal towns to each other, to Jerusalem and to the line running from Damascus to Arabia.

At the same time, the population of Palestine was rising dramatically. From a mere 250,000 at the beginning of the nineteenth century, it had tripled by 1914. Much of this increase was due to the rising birth rate, improved public health and lower infant mortality. There were other factors, too – and this is where the rosy picture takes on a somewhat darker hue.

Immigration

As well as a flood of pilgrims, including the Emperor of Germany, European immigrants arrived from France, Russia and Germany. Some have termed the incoming wave of non-Muslims as an 'unarmed crusade'. Many Christians came for religious reasons, establishing and maintaining monasteries, schools, surgeries and missions. They came singly or in small family or other groups. The Sultan expressly forbade the immigration of large, cohesive groups for fear they would disrupt existing social and administrative patterns. His ban, reissued several times, was easily avoided.

The Sultan's prohibition was aimed at a specific sector of immigrant, the European Jews. As we have seen, there had been Jews in Palestine since time immemorial. Despite the Diaspora and periodic persecution, a handful had remained in specific settlements, notably in Jerusalem and in the Galilee region. Recently, their numbers had been growing. A census taken in 1844, for instance, revealed that they had become Jerusalem's largest religious group. Even so, they comprised no more than 15 per cent of Palestine's total population. In the years immediately before World War I, however, the situation was beginning to change noticeably.

The number of Palestinian Jews doubled between 1840 and 1870. In 1880 it had reached 24,000, by 1900 it was perhaps around 60,000, and some estimates claim that by 1914 it was as high as 100,000. At the same time, Jewish families were living away from traditional areas of settlement and engaging in a far wider range of occupations than had hitherto been the case. Understandably, tension between the Muslim and Jewish communities rose.

Zionism

After the Diaspora

Following the Diaspora, as we have seen, the Jews survived in relatively isolated communities around the world. As a distinctive minority, they were an obvious target for racial hatred and were subjected to almost continual discrimination and ill-informed hostility from both Christians and Muslims. From time to time this flared into full-scale slaughter, as happened in Arabia in the seventh century, all over Germany at the time of the Crusades, and periodically throughout Europe and the Middle East thereafter.

Prejudice gained official support when the Roman Catholic Church condemned the Jewish people as the 'killers of Christ'. An example of the sort of wild accusation Jews had to put up with was the charge of 'blood libel' – using the blood of a slaughtered child for ritual purposes. In the nineteenth century, an unholy alliance of the political right, the Roman Catholics, and the Orthodox Church blamed them for conspiring to bring about the excesses of the French Revolution. In Russia, popular misconception held them responsible for the assassination of Tsar Alexander II in 1882, leading to fierce pogroms (anti-Semitic violence).

For centuries, persecution probably made Jewish communities more determined to maintain their faith and way of life. Then in the first half of the nineteenth century, a new attitude began to stir Jewish communities, particularly those in Eastern Europe. Instead of accepting persecution, they could do something about it: not by meeting violence with violence but by moving themselves out of the firing line. The movement that emerged was known as Zionism.

Intellectual foundations

Zionism was a drive to restore the Jewish people to the land their distant ancestors had occupied in Biblical times. Zion was Mount Zion in Jerusalem, a symbol of the Jewish homeland since the sixth century BC. Its emergence owed much to three factors: nationalism, imperialism and a Jewish religious movement that believed that the Jews could redeem themselves and hasten the arrival of the Messiah if they returned to the Holy Land and prepared it for His arrival.

Nationalism had been around since the late Middle Ages but it was given fresh impetus when the French Revolutionary armies broke up existing empires and encouraged national self-determination. The development gathered momentum over the course of the century that followed, leading to the establishment of the Kingdom of Italy, a united Germany, and many smaller independent states like Belgium, Greece and Serbia. With such templates before them, Jewish intellectuals wondered why their people too should not have a state of their own. The trouble was, where and how?

This is where imperialism came in. Just as the Jews saw new nations emerging all around them, so too they saw new empires being created and old ones expanding. The principal motives for the acquisition of these empires were commercial and political. They were justified, however, on less materialistic grounds. Scrupulous imperialists tended to claim that as Europeans were more politically, technologically and perhaps even morally advanced than the peoples they governed, it was their duty – 'the white man's burden' – to civilize them. The less scrupulous preferred a crude paraphrase of Darwin's thesis (1859): 'the survival of the fittest'. This was certainly the attitude of some Zionists, whose attitude towards the native Palestinian Arabs was anything but complimentary. This is implicit in the extraordinary Zionist slogan: 'A land without people for a people without land'. No one disputed the second half of the catchphrase, but to dismiss the 615,000 Muslim Arabs and 70,000 Christians living in Palestine in 1914 as non-existent was racist arrogance.

In the minds of some Orthodox Jews, nationalistic and imperialist impulses mixed with the theological idea of redemption. No longer did they have to wait for God to send his Messiah and deliver the Jews and all others from wickedness – instead the Jews could prove their eagerness for such deliverance by returning to the Holy Land, where the Messiah would appear, and preparing it for him. Such thinking appeared as early as 1834 in a book by the Serbian Jew, Yehuda hai Alkalai, who called for Jewish colonies in Palestine. In the years that followed, the call was taken up and expanded upon by other Jewish writers. It led in 1882 to the foundation of the *Hovevei Zion* (Lovers of Zion) movement, begun by a group of Jewish exiles meeting in Constantinople. They called unequivocally for 'a home in our country' that had been given to them by God – a gift 'registered in the archives of history'. By 'our country', of course, they meant Palestine.

The Jewish State

Until the 1890s, Zionism was primarily a religious and economic movement. Theodore Herzl made it a political one. An Austrian Jew working as a journalist and playwright, Herzl covered France's anti-Semitic Dreyfus scandal of 1894–5 for his newspaper. The story convinced him that the 'Jewish problem' could be solved only by the creation of a Jewish national homeland. He set out his ideas in a small but highly influential book, *The Jewish State* (1896). Interestingly, he did not specifically plump for Palestine as the place where this state might be established. A sparsely populated area of Argentina was one option and later a region in East Africa was suggested. For obvious reasons, neither was acceptable to religious Zionists.

The year after Herzl's publication, a World Zionist Organization held its first meeting in Basle, Switzerland. The mood was positively pro-Palestine and a mission was sent out to explore the ground. Its reply encapsulates with poetic precision what would become the tragedy of that land: 'The bride is beautiful but she is married to another man'. In other words, the region was well-suited to settlement but was already inhabited. Such sentiments might well have been expressed by British pioneers upon reaching the land they were to call Rhodesia; just as it did not prevent them going ahead with their settlement plans, neither did it stop the Zionists.

Seeking official backing for his dream, Herzl made several visits to the Ottoman sultan. At one stage, in what might appear a parody of archetypal Jewishness, he even offered to buy Palestine! Deeply affronted, the Sultan said the territory was not his to sell. Herzl's requests for special status for Jewish immigrants also came to nothing. In fact, in 1900, the Ottoman government even banned Jewish settlements in Palestine.

Istanbul's hostility to extensive Jewish immigration into Palestine had little practical outcome partly due to conditions on the ground and partly because Herzl had more success getting backing from the major European powers. The German Kaiser, who developed a close relationship with Istanbul in the years before World War I, was attracted by the idea of a Jewish Palestine pledged to support Germany commercially and politically. The British government had doubts about Palestine as a Jewish homeland, but British Jewry was rich and influential and there was always the hope that a friendly Palestine would further secure Britain's position in the Middle East. Furthermore, after a vicious pogrom in 1903, in which dozens of Russian Jews were killed and wounded, the Russian government came to see Jewish emigration to Palestine as a useful way to lessen domestic tensions.

Colonization

The steady trickle of Jewish immigration into Palestine in the earlier years of the nineteenth century swelled markedly from about 1880 onwards. The Jews recognize two waves, known as the First and Second Aliyah (going up): 1882–1903 and 1904–13. As we have seen, although the numbers were not huge, by 1914 Jews were an appreciable minority – perhaps one seventh – of the Palestinian population. More significant than their numbers, however, was what they were doing.

With the help of super-rich individuals such as Baron Edmund de Rothschild, followed later by organizations such as the Jewish National Fund (1905) and the Palestine Land Development Fund (1908), Jewish settlers were able to establish institutions, set up businesses, buy the best land and use it to grow the most profitable crops. It was up to five years, for instance, before a newly-planted orange grove bore commercial quantities of fruit; few Arab farmers could afford to wait that long. A Jewish agricultural school was set up in 1870, the same year as Jewish settlers first made their homes on the coastal plain. Other institutions and settlements followed: de Rothschild funded a whole new village in 1882, a Hebrew high school opened in Jaffa in 1906, Tel Aviv was founded on land bought from the Turks in 1909, and two years later the first Jewish hospital opened. By now other Palestinian communities were expressing alarm at what was beginning to look like an attempt to create a state within a state.

Confrontation

Confrontation between Jews and Arabs was not inevitable. Herzl expressed a wish that two substantially-sized communities would be able to live together in harmony, although the realism of this vision has to be questioned. Early friction between immigrants and the indigenous population arose not out of racist or even religious hatred but because of simple misunderstandings over questions such as the precise boundaries of the land Jews had purchased. By 1914, although Jews owned only about two per cent of the land in Palestine, the pattern of their purchases was causing resentment.

Some Jewish immigrants had absorbed Zionist propaganda about their supremacy to the local people and about the land being theirs by God-given right. Moreover, the new arrivals were often separatist. The original Palestinian Jews had been city dwellers, living largely within the communities of Gaza, Hebron, Jaffa, Jerusalem and elsewhere. The new arrivals planted exclusive, self-contained colonies such as Tel Aviv. By the end of World War I there were 47 of them.

One of the earliest manifestations of hostility towards Jewish immigration and land settlement was the choice of two anti-Jewish deputies to represent Jerusalem at the first Ottoman parliament, 1876–7. In 1886, Arab peasant farmers attacked a Jewish settlement after a squabble over land; the following year a Jewish woman was killed as the result of a similar confrontation. By the 1890s both Roman Catholic and Muslim leaders were petitioning Istanbul, asking the Sultan to do something about the flood of Jewish immigrants that was distorting the traditional fabric of the country. There was another outbreak of Arab–Jewish violence in 1891. Tensions rose again with the upsurge in Arab nationalism that followed a change of regime in Istanbul, 1908–9.

Conflicting nationalisms

Arab nationalism

In the second half of the nineteenth century, as nationalism burned bright across Europe, its enervating beams had stirred hearts in the Middle East, too. From the 1860s onwards, Arab intellectuals began to talk of an Arab nation. The romantic concept rested on three legs – two historical, one linguistic. The first was the shared past of the people who had spread Islam; the second the common heritage of an empire (the Caliphate) that at its height had been larger than that of the Romans; and the third a common language.

The Arab 'awakening' found its first voices in literary and scientific societies. One of its earliest focal points was the Syrian Protestant College of Beirut, later to become the American University of that city. The movement was given a pronounced fillip when, in 1908–9, an opposition group known as the Young Turks forced the sultan to accept constitutional rule and then to abdicate when he tried to backtrack. The Young Turks had acted in the name of nationalism, but since only 30 per cent of the sultan's subjects were Turks, the message relayed across the Arab world was not the same as that heard in Istanbul and Anatolia. To the intellectuals of Cairo, Damascus and Baghdad, nationalism meant rejection of Ottoman rule and the gathering of all Arab peoples into a huge Arab nation.

Or did it? Could a nation state of such diversity as the Arab-speaking world really be created on the basis of a common language and faith? Was it genuinely realistic to think of the citizens of Morocco, Syria and Arabia living as harmoniously together as those of, say, Provence, Brittany and Burgundy, or even Texas, New York and California? The truth was then, as it is today, that Arab nationalism was a chimera, a beautiful dream rather than a realistic possibility. Within the Arab-speaking world, other nationalisms were a far more realistic possibility.

Palestinians?

Although few would deny the existence of Palestinian nationalism today, there is widespread disagreement over when it came into being. Roughly speaking, there are three schools of thought. Most Israelis maintain that before the 1960s the idea of a Palestinian nation had not existed and it came into being only as a reaction to the creation and expansion of Israel. Of course, such a position helps justify Jewish immigration into Palestine and the creation of the State of Israel. In establishing a country where one had not existed before, the argument runs, the Jews were doing little more than others, like the Americans, who had built nations in tribal lands.

It goes without saying that the majority of Palestinian historians deny this claim. The more hard-line among them insist that the Palestinian nation has existed since time immemorial, tracing its roots, like the Jews, to Biblical times. Such a position is difficult to accept: there may have been a land generally known as Palestine all that time, but territory and name alone do not make a nation. A great deal more realistic is an alternative view – that the Palestinian nation has emerged gradually over the last 200 years.

A suggested starting point is the 1834 revolt against the invading Egyptians (see pp. 16–17). The movement united all sections of Palestinian society in a common cause for the first time, thereby creating the sort of shared heritage nationhood requires. Ottoman reforms and nineteenth-century economic development added to a vague sense of national cohesion. Far more influential was resentment at Jewish encroachment. Like the 1834 rebellion, the perceived threat to the traditional way of life led increasing numbers of educated Palestinians to think in terms of a Palestinian nation. This found concrete expression in Arabic newspapers intended for a specifically Palestinian readership. There was no Palestinian head of state, flag, anthem or even national government, but the soil had been prepared in which such things would grow.

The Impact of war

Taking sides

World War I changed Palestine for ever. The region's inhabitants had little or no direct interest in the causes of the conflict but were drawn into it because of their Turkish overlords. At the beginning of 1914, Turkey was not allied to any of the major powers. Recently, it had been turning away from its traditional friendship with Britain and drawing closer to Germany. German finance was behind the ongoing project for a Berlin to Baghdad railway, and German officers were helping to modernize the Turkish army. Both Berlin and Istanbul shared a mistrust of Russian imperial ambitions. As a consequence, following a secret treaty with Germany and a series of provocative blunders by the Allies, in early November 1914, Turkey joined the war against Britain, France and Russia.

The Turks had been finding it difficult enough holding together their shrinking empire in peace-time; the strain of war broke it completely. Over the next four years they faced an Anglo-French naval blockade of their coastlines, an Anglo-Indian force invading from southern Mesopotamia (Iraq), a brutal campaign with Russia in the Caucus region, allied occupation of the Gallipoli Peninsular, and a British invasion from Egypt closely linked to a British-assisted Arab revolt beginning in the Hejaz (Western Arabia). As far as Palestine was concerned, the last two were crucial.

Vague promises

The Middle East was vital to Britain because of the region's strategic position on the route to British possessions in India and the Far East, and because its oil was used to power British warships and an increasing proportion of British industry. With huge numbers of British troops tied down on the Western Front, British diplomats looked around for allies in their campaign against the Turkish Empire. The Arabs, always resentful of Turkish overlordship and now nationalistic as well, were an obvious target.

Thus, in 1915–16, Sir Henry McMahon, the British Consul-General in Egypt, engaged in a lengthy correspondence with Hussein, the clever but enigmatic Grand Sharif or Emir (a sort of hereditary governor) of Mecca. As head of the Hashemites, a clan descended from the Prophet Mohammed, and guardian of the Muslim holy cities of Mecca and Medina, Hussein had as good a claim as anyone to speak for the Islamic Arab 'nation'. Since his allegiance to the Ottomans was known to be shaky, McMahon believed he could be persuaded to throw in his lot with the allies.

The Consul-General was right. Speaking for the British government, Sir Henry said it would support Arab independence and help the Arabs establish such states as they thought fit out of the territory in which they lived. Specifically, 'portions of Syria lying to the west of the districts of Damascus, Homs, Hama and Aleppo' were excluded from the agreement as Sir Henry felt that they 'cannot be said to be purely Arab' (Sir Henry McMahon, letter to the Sharif of Mecca, 24 October 1915). The correspondence was not accompanied by maps.

The Grand Sharif accepted the terms and, led by his son Faisal and assisted and perhaps even inspired by the able and eccentric self-publicist T.E. Lawrence 'of Arabia', the Arabs rose up in the Hejaz and drove north to link up with British forces that had advanced into Palestine from Egypt. General Allenby was in Jerusalem by Christmas 1917 and had advanced north to Damascus and Aleppo by the end of the war.

Outside Arabia, full Arab independence did not follow. And even when it eventually did, Palestine was not included. Politicians and scholars returned to Sir Henry's letter. Had the diplomat been thinking of Palestine when he excluded certain regions from Arab rule? If so, either his geography was somewhat awry or the true meaning had been hidden in translation between English, a fairly specific language, and the more poetic Arabic. The Arabs felt betrayed.

Double-dealing

Six months after Sir Henry's promise to support Arab independence, the vigorous British diplomat Sir Mark Sykes negotiated a secret understanding with his French counterpart François Georges-Picot. Worried that Arab portions of the disintegrating Turkish Empire might come under Russian influence, the Sykes–Picot Agreement divided the Middle East into five parts. Britain and France were each to have an area they controlled directly, and another that lay within their 'sphere of influence'. The independent Arab states promised by McMahon were included, somewhat paradoxically, within these spheres of Influence. Palestine, labelled 'international sphere' on the accompanying map, featured in neither.

To confuse the situation even further, on 2 November 1917, the British Foreign Secretary, Arthur James Balfour, declared that, 'His Majesty's Government viewed with favour the establishment in Palestine of a national home for the Jewish people'. All sorts of reasons have been put forward for this statement, including a crafty plan by the British government to bring the 'international zone' of the Sykes–Picot Agreement within its sphere of influence.

In the end, though, Balfour's motive was irrelevant. What mattered was that the world's foremost imperial power appeared to have given it's blessing to Zionism. In so doing, although it had used 'homeland' instead of the more confrontational 'state', it had further reneged on its agreement with the Arabs. At the same time, it had raised the hopes and expectations of Jews living in Palestine or hoping to move there, and dealt a bitter blow to the Palestinian Arabs. Small wonder, therefore, that the 18-word sentence quoted above is often held up as British diplomacy's biggest single blunder of modern times.

03

the mandate

This chapter will cover:
- Palestine's emergence as an embryonic state after World War I
- British government of the Palestinian 'mandate'
- mounting Arab–Jewish–British mistrust and violence
- attempts to solve the 'Palestine problem' before 1945.

In the 17 years that separated the end of World War I from the end of World War II, Palestine changed from being a problematic district within the Turkish empire to a disputed land discussed and argued over throughout the world. This was partly because, under British rule, the Arab–Jew tensions just becoming visible in 1914 sprouted into an armed conflict. The dangerous situation was greatly complicated by events in Europe, namely the systematic attempt by the Nazis to wipe out European Jewry. As a consequence, by late 1945, Palestine was close to being torn apart in a three-way battle between the British, the Arabs and the Jews.

Peace-making

Legacy of war

Palestine had a hard time during World War I. As an Ottoman territory, its overseas trade was disrupted by allied naval power. Poverty increased and all sectors of the population suffered from outbreaks of typhus and cholera. Fighting, notably the advance of British and Arab forces across Palestine in 1917, caused inevitable hardship, loss and suffering. Many Jews who had retained their Russian citizenship (a number had done so to avoid conscription into the Ottoman Army) were forcibly deported. The population of the entire territory fell by an estimated 160,000. It was with a degree of relief, therefore, that all those living in Palestine heard that Turkey had accepted defeat on 30 October 1918.

The relief was coupled with anxious anticipation. What would happen to their land? The only fact locals could be sure of was that they themselves would probably have little say in whatever was decided. Would their territory become an independent Arab state, as Grand Sharif Hussein said Britain had promised? If so, then how could this be reconciled with the Balfour Declaration of support for a Jewish 'homeland' in Palestine? And what about the Anglo-French Sykes–Picot Agreement to carve up ex-Ottoman territories in the Middle East between them, leaving Palestine as some sort of international protectorate? In the end, an attempt was made to implement all three policies – and the result, understandably, was an unholy mess.

figure 3 the Middle East mandates

Britain's mandate

The several separate treaties that followed World War I, broadly known as the Versailles Settlement, were supposed to be based upon US President Wilson's principle of national self-determination. In practice, the principle raised as many difficulties as it solved. What did self-determination mean in Palestine, for instance? To find out, Wilson asked the King-Crane Commission (1919) to investigate and report back to him. Not surprisingly, the Commission declared that the situation was extremely tricky: the Arabs, comprising 90 per cent of the population, wanted Palestine joined to the emerging Syria or set up as an independent entity, while the Zionist Jews pressed for it to become their homeland. Left in a quandary, Wilson accepted the status quo. He was not the first politician stymied by the Palestinian situation, nor by any means the last.

The status quo at the end of the war was that British troops occupied Palestine, making it a de facto addition to their empire. Their imperialist land-grabbing was given a fig leaf of respectability by the 'mandate' system. Backed by the newly-created League of Nations, mandates were territories deemed suitable for democratic independence after a period of assistance and tutelage by an established Western democracy. That meant Britain and France. The latter took responsibility for Syria and Lebanon, Britain for Iraq and a large Palestine that extended across the River Jordan (see Figure 3). In fact, the Palestinian mandate involved the twin tasks of preparing the country for independence while also fulfilling the Balfour Declaration's promise of giving the Jews a homeland there.

The ill-thought-out Palestinian scheme ran into difficulties almost immediately. Not only did tension between Jews and Arabs rise dramatically as a fresh wave of Jewish immigrants descended on the country, but circumstances obliged the British to divide the country in two. In 1921, Prince Abdullah, Grand Sharif Hussein's second son, turned up with a small army in the Palestinian territory on the eastern bank of the River Jordan. Having been replaced by his elder brother as King of Iraq, he was on his way north to try his luck in Syria. He got no further than the tiny settlement of Aman. Here he received a British proposal that he become king of the mandate territory he occupied. Thus, in an extraordinarily cavalier piece of state-making, the British divided their Palestinian mandate. Territory to the west of the River Jordan remained as Palestine, while that on the other side of the river became the new mandate of Transjordan. Given independence after World War II, it emerged as the Hashemite Kingdom of Jordan.

Going nowhere

British administrators carried out the logistical side of their mandated duties with laudable efficiency. Their efforts to improve life in Palestine attracted Arab immigrants as well as Jews. They modernized transport by expanding the rail network and building roads; they built schools and sewage treatment plants; laid water pipelines and increased the provision of electricity. Medical services improved too, leading to lower child mortality and an increase in the population. Palestine's relative stability and security during the 1920s and early 1930s allowed industry and commerce to continue the expansion begun before World War I.

Material progress was not matched by any similar progress in the political sphere. Britain's mandate from the League of Nations had included neither time limit nor specific targets for independent institutions. That was just as well, for no target would have been attainable. Arab opinion, as voiced by the unelected Palestinian National Congress, rejected the mandate as long as it incorporated the hated Balfour Declaration. The Jews refused to endorse an elected all-Palestine government for fear it would ride roughshod over the aims and aspirations of the Jewish minority.

As a consequence, despite many meetings and proposals and much talking, there was very little progress towards independence. The Arabs ran their own local affairs and the Jews ran theirs. Somewhere in the middle, spending a fortune on translating between three official languages (Arabic, Hebrew and English) but enjoying three days of holiday per week (the Muslims' Friday, the Jews' Saturday and the Christian's Sunday), the British bureaucracy attempted to hold the ring while dealing with issues like transport and immigration that required a mandate-wide policy.

Breakdown

1920s – uneasy peace

Although during the early years of mandate there was less violence in Palestine than in either Syria or Iraq, several factors were making some sort of future bloodletting highly likely. The lack of a date or even preconditions for British occupation to end led to mounting hostility in both communities, but especially among the Arabs. Indeed, they were beginning to talk of 1920 as their 'Year of Catastrophe'. What right had foreigners, they asked, either to divide their land or force them to accept a state within a state?

The British government's appointment of Sir Herbert Samuel, a Jew and an openly enthusiastic Zionist, as Palestine's first all-powerful High Commissioner hardly displayed tactful even-handedness. Sceptical Arabs believed the British government was so inherently pro-Zionist that it intended to hang on to Palestine until sufficient Jewish immigrants had arrived to make them the majority of the population. Nor were Jewish Palestinians delighted with their British overlords. The more extreme among them, in particular, were infuriated by the decision to make Transjordan a separate mandate because the move reduced the chances of recreating the ancient Judean Kingdom of David that bestraddled the River Jordan (see p. 5).

Meanwhile, streams of Jewish immigrants continued to flood into Palestine. The Jewish population of the mandate probably doubled in the ten years after World War I. By 1922, they made up 11 per cent of an overall population that had risen to around 750,000. After an initial rush, the British, worried by the Arab reaction, imposed limits on immigration. Nevertheless, by 1928 Jews accounted for 16 per cent of Palestinians.

More importantly, ten years after the end of World War I, Jews owned 4.2 per cent of Palestinian land. This may not sound much, but a good deal of it was in areas where the soil was fertile and suitable for agriculture. These were comparatively rare before the introduction of large-scale irrigation. Land purchases were a regular source of friction, too. This was not because they were done illegally or by force but because, in the semi-feudal society of rural Palestine, land rights were often assumed rather than documented. Moreover, much land was bought from absentee Arab landlords who had little knowledge of or interest in their tenants. Such sales led to Arab peasants being turned off land they and their ancestors had farmed for generations.

Embryonic institutions

During the 1920s, the Jews rapidly established the embryonic apparatus of a distinctively Jewish state: a Jewish National Assembly, trade unions, schools, industrial enterprises, a university, and so forth. They even had their own fighting force, the Haganah – labelled a 'defence force' by Jewish historians and a 'terrorist organization' by Arab ones (see pp. 42–3).

Unlike the immigrant Jews, the Palestinian Arabs did not benefit from a clean slate when it came to organizing themselves and establishing institutions. The territory had been served by an official and semi-official administrative network for centuries but this did not always harmonize with British plans. The imperial power, for instance, set up a Palestinian Arab Congress that was empowered to choose a Palestinian Arab Executive. But when the latter boycotted the mandate concept because it incorporated the Balfour Declaration, Anglo-Arab cooperation was severely shaken.

The complexity of the situation is reflected in the fact that a Supreme Muslim Council operated in parallel with the Palestinian Arab Executive. The Council was headed by Amin al-Husseini, Grand Mufti (expert on Muslim religious law) of Jerusalem. To make matters even more difficult, his position was hotly disputed after a very dubious election had been overruled by British fiat. He also suffered from traditional rivalry with the an-Nashasibi family. Husseini supported the Arab Executive, for example, while the Nashasibis preferred to operate through yet another rival organization, the National Defence Party. When ancient town–country, tribal and religious divisions are added to the mix, it is not difficult to see why the Palestinian Arabs failed to present a united front against the Jews and the British.

Early violence

In 1920, during fairly widespread anti-Jewish riots, Bedouin tribesmen attacked a Jewish settlement in Upper Galilee and killed six settlers. The following May, inter-community violence left almost 100 dead, equally distributed between Jews and

Arabs, and several hundred injured. There was further fighting towards the end of the year. The trouble provoked two responses. First, the British temporarily limited immigration into Palestine – there was actually a net emigration from the mandate in 1927. Second, the Jewish community established the Haganah (see pp. 42–3). Thereafter, the situation remained tense but calm until the end of the decade.

The uneasy post-war peace collapsed in 1929. Each side blamed the other. The Jews and most of the British criticized the Grand Mufti and a journalist named Arif al-Arif for stirring up anti-Jewish feeling among the Arab population. The Arabs said they were responding to an aggressive call by the Zionist extremist Ze'ev Jabotinsky for the massive increase in Jewish immigration necessary for the formation of an all-Jewish state in Palestine. Within Jerusalem, tension had been building over several months because of the erection of screens to separate Jewish men and women at the Wailing (Western) Wall of Temple Mount (see p. 14). The Wall, it will be recalled, was sacred Muslim property and any form of furniture there (including screens) was supposedly banned by mandate law. When a Jewish boy was stabbed to death after kicking a football into an Arab garden, his funeral provoked demonstrations and eventually, in August 1929, a full-scale, bloody riot.

Fired-up Arab peasants armed with a variety of weapons descended on Jerusalem and, in the ensuing orgy of murder, rape and pillage, slaughtered 133 Jews. Before order was restored, 116 Arabs also lay dead, a few killed by Jewish vigilantes but most by the gunfire of the British security forces. Later, further Arabs died in a Jewish reprisal attack. Whatever slight hope there had been of Jews and Arabs living together in a single harmonious Palestine was all but gone; there was a grim inevitability about what followed.

Mission impossible

1930s

During the 1930s, the situation in Palestine became simultaneously more complex and more intractable. It became more complex as Palestinian Arabs felt increasingly threatened by growing Jewish immigration – a British census of 1931 revealed that the mandate's population was now over 1 million, of which 16.9 per cent was Jewish. The nature of this Zionist community was important, too. Particularly after the Nazis took power in Germany and connived at the repatriation of many German Jews to Palestine, Palestinian Jews were relatively well educated, politically sophisticated, united in their objectives and, above all, internationally funded. In comparison, after centuries of relative cultural, political and economic stagnation under Ottoman domination, the deeply fragmented Palestinian Arab community was only slowly losing its parochial, semi-feudal mentality. Although numerically superior, in almost all other respects it was anything but the dominant force.

A British committee report, blaming excessive Jewish immigration for the 1929 bloodshed, suggested that only another 50,000 Jews be allowed to enter Palestine. This target was soon overturned. 30,000 German Jews arrived in 1933, rising to 61,000 in 1935. By World War II the Jewish community in Palestine numbered around 467,000, almost one-third of the total population. It owned around six per cent of the land and had established some 300 Zionist colonies.

The 1929 violence provoked a split among Palestinian Jews. The majority followed the more moderate ('Labour') leaders of the World Zionist Organization, Chaim Weizmann in London and David Ben-Gurion in Palestine. They sought a socialist Jewish state in Palestine separate from a Palestinian Arab one. The Haganah would be needed to defend this state, but force was not an integral part of it.

Jabotinsky's was the more extreme, minority view. He and his World Union of Zionist Revisionists had set up a militant security force of their own, the Irgun. Their policy, later known as the 'iron wall', was based on four principles. First, the Jews were the standard-bearers of a superior Western civilization into the Middle East. Second, Zion should comprise all Palestine on both banks of the Jordan ('Greater Israel'). Third, the Arabs would never voluntarily accept this. Fourth, the only answer, therefore, was force: Zionists had to carve out their state and secure it behind an iron wall. Only when the Arabs knew they could never win, would they accept the presence of the Jewish state in the Middle East. When we wonder why peace between Palestinians and Israelis is so elusive, we have only to look to this inflexible Revisionist doctrine to grasp at least part of the answer.

Palestinian uprising

The later 1930s were dominated by a massive uprising of the Palestinian Arabs against the whole mandate apparatus. Although perhaps deliberately started by Grand Mufti Husseini, it soon acquired an instinctive, chaotic momentum of its own. Consequently, it has been likened to the 1834 revolt against the Egyptian Mamluks and to the more recent Intifada uprisings (see p. 156 and 199). Paradoxically, the revolt of 1936–9 played an important part in strengthening a sense of Palestinian nationalism while at the same time fragmenting that nation's social and political structure.

The uprising took place against a background of rising three-way – Arab–Jewish–British – violence. It was sparked by rumours of planned Jewish construction work around Jerusalem's Temple Mount and the British killing in battle of a Syrian freedom fighter/guerrilla named Sheikh Izz al-Din al-Qassam. Arab resistance took the form of a general strike, which left its own supporters deeply impoverished, a refusal to pay tax, and sporadic violent attacks against Zionist communities, the British and even Christian Arabs. By 1938–9, the revolt and the tough British response had so disrupted the Arab community that fighting between rival villages was as violent as that against their common enemies.

At first Arab leadership was exercised by the traditional notable class, especially Grand Mufti Husseini. Already president of the Supreme Muslim Council, in 1936 he became president of a newly-created Arab Higher Committee. His authority did not last beyond 1937, when, wanted by the British after the assassination of a British commissioner, he fled in disguise to Lebanon where the French put him under house arrest. His Higher Committee was forcibly dissolved along with other Arab political organizations. Rumours that the Arab revolt had received Nazi funding were given some credence when, during World War II, the Grand Mufti cooperated with the regimes of both Hitler and Mussolini.

By the end of the revolt a new class of radicalized Palestinian Arabs had emerged. Its members were usually young men not related by blood or temperament to the community's traditional, Jerusalem-based ruling class. They were urban, wage-earning (if in work), aggressively violent and often employed Muslim terminology. The kafiya, later made famous by Yasser Arafat, was their badge of resistance and their loyalty was to the red, black and green of the Palestinian flag.

Partition

After a fairly low-key initial response, in 1937 the British set about quashing the revolt with determination. Martial law was imposed and the Palestine garrison increased to over 20,000 troops. Far more controversial and destructive of Anglo-Arab relations was cooperation with Jewish volunteers in Special Night Squads that attacked Arab villages suspected of harbouring rebels. Within four years perhaps 10,000 Arabs were killed (albeit a fair proportion at the hands of other Arabs) and 15,000 wounded.

Jewish cooperation with the British was by no means guaranteed. The Revisionist faction, regarding British attempts at even-handedness as hostility, reacted to the hanging of an Irgun member in 1938 by blowing up a bus in Haifa, killing 74 passengers and bystanders. At the same time, the Irgun pressed on with its own private battles with the Palestinian Arabs, killing dozens while picking up comparatively few casualties itself. By now the chances of Arabs and Jews living together in a single Palestinian state, never great, had vanished.

This was recognized by the British Royal Commission (usually known as the Peel Commission) which examined the Palestine situation over the winter of 1936–7. Its recommendations, published in July 1937, were headed by a new principle: partition. The British had already resorted to this in Ireland, where sectarian differences had seemed beyond reconciliation, and they were to do the same when separating Pakistan from India at the time of independence. Although superficially attractive as a way of solving a difficult problem, in fact partition was a way of avoiding that problem rather than solving it. Britain's mandate had been to create a single Palestine, not two. Partition would mean creating minority communities in either state or a near impossible – even forced – movement of peoples from one region to another.

The Peel Commission suggested a three-way split: (1) a Jewish state comprising about one third of the land of Palestine but with almost half the mandate's population of Arabs; (2) a larger Arab state; (3) a special zone controlled by the League of Nations (in effect Britain) that included Jerusalem and its surrounding holy sites. Interestingly, a somewhat similar partition plan had been agreed 19 years earlier by Chaim Weizmann and Prince Faisal but it had been dropped after rejection by other Arab leaders. Acceptance then would have avoided an immense amount of blood and tears.

Ben-Gurion, the most influential Jewish leader, gave the latest British proposal a cautious welcome. It did, after all, offer his people a nation state of their own. The Revisionists, on the other hand, rejected it outright as a sell-out. Likewise, the Arab Higher Committee turned down the proposal flat. What right had a Western power, they asked, to descend on their land, allow hundreds of thousands of strangers to settle there and then, when the locals objected to the influx, give away a large chunk of territory to the newcomers so that they could have a state of their own? This far from illogical position, spiced with religious overtones, remains that of militant Palestinians to this day.

World War II

Changing course

By 1938, as the British were struggling to regain control of the upland villages of eastern Palestine, it was becoming clear to the government in London that it would soon be involved in war on a vastly greater scale with the fascist regimes of Germany and Italy. If – when – this happened, the last thing Britain wanted was a row with the Arab world that might provoke a cut in oil supplies and even some sort of fascist-Arab alliance based on Nazi promises of full Arab independence. (Precisely the sort of deal Britain had struck to get Arab support during World War I!) Furthermore, there was the possible meeting of minds between Germans and Arabs over the Jewish 'problem'.

The international situation, coupled with yet another report from the mandate, led to a conference, a debate in Parliament and a White Paper that signalled further change in British policy. Partition was ditched. In its place, Britain proposed full independence for a united mandate in ten years' time, Jewish immigration limited to 15,000 a year for five years and thereafter only with Arab consent, and a limit on land sales. As might have been expected, this pleased no one. The majority of Jews were particularly disappointed at the way their dream of independence had been dashed.

War efforts

Moderate Arabs and Jews agreed on one thing: the threat posed by the fascist Axis was worse than anything Britain could throw at them. On the outbreak of war, inter-community conflict died down and large numbers from either side agreed to support Britain and its allies in their struggle. As many as 27,000 Jews and 25,000 Arabs (particularly the famous Arab Legion) fought with the British Army. With funds pouring into the mandate to support the 280,000 allied service personnel based there, after 1941 the Palestinian economy roared into double-figure expansion. The Jewish sector did particularly well, developing its industry to meet allied war needs.

There were exceptions to this comparative harmony. One was the Grand Mufti (see p. 34). Revisionist Zionists, whose main instrument of guerrilla rebellion remained the Irgun, also maintained their hostility towards Britain. One notorious sect, the Stern Gang, actually tried to open negotiations with the Nazis. Their assassination of a Zionist-inclined British minister in Cairo in 1944 did not win them many friends, either. Indeed, by this date the Haganah and Irgun were in open conflict, the former handing over 1,000 of their Jewish rivals to the British.

Despite the British limit, large numbers of desperate Jewish immigrants continued to pour into Palestine from Nazi-threatened Europe. Perhaps as many as 40,000 got in somehow in 1940. Dreading an Arab backlash, Britain tried hard to maintain its quota system, often with tragic results. One incident in particular caught the world's attention. It involved the ancient and unseaworthy steamship *Struma*, which in December 1941 left the Romanian port of Constanza for Palestine with 769 Jewish refugees on board. The ship's engines gave out *en route* and she was towed into Istanbul where all but a handful of passengers were denied entry visas for Palestine. Towed back out to sea, the *Struma* drifted helplessly until sunk by a Russian torpedo with the loss of virtually everyone on board.

Another effect of the war was to draw the United States deeply into Middle Eastern politics for the first time. Like Britain, the US needed Arab oil and poured money into Saudi Arabia to keep it stable and on side. Nevertheless, the pro-Arab stance of President F.D. Roosevelt ran contrary to a growing pro-Zionist feeling of the US at large. Following a visit of Ben-Gurion and Chaim Weizmann to the US, a programme of support for the Zionist project (the Biltmore Programme) gained widespread backing, even from Congress and presidential election candidates.

Into the abyss

In the end, World War II did little more than put the Palestinian crisis on hold. If anything, the situation in 1945 was worse than it had been in 1939. As the full extent of the horrifying Nazi slaughter of some 6 million European Jews became known, a worldwide tide of support for Zionism ran strongly. Jews everywhere were more determined than ever to carve out a secure homeland for their people, whatever the cost. Rulers of neighbouring Arab states made the appropriate pro-Palestinian noises while watching the situation carefully to see what political opportunities it might offer. Britain, bankrupt and exhausted by almost six years of total war, had no stomach for further conflict in Palestine and wanted out.

Somewhere in the middle of this venomously complex equation were the Palestinian Arabs. Although most were better off than they had been, the majority were still poor. In the towns they were small shopkeepers or wage-earners. In the countryside they were landless or farmed small parcels of stony soil. They lacked unity and leadership. In short, they were totally unprepared for the storm gathering on the horizon.

In depth: Mohammed Amin al-Husseini (1893–1974), Grand Mufti of Jerusalem

Born into a respected, aristocratic Palestinian family, (Haj) Mohammed Amin al-Husseini was the most influential figure in Palestinian politics between the World Wars. His fervent Arab nationalism won him many supporters, but his links with the Nazis and their policies has left a stain on his reputation that Israeli propagandists were not slow to emphasize.

After dabbling in law at Cairo University and administration in Istanbul, al-Husseini made a pilgrimage to Mecca before joining the Ottoman Army as an artillery officer in 1914. He returned to Jerusalem on disability leave two years later, changed sides, and worked for the British. After the war he campaigned for Palestine to be incorporated within a Greater Syria. When this idea collapsed, he adopted the cause of Palestinian nationalism and the expulsion of Jews from the mandate.

Sentenced to imprisonment by the British for stirring up racial hatred, al-Husseini took refuge abroad before being pardoned and, in an extraordinary piece of imperial high-handedness, appointed Grand Mufti of Jerusalem by High Commissioner Sir

Herbert Samuel. Simultaneously president of the Supreme Muslim Council, with control over Sharia (Islamic) courts and the appointment of teachers and preachers, al-Husseini had become the most powerful Arab in the mandate. The striking gold-covering of Jerusalem's Dome of the Rock owes much to his fundraising at this time.

Jewish sources accused the Grand Mufti of provoking the 1929 massacre of Jews in Hebron but a British enquiry found no evidence for this. During the 1936 Arab Revolt, however, al-Husseini's anti-Semitic and anti-British inflammatory pronouncements were widely attested and he escaped arrest by fleeing to Syria and then Iraq. By this time he had established links with Hitler's Nazis, whose anti-Semitism he hoped to exploit for Palestinian ends. During World War II, he worked with pro-fascist elements in Iraq, mixed with Nazi leaders in Germany, and supposedly recruited Bosnian Muslims for the Waffen SS in Yugoslavia.

In 1945, the exiled Grand Mufti fled to Cairo via Switzerland and France. Greeted as a hero, he continued his ruthless campaign for the creation of an independent Arab Palestine. However, his power and influence rapidly dwindled after the Arab League by-passed him and his forces disintegrated during the 1948 war with Israel. By the time of his death, leadership of the Palestinian cause had passed to a distant cousin popularly known as Yasser Arafat.

In depth: Haganah and Irgun

The Haganah began as a small group of volunteer settlement guards known as the Guild of Watchmen. During the 1920s, the Guild grew into a large but still illegal and relatively ill-coordinated collection of poorly-armed defence units. Following the 1929 massacre (see p. 35), the Haganah was developed into a serious force of several thousand, with organized training and its own weapons' workshops.

In 1931, Haganah's more right-wing elements set up the Irgun movement (see opposite). During the 1936–9 Arab Revolt, the 10,000-strong Haganah received semi-official recognition from the British whom it helped in their struggle to hold down the Arab population. The training and experience gained at this time was to prove invaluable in Israel's 1948–9 War of Independence.

During World War II, the Haganah defied the British by continuing to facilitate illegal entry of Jewish refugees into Palestine. At the same time, it threw its weight behind the anti-fascist war effort and was eventually allowed to form a distinct Jewish Brigade of the British Army. From 1945–8, the Haganah switched to anti-British tactics of sabotage and terrorist-style bombings before being transformed into the Israeli Defence Force (IDF). By this time, two future prime ministers of Israel, Yitzhak Rabin and Ariel Sharon, as well as future Defence Minister Moshe Dayan, had all passed through its ranks.

The Haganah was closely associated with the socialist ethos of the majority of Jewish immigrants who arrived in Palestine during the first part of the twentieth century. This political stance, together with the Haganah's reluctance to use brute force, irritated hard-line Zionists who, in 1931, left to form the Irgun (or Etzel) group. Opposed to both socialism and restraint, Irgun's members included future Israeli Prime Minister Menachem Begin.

From the beginning, Irgun organized clandestine attacks on Arab targets, claiming over 250 'enemy' deaths by September 1939. Like the Haganah, Irgun also organized illegal immigration into Palestine. From 1940–43, Irgun joined Haganah in suspending anti-British activities, although these were continued by extremist splinter groups such as the Stern Gang. In 1948, Irgun resumed its attacks on the occupying power, the most notorious being the bombing of Jerusalem's King David Hotel (see p. 46). At the same time, its gunmen deliberately terrorized Arabs into leaving areas intended for incorporation into the State of Israel. Its best-known operations were the massacre of Deir Yassin and the attack on Jaffa.

04

Israel

This chapter will cover:
- the situation in Palestine at the end of World War II
- Britain's decision to hand over the 'Palestine problem' to the UN
- unofficial war between Jews and Arabs, 1947–8
- formation of the State of Israel and its war with Palestinians and other Arabs
- the destruction of the embryonic Palestinian nation.

The dying mandate

Palestine in 1945

Almost as soon as World War II ended, Palestinian politics reverted to something close to its pre-war courses. Grand Mufti Husseini, the nominal leader of the Palestinian Arabs, was making his way back to the Arab world and calling for an independent Palestine and the destruction of the Jewish community there. As before, Muslim Arabs were deeply resentful of what they saw as a Western-backed attempt by the Jews to take over Arab land, and remained fearful of where this might lead.

Palestinian Jews of all persuasions had been quick to settle their wartime differences and were waiting impatiently to see precisely what Britain would do. Ernest Bevin, the Foreign Secretary in Britain's recently-elected Labour government wondered, as had many of his predecessors in that office, whether there was any way of honouring the Balfour Declaration while still keeping in with the Arabs. He soon realized there was not.

Although the essence of the Palestine situation was the same as before the war – two peoples but only one land – several of the surrounding circumstances had changed significantly. Britain's imperial commitments were now more than it needed or could cope with, and it wanted to shed as many of them as possible. The League of Nations, by whose mandate Britain was still in Palestine, was defunct and about to be formally abolished. Palestine's neighbours were all either independent or about to become so. (Transjordan, the last, had to wait until 1948.) In March 1945, with British backing, Egypt organized an Arab League that comprised itself, Syria, Saudi Arabia, Transjordan, Iraq, Lebanon, and Yemen. The League's primary purpose was to foster unity and cooperation among Arab peoples and at first its activities were largely cultural, social and economic. Nevertheless, the League established a Higher Committee to lobby against Zionism and welcomed a spokesperson from the Palestinian people.

Two other factors profoundly influenced the Palestinian situation. One was the Nazi Holocaust in which some 6 million European Jews had perished. This had had a double effect: raising a massive worldwide tide of sympathy for the Jewish people, and making the Jews themselves utterly determined that they would not allow anything even vaguely similar to occur ever again. Both militated in favour of the Jewish 'homeland' becoming a fully-fledged state. Finally, there was the new global importance, power and influence of the United States of America. US input into the Palestine question was bound to be significant, although President Truman had to play a double game. For strategic and commercial reasons – essentially keeping out the Soviets and maintaining an uninterrupted supply of oil – the administration favoured a pro-Arab stance. American public opinion, however, was fiercely pro-Jewish. Truman had to tread carefully.

Attack on Britain

Foreign Secretary Bevin soon saw that allowing unlimited Jewish immigration into Palestine would only make Britain's task there ever harder, so he abandoned his party's traditional pro-Jewish stance and imposed a monthly ceiling of 1,500 Jewish immigrants into Palestine. The move infuriated Palestine's Jewish community. While an estimated 250,000 Jews hung about in wretched camps around Europe waiting to be taken to the 'homeland', the Royal Navy was barring shipload after shipload of immigrants from entry. Some – including those on board the famous *Exodus* – were returned to Europe, others were interned in makeshift camps in Cyprus.

The Jewish community, headed by Jewish Agency President David Ben-Gurion, responded by organizing illicit immigration and waging a ferocious campaign against the British. Its aim was to make their presence in Palestine so unpleasant that they would withdraw and leave the Jews to set up a homeland on their own. The Haganah worked more or less closely with the Irgun and Lehi guerrilla organizations to target anything British. Railways were cut and bombs damaged airfields, bridges, oil refineries, radar installations, police stations and a host of other symbols of imperial occupation.

The two most dramatic attacks were dynamiting Acre jail to free prisoners and bombing the British security headquarters in the King David Hotel, Jerusalem (22 July 1946). The 91 people killed included British, Jews and Arabs. By the end of 1946, Jewish violence had claimed 373 lives, 300 of whom were civilians. When, later in the century, Jews found themselves the targets of similar outrages perpetrated by Arabs, the cruel irony of the situation was plain to all. Back in 1945–6, though, Arab violence was largely confined to attacks on fellow Arabs who sold land to the Jews.

Enter the UN

Vain proposals

By the end of 1945 President Truman was seeking popular approval in the US by asking Britain to accept at least 150,000 more Jewish immigrants into Palestine. Although the imposition of martial law and other strict security measures were failing to halt the Jewish terror campaign, Britain refused to allow more immigrants until the Haganah called a ceasefire. It would not. Deadlock. When an Anglo-American committee of investigation also called for the immigration limit to be raised, the British government again refused, and the Arab community responded with a strike.

Another set of Anglo-American proposals, this time suggesting a federal Palestine based on provinces, was rejected by Jews and Arabs. By now the Grand Mufti was back in Egypt and trying, with other members of his family, to put together some sort of unity among the fragmented Palestinian Arabs through an Arab Higher Executive. He met with little success. Finally, worn down by Jewish guerrilla violence, international condemnation and the intransigence of both sides, Britain invited the newly-established United Nations to investigate the Palestinian problem and come up with a solution.

The United Nations Special Committee on Palestine (UNSCOP) produced majority and minority reports in September 1947. The former proposed a partition of Palestine not unlike that put forward by the Peel Commission: separate Jewish and Arab states, united in an economic union, with Jerusalem and its environs under international control. The latter resurrected the federation idea. The USA, the USSR and the Jewish Agency accepted the partition plan, the Palestinians, the Arab League and Britain rejected it. Shortly afterwards, the British government announced that, whatever happened, it was pulling out of Palestine in six months' time. In November, after intensive lobbying from the US, the partition plan was put before the UN General Assembly where 33 nations voted in favour, and ten against. Tragically, UN intervention had polarized the position in Palestine rather than placated it. The vote was for war.

Two states and none

Ben-Gurion and the majority of the Jewish leadership in Palestine did not believe for one second that the UNSCOP majority plan was the last word on the subject. They accepted it because it offered them a UN-sanctioned state as a launching pad for further expansion. The plan was just as unacceptable to the Arabs as the other suggested partitions had been because it took away, without consent, land that was rightfully and legally theirs.

The situation was this: In 1947 the Jews owned some seven per cent of the land of Palestine, including much of the best farmland. They had bought it in Ottoman times, picked it up after the Ottoman withdrawal or purchased it from Arab landlords, many of whom had been absentee. The Jewish population was around 600,000, the Arab about 1.2 million. Yet the UNSCOP proposal was for the new Jewish state ('Israel') to have 56.5 per cent of the land of Palestine and the Arab state a mere 43.5 per cent. Some 80 per cent of the land of the new Jewish state would be Arab-owned, including over 85 per cent of the Arabs' orange groves.

Another sticking point over the UN plan was Jerusalem. The committee decided that since neither Jew nor Muslim would surrender control over so holy a city, it should be placed under permanent international trusteeship. A quick glance at the map (see Figure 4) shows why such a proposal appeared to favour Muslims over Jews – the city was envisaged as an enclave within the Arab state. In other words, in order to visit the Wailing Walls and other holy sites, Jews would have to pass through or over hostile territory.

The same map reveals another flaw with the UNSCOP plan: the frontiers. The proposed Jewish state was in three scarcely-linked blocks. The northernmost, around the Sea of Galilee, had good access to fresh water; the central part contained most of the fertile coastal plain; the southern, largest sector was largely made up of the Negev Desert. The three were linked by the narrowest of corridors. Similarly, the Arab state was in three, although its tri-partite nature and the infertility of the terrain, which included most of the hilly West Bank, rendered it too unviable as a state.

Practicalities aside, the Arabs repeated time and again that they had more fundamental objections to the plan. First, it denied the principle of self-determination; second, the two-state solution required them to give up something they *had* while the Jews

figure 4 the UN's proposed two-state solution, 1947

were required to give up only something they *wanted*. Whether or not the partition plan was a gesture of repentance by the powers that had failed to protect the Jews against the Nazis, in Arab eyes it was simply unacceptable.

War

Civil strife

The war that followed the vote in the United Nations' General Assembly was waged in two parts. The first (November 1947 to May 1948) was an unofficial conflict, fought between Jews and Arabs while Palestine was still technically under British control. The second (May 1948 to July 1949) was an international confrontation between the new state of Israel and its Arab enemies. During the first it looked for a time as if the Arabs might triumph; the second saw the State of Israel emerge as a fixture on the world map and the embryonic nation of Palestinian Arabs scattered and all but destroyed. Small wonder, then, that the Jews remember the struggle as the War of Independence while to Palestinian Arabs is it simply *Al Nakba*, the Disaster.

Having fixed 15 May 1948 as the date when its forces would be withdrawn from Palestine, Britain was prepared to do no more than protect its own interests in order to keep casualties and economic loss to a minimum. Into the vacuum thus created stepped Jewish and Arab militias. The Zionist campaign was predominantly masterminded by the Jewish Agency, headed by Ben-Gurion, which controlled the disciplined and relatively experienced Haganah forces numbering at least 40,000. The Irgun, Stern Gang and other guerrilla groups worked more or less together with the official forces.

The internal and external Arab forces were ill-coordinated but, initially at least, relatively numerous and determined. The Arab League paid for an Arab Liberation Army and gave command to Fawzi al-Din al-Qa'wuqji, a charismatic but militarily suspect veteran of the 1936 Arab Revolt. Although he eventually commanded about 6,000 men, he had little respect for local Arab fighters, refused their requests for assistance and even cooperated with the Haganah against fellow Arabs. Meanwhile, the Grand Mufti had moved to Lebanon to be nearer the action and had given his heroic nephew, Abdul Qadir al-Husseini, command of a volunteer Holy War Army. Some 2,000 Muslim Brotherhood volunteers also moved into Palestine from Egypt These forces were supplemented by local village guards and other warbands assembled to defend lives and property against Jewish depredations.

Plan D

The fighting was sporadic but bitter and both sides perpetrated horrific war crimes. The Jews' weakest point was Jerusalem, where thousands of co-religionists were besieged by al-Husseini's men. Elsewhere the Haganah and Irgun implemented a policy of 'aggressive defence', clearing Arabs from areas allocated to the State of Israel. This ruthless and often cruel process was what has come to be called 'ethnic cleansing'. Starting along the coastal plain and later moving north, the tactic was either to force Arab families to pack up their belongings and leave or to scare them into doing so by perpetrating some atrocity and then deliberately exaggerating its scale. As the deaths and casualties on either side rose into the thousands, neither a UN arms embargo nor repeated calls for a truce from the US managed to stop the bloodshed.

By the late spring of 1948, the under-equipped Jewish forces were under serious pressure. At this stage Ben-Gurion decided to launch Plan D, a strategy that had been devised for when the British eventually pulled out. It involved not only seizing territory assigned to Israel by the UN but also moving into areas allocated to the Arab state. The first target was to open up a corridor through Arab lands to Jerusalem.

It was during this campaign that Jewish guerrilla forces sacked the Arab village of Deir Yassin, which had made a non-belligerency pact with local Jews. After the withdrawal of Palestinian Arab irregulars from the area, the Irgun under Menachem Begin and the Lehi under Yitzhak Shamir, moved in and slaughtered large numbers of men, women and children. Original reports spoke of over 250 killed, although modern research has suggested that the true figure was less than half that number.

At the time, it was in the interests of both sides to exaggerate the scale of the outrage: Jews did so to terrify other Arab villagers into fleeing lest they be the next victims, and Arabs did so in order to persuade the world that they were innocent victims of Jewish barbarity. The importance of the Deir Yassin massacre, therefore, was not so much in what happened – there were similar tit-for-tat outrages going on all over Palestine – as in its effect as propaganda. By the end of April 1948, just as Ben-Gurion and his provisional government in Tel Aviv had planned, perhaps 200,000 Arabs had fled their homes in areas coveted by the Jews (see Figure 5).

figure 5 the Arab–Israeli War, 1948–9

Israel and war

The British finally pulled out of Palestine on 15 May 1948. The previous day, at 16:00 hours local time, Ben-Gurion's Zionist Provisional State Council declared the State of Israel to be in existence. It was immediately recognized by the US administration of President Truman and not long afterwards by the Soviet Union. This rare act of accord by the two rival superpowers was bad news for the Arab world and particularly distressing for the Palestinian Arabs. (Henceforth the latter will be called simply 'Palestinians' and their adversaries 'Israelis'.)

As expected, the Arab League condemned the Israeli announcement and shortly afterwards small armies from Transjordan, Egypt, Syria, Lebanon and Iraq, as well as token forces from elsewhere in the Arab world, began arriving in Palestine to crush the impostor. On the surface it looked like an impressive display of Arab unity and the Israelis were not slow to make the most of the David vs. Goliath image. The truth, however, was a great deal more complex.

Unity and disunity

Unfortunately for the Palestinians, few, if any Arab states were really interested in helping them. Three neighbouring countries – Egypt, Transjordan and Syria – all saw the chaos on their borders as an opportunity for territorial expansion of their own. Most startling had been secret meetings between Abdullah, King of the newly-independent Transjordan, and a Ukrainian-born, US-educated Zionist politician named Golda Meir.

Abdullah, having picked up his own kingdom through a stroke of British hard-nosed political chicanery, was nothing if not a realist. He dreamed of one day ruling a Greater Syria that united his own state with the Syrian one to the north and Palestinian territory to the west of the Jordan River. The last thing he wanted was a flourishing Arab Palestine and he shared the Israelis' detestation of Grand Mufti al-Husseini. Consequently, he had no problem reaching an agreement with the equally realistic Mrs Meir. In the event of full-scale war between Israel and the Palestinians, he should take over Palestinian territory on the West Bank of the Jordan and leave the Israelis to grab what they could of the rest. The status of Jerusalem was left open.

In an effort to tie the hands of a monarch they did not trust, the other warring Arab states appointed Transjordan's King Abdullah Command-in-Chief of the Arab forces. The military title was meaningless. The King produced no overall strategic plan and his allies refused him permission to ascertain precisely the state of their forces. These were not as sizeable as might have been expected, either. In mid-1948 it is estimated that the non-Palestinian Arabs managed to put about 23,000 troops into the field. The better trained Israel Defence Force (IDF), created by forcing the experienced Haganah, Irgun and smaller groups to amalgamate, then stood at around 35,000. This eventually rose to over 96,000, at least double that of the increased Arab armies. Particularly after the rearmament of the summer of 1948 (when weapons and ammunition of all kinds came in from Soviet-backed Czechoslovakia, France and private US sponsors), the IDF was better armed than the Arabs. It even secretly acquired three US Flying Fortress bombers with which it was able to attack Cairo.

Despite cultural differences between Jews originating from Europe (Ashkenazi) and those from Oriental lands (Sephardi), all Israelis knew that they were fighting for their very existence. This gave them a ruthless determination, sometimes known as the 'Holocaust syndrome'. Israelis had seen what had happened to the meek and conforming Jews who had trusted others – they had been exterminated. The 'fighting Jew' would never let this happen. Their toughness might make them feared – hated even – but it would keep them safe.

To the first generation of Israelis, the end justified the means – even if it meant attacking their own unarmed trucks in order to provoke further fighting with Egypt; even if it meant Haganah troops of future Prime Minister Yitzhak Rabin killing Irgun fighters who had rejected a unified command (another future prime minister, Menachem Begin, survived the attack); even if it meant extremist assassins commanded by yet another future prime minister, Yitzhak Shamir, killing the UN mediator because he seemed too pro-Arab; even if it meant Moche Dayan's forces terrorizing Arab villages outside Israel so that their inhabitants would learn to live in fear of their neighbours. All of these acts of desperate cruelty actually happened. Understandable but nevertheless abhorrent, they built the wall of hatred and mistrust that has yet to be broken.

Faced with overly Israeli unity, the motley Arab forces stood little chance. Apart from Egypt, their states were largely new creations. They were politically unstable (the Egyptian prime minister was assassinated in 1949 and the country had nine further changes of government over the next three years) and unable to cope with the strains of full-scale, long-distance warfare. Moreover, although some troops might have been inspired by feelings of Arab or Muslim unity, their leaders were not. The Grand Mufti, Palestine's nominal leader, did not get on with the Arab League. The aim of the Egyptians was to seize as much land as possible on the Sinai side of the Suez Canal. The Syrians wanted the fertile land in the Golan Heights and around the Sea of Galilee. The Saudis sent one paltry battalion; the Lebanese and Iraqis were there largely because it was politically less trouble than not being there. As we have seen, Commander-in-Chief Abdullah wanted only a limited campaign to take Palestinian land on the West Bank.

Palestine destroyed

Phase 1

During the first phase of the international war, which lasted until a UN-brokered truce on 11 June 1949, neither side gained the upper hand. Indeed, the Israelis found themselves hard-pressed on all fronts. They suffered from a lack of suitable aircraft, making do by rebuilding and adapting old World War II Messchershmits, Spitfires and spotter aircraft. Without either heavy armour or artillery at this stage, they were at a distinct disadvantage when confronting the better-equipped Egyptians in the south. In the streets and outlying districts of Jerusalem they also met a better-organized and armed fighting force in the British-trained Transjordanian Arab Legion.

The truce was arranged by Count Bernadotte, a UN official from Sweden. By agreeing to the month-long break in the fighting, the Arab forces lost the initiative and with it their chance of bringing the Israelis to their knees. The interval enabled the Ben-Gurion government and its high command to reorganize, re-train and reinforce. When the truce was broken on 8 July, the Israelis were able to go on the offensive to devastating effect.

Phase 2

Interrupted by a second truce between 18 July and 15 October, the war dragged on into 1949. In reality, by the previous autumn the Arab forces had lost the stomach for a fight and the conflict had become largely an Israeli mopping up operation. The acts of terror continued, one being the Israeli assassination of Count Bernadotte because he was thought to favour the Arabs. It was a tragic, unnecessary end for a man who had personally been responsible for saving many Jews from the Nazi Holocaust.

Far too late, in September 1948 the Grand Mufti and his Arab Higher Committee announced the formation of a Government of All Palestine with the Mufti as president, Jerusalem as its capital and Gaza as its seat of government. The empty gesture raised little enthusiasm and evoked even less worldwide response. Abdullah emphasized the point by setting up a larger rival Palestinian Congress in Aman. Meanwhile, Israeli forces crossed the Negev desert to Eilat, advanced into southern Lebanon, took the western half of Jerusalem and were only prevented by the intervention of the RAF from occupying the Sinai. By the spring of 1949 the Israelis possessed over three-quarters of the territory that the UN had allocated to the state of Palestine. The only exceptions were a Egyptian-held coastal strip around Gaza and the West Bank, which was now in Transjordanian hands.

Israel agreed truces with Egypt in February 1949, with Lebanon in March, Transjordan in April and Syria in July. Jerusalem was divided between an Israeli west and a Transjordanian east with a demilitarized zone between them. A similar zone ran between Israel and Syria in the north. Over time the truces matured into more durable armistices with every state except Iraq. No proper peace treaties were signed, however, implying that the fighting was by no means over. All that the war of 1948–9 had achieved, in fact, was the morphing of the 'Palestine question' into the equally insoluble 'Israeli–Palestinian conflict'.

In depth: David Ben-Gurion (1006 1973)

Arriving in Palestine in 1906, David Ben-Gurion (born David Gruen) went on to mastermind the formation of the State of Israel and become the country's first prime minister. For his many achievements he is revered in Israel as the 'Father of the Nation'.

During his youth in Russian-occupied Poland, the young Ben-Gurion became aware of European anti-Semitism and the exciting dreams of the early Zionists. Palestine was the obvious destination for a young man fired by Zionist enthusiasm, and before World War I he worked there as an agricultural labourer. In 1915, the Ottoman authorities threw him out on account of his cocktail of socialist and Zionist views. He travelled to the USA, where he campaigned vigorously for the Zionist cause before joining the British Army's Arab Legion. Re-settled in Palestine after the war, he devoted his considerable talents to the creation of an independent Jewish state out of the British mandate. To this end he founded and led the Histadrut, a union of Jewish workers in Palestine, and the socialist Israeli Workers' Party (Mapai), which he also headed. By 1935 he was the dominant figure in the international Zionist Executive and Palestine's Jewish Agency.

Originally hostile to Palestinian Arabs as the principal stumbling block on the path towards a Jewish state, from 1940 onwards Ben-Gurion was suspicious of the Arab-friendly British. After the end of World War II, while publicly condemning the extremes of groups like the Irgun, he pursued a policy of 'fighting Zionism' that led to Britain handing over the future of Palestine to the UN and the eventual foundation of Israel in May 1948. Taking the posts of prime minister and minister of defence, he insisted that all Jewish fighting forces amalgamate into the IDF. That done, he masterminded the campaign that saw Israel assimilate most of the land the UN had allocated to an Arab state.

After the War of Independence, the extraordinarily hard-working and enthusiastic Ben-Gurion continued his double role as prime minister and defence minister to 1953 and again from 1955 to 1963. His policies were straightforward and direct: strengthen Israel through immigration, irrigation, education, industrial development and, above all, hard manual work; and come down heavily on any Arab state that threatened the country's security. On retirement – hastened by suspicion of clandestine anti-Western operations in Egypt – he devoted his time to writing and research. He was recognized by the influential Time magazine as one of the leading figures of the twentieth century and Israel's major airport is named in his honour.

In depth: *Al Nakba*

Israelis like Prime Minister Golda Meir, wanting to justify what happened in 1948–9, claimed that a Palestinian nation had never existed before the later twentieth century. Until then, there had simply been Arabs living in an administrative district known as Palestine, without distinctive national religious, social, cultural or historical traditions.

Most historians now disagree with this thesis. A sense of Palestinian nationhood had been evolving since the early nineteenth century, originally in opposition to outside intervention. The British mandate, reintroducing the ancient concept of Palestine as a distinct entity and offering it future independence, considerably boosted nationalist sentiment. It was further enhanced by the 1936 Arab Revolt against the British and by the wishes of the Jews to break up Palestine or even fashion it as a Zionist state. Lack of leadership and a fragmented social set up prevented the Palestinians from realizing their ideal before *Al Nakba*, the Disaster, of 1948–9 set it back half a century and more.

The war that led to the creation of Israel saw the destruction of 360 Arab villages and 14 Arab towns. About 70 per cent of Palestinians (those people who might have expected to live in a UN-fashioned Palestinian Arab state) had become refugees. Some were forcibly evicted from their homes, others left because they feared what would happen to them if they did not. After the war, around 165,000 remained as a second-class minority within Israel. The number forced to become refugees was disputed. The Israelis said 520,000, the British between 600,000 and 760,000, and in 1949 the United Nations registered 726,000.

Whichever figure is correct, the scale of the exodus was staggering. A whole society was dispersed: men, women and children, healthy and infirm, rich and poor. Some families herded before them livestock they had been able to rescue. Others managed to get away with just a few household possessions, dragging them in carts or squeezing them into buses and lorries as they headed for the safety of the border and life in a makeshift camp. Over 200,000 crammed into the Gaza Strip, more than 300,000 ended up in the West Bank, perhaps 100,000 made it to Lebanon, another 100,000 to Syria and around the same number to Transjordan.

Scattered, temporarily housed in tents and rough shelters, without running water and proper sanitation, deprived of schools and medical facilities, the Palestinian nation came of age. It was an understandably bitter and angry people, too, and one that would not – could not – forget. In time, therefore, their Disaster became the whole world's.

05

battle lines

This chapter will cover:
- the new State of Israel
- the fate of the Palestinians after the war of 1948–9
- the impact of the war on the Middle East and beyond.

To most Jewish people living in the Middle East and elsewhere, the war of 1948–9 had been an outstanding success, almost a miracle. True, losses had been high. With 6,000 killed and 30,000 wounded – 4.6 per cent of its population – Israel's first war would be its costliest. But the outcome had been remarkable: the birth, survival and widespread acceptance of the State of Israel. The 'homeland' was no longer a dream, an aspiration or even a target – it was a living, tangible reality. Tragically, though, partly because of the way the state had been forged and partly because of the way it conducted itself during its first years of existence, this was by no means the end of the story. Rather, it was merely the close of a chapter – and those that followed were sadder, more harrowing and infinitely more complicated.

The winners...

Israel

Having absorbed 77 per cent of the UN's proposed Palestinian state, Israel was some 21 per cent larger than the country envisaged by the 1948 partition plan (see p. 48). Unlike that state, the new Israel had defensible frontiers – though not as defensible as some in the military would have liked. The population comprised 717,700 Jews (with Ashkenazi outnumbering Sephardi 6:1) and 165,000 Arabs (almost one fifth of whom were Christian).

Strict Zionists claimed that Israel was not a new country but simply the restoration of a very old one. That belief, together with British influence and the need for flexibility, persuaded the Israeli governing élite not to draw up a written constitution. Instead, the country's parliamentary system evolved through legislation, practice and executive orders.

The cabinet, invariably a coalition, was the lynch pin of Israeli government. The country's central democratic body was the Knesset, a 120-seat representative assembly. Normally elected every four years on a proportional basis, it ensured reasonably fair representation for Israel's Jewish and Arab populations, each of which was politically and religiously extremely diverse. All adult citizens had the vote and Hebrew and Arabic were recognized as official languages. Proportional representation produced a multiplicity of parties. The largest, Mapai (Labour – see p. 105), provided Israel with its first (David Ben-Gurion) and second (Moshe Sharett) prime ministers. Further left was the Mapam Party, while Herut inherited the right-wing mantle of the Irgun. The Knesset elected Chaim Weizmann to the largely honorary position of president.

Experience had taught the leaders of the Jewish community to temper Zionistic idealism with practical pragmatism. Thus, as there was no written constitution, so there was no Bill of Rights. The independent judicial system operated through municipal, religious and military courts inherited from the mandate. The law derived from Ottoman and British traditions, adapted by religion, precedent and legislation.

As one might expect in a country born in war, the military played a far larger part in Israeli life than in many Western states from which most of its traditions derived. Military service was compulsory for all non-Arabs and in matters of budget, planning, transport and foreign policy, the needs of the IDF and the security services generally had priority.

Ben-Gurion

David Ben-Gurion dominated Israeli politics for the first 15 years of the country's existence. As prime minister for all but two years during that period, he determined key policies that decided how the country saw itself, how it presented itself to the outside world and, most importantly, its relations with the people upon whom it had stolen such a decisive march – the Palestinians.

The key to Ben-Gurion's thinking was that Israel, surrounded by enemies and harbouring potentially dangerous minorities within, could not afford to relax its guard for one moment. Everything had to be geared to maintaining what had been won and, where possible, to strengthening it. Domestically his policy may be divided into four strands: (1) minimizing the internal Arab threat by relocating some of Israel's Arabs away from the borders and keeping others under military rule; (2) developing economic self-sufficiency; (3) building up the country's resources, especially its agriculture through irrigation; (4) encouraging as many Jews as possible from the worldwide community to return to the homeland.

The 1950 Law of Return, which granted citizenship to all immigrant Jews, was a key instrument in doubling Israel's population by 1952. Some of the new immigrants came from

Europe but a high proportion were refugees from Arab lands where, after the war of 1948, they found themselves shunned and even persecuted. As one might expect, immigration on such a vast scale produced problems. There was a serious shortage of housing (see below) and defining Jewishness was sometimes a tricky business. Moreover, most Sephardi Jews had been raised very differently from their European counterparts. They were usually less well educated and their attitudes were urban and socially conservative. In business, politics and administration, they found themselves occupying a sort of intermediate position between the Ashkenazi and Arabs, leading to political tensions.

Housing was a thorny issue, too. When the Knesset allowed the state to appropriate abandoned Palestinian property, thousands of empty houses were given to immigrants. Even so, there were not enough to go around. Sprawling shanty towns of makeshift shelters spread out around major cities and in 1951 there were still 100,000 Israelis living in tents. Most of these were recent Sephardi immigrants.

Self-sufficiency did not come easily. Israel had to cope with an Arab boycott (see p. 77) and at least one major irrigation scheme met with serious political objections (see p. 85). Even so, the armistice line of 1949 (see p. 56) was soon known as the 'Green Line' because the fertility on the Israeli side contrasted so starkly with the barren waste opposite. The economy also benefited from the substantial donations made to individuals and institutions by overseas Jewish groups, especially American. By 1952 Israel was also in receipt of hefty overseas aid. The most controversial donations came from West Germany: the right-wing Herut Party violently condemned them as 'blood money'.

...and the losers

Palestine

The war of 1948–9 erased the name 'Palestine' from maps printed outside Arab lands. The lion's share of what had been Palestine had been swallowed up by Israel. Around 40 per cent of the land it had absorbed (or stolen, depending on one's viewpoint) had only months previously been Arab-owned. In the north, a demilitarized zone separated Israel from Syria, which coveted half the Sea of Galilee and land nearby. As agreed with Israel before the war, Transjordan had occupied the adjacent part of Palestine known as the West Bank. A year after his armistice with Israel, King Abdullah held a dubious consultation in the West Bank before annexing it formally to his re-named Kingdom of Jordan. The move was accepted by Britain and the US, but rejected by Israel and all Arab states except Iraq. The city of Jerusalem remained divided between Israel and Jordan.

In the south-west, Palestine had been carved up by Israel and Egypt, the latter taking the Gaza Strip. The Egyptians also cast covetous eyes over the neighbouring Negev (see Figure 5). An Egyptian-backed attempt by Mufti Husseini (whose reputation stood even lower after the 1948–9 debacle) to form a sort of mini-Palestine in Gaza, came to nothing: the exiled and ageing cleric remained the putative ruler of a state that simply did not exist.

Palestinian diaspora

What of the Palestinian people themselves? Broadly speaking, they may be divided into three. Those left within Israel, those who had fled or emigrated to more distant lands, and those for whom home was now a refugee camp in the Gaza Strip, the West Bank, Jordan, Syria or Lebanon.

Many of the relatively small middle class of Palestinians – the teachers, doctors, better-off businessmen – managed to get away from the frontier areas and start new lives in cities elsewhere in the Arab world or even further afield. Kuwait became the largest community, hosting some 400,000 Palestinians by 1990. Quite large numbers found their way to the US, where the Palestinian diaspora grew to over 100,000. These better-educated and generally wealthier refugees were not always popular or well-treated in their new homes (hard-working immigrants rarely are) but at least they had a future. They had a past, too, which not all were prepared to forget: it was from middle-class exiles that a new Palestinian leadership would eventually emerge.

Israel's Palestinians

Around ten per cent of all Palestinian Arabs remained behind and eventually became citizens of Israel where they made up some 15 per cent of the population. Clustered in Galilee and between Jerusalem and the coast, theirs was a difficult existence on the margin of two communities. This is witnessed by the names by which they were known, the 'Arab citizens of Israel', 'Palestinian Israelis' and 'Israeli Arabs'.

For at least 20 years, Israel's Palestinians remained a shocked, leaderless, depressed and isolated minority. Families had become separated by the Green Line, which they might not cross. Their communities were subjected to military control, limiting the ability to assemble or travel without permission. During the fighting of 1948–9, many thousands had abandoned their original homesteads in search of safety and in most cases they were unable to return. Thus they became refugees within their own country. Even harder to bear, they were regarded with suspicion, even as traitors, by Arabs living elsewhere.

The position of Israel's Palestinians on the political margins is illustrated by the fact that only the Israeli Communist party accepted both Arab and Jewish members. No Arab became a member of the ruling coalition. Exemption from the draft meant they missed out on the privileges afforded to veterans. To political and social exclusion was added economic discrimination. Arabs were not allowed to form cooperatives and their settlements had less adequate water and electricity supplies than their Jewish neighbours. Not afforded sufficient building land, the crowded dwellings erected for their swelling population were often put up illegally and therefore under continual threat of demolition.

Hard though life was for Israel's Palestinians, their suffering was relative. Their standard of living might have been lower than that of most Israelis but it was still way above that of the refugees. The same can be said of the education they received. As a consequence, the third generation of Israeli Palestinians, while maintaining a distinct Arab identity, began to identify more closely with the state into which they had been born than with the land beyond the Green Line.

The camps

The Palestinian refugees, marooned beyond Israel's frontiers, were gathered together by relief and other agencies and settled in vast tented camps: four on the East Bank of the River Jordan, 19 on the West Bank; 15 in Lebanon; eight crammed into the Gaza Strip; nine in Syria (see Figure 6). Over time, some of the original, temporary camps were emptied and their occupants

figure 6 the main Palestinian refugee camps

moved on. Syria's Lattakia camp is a good example. Housing Palestinians originally from Jaffa and villages of northern Palestine, it was founded in 1955–6 on the edge of the Mediterranean town whose name it bears. Its occupants earned what they could from fishing, casual labour in the port and tourism.

Depending on their point of view, outsiders saw the camps as either a ring of shame or of dangerous hatred around the newly-fledged Israel. Almost 60 years later, with some exceptions and additions, they were still there: hotbeds of hatred, bitterness, prejudice, hopelessness and fantastic dreams – a nation in waiting. Over time it was this sense of being in limbo that the refugees found most debilitating. In just a few months they had fallen from being founder members of a new country to being merely stateless 'Arab refugees', at best pitied, at worst derided as unwanted intruders.

Dreams and despair

Generally those least able to help themselves ended up in the camps. They were the families without connections, without money, without education. Some were illiterate or semi-literate peasant farming folk, others were unskilled labourers and their dependents.

Where such refugees settled, and the conditions they met with, depended largely on where they had started from. Those who moved north, into Lebanon, probably fared best. From the six camps scattered around Beirut, the prospects of employment, much of it in industry, were quite good when Lebanon's economy boomed during the later 1950s and into the 1960s. Conditions were worst in the Gaza Strip, where the population density was highest, the facilities least and the chances of employment lowest (see p. 72). The situation within the Syrian and Jordanian camps was better than within the Gazan ones, but still deplorable.

The influx of huge numbers of refugees presented Jordan's King Abdullah with a problem. His native Jordanians were suddenly outnumbered by immigrants in the ratio 2:1, not something he had foreseen when making his pact with Israel (see pp. 53–4). The newcomers were generally better educated too, for although the mandate schools had not been wonderful, they were better than anything the King had provided for his subjects.

Abdullah responded by claiming to be the true leader of the Palestinians. This was in a sense true since he hoped to rule a Pan-Arab country that included his own state (incorporating the West Bank), Syria, Lebanon and perhaps even Iraq. The majority of the refugees inside Jordan were given Jordanian citizenship and their education was designed to raise them as Jordanians rather than Palestinians. To support this programme of Jordanization, Palestinian nationalist organizations and media were banned, as were all political parties. Although 25 per cent of Jordan's East Bank population lived in the camps, they provided not one member of the country's consultative parliament in the period 1950–65.

The 'Lost Garden of Palestine'

On the West Bank, attempts at Jordanization were less successful. The population here had risen from 400,000 to 700,000; the new arrivals being distributed fairly equally between towns, villages and camps. The strain on local services was immense and there was constant feuding between the original inhabitants and the refugees. The situation, like that in Gaza, was made worse by lack of leadership. The better off and educated Palestinians with marketable skills had not remained with the traumatized masses. The leadership drain did not stop, either: between 1950 and 1954 a further 100,000 West Bankers emigrated from the forlorn hillsides.

Dismayed and dispirited by their own weakness, for a time Palestinians took hope in Nasser's talk of reviving Arab nationalism (see p. 86) – the Arab nation would unite, drive out the imperialists and Zionists, and the people of Palestine would be free to return home. But nothing happened. Nasser, quite logically, put his own people's interests before others. When it came to executive decisions, so too did other regional heads of state. For all of them, 'Palestine for the Palestinians' was good rhetoric but bad policy.

Where did that leave the Palestinians, a people with no state and no leader? It left them with memories that merged with their dreams. Determined to cling on to their heritage, they assiduously preserved the names and customs of their former life. The homeland from which they were excluded became the 'Lost Garden of Palestine' to which one day, somehow they would return. Slowly, the men chatting in the streets of Nablus and the refugee women gathering in the markets or outside the tents began to realize a vital lesson. No one – not the Americans, not the Russians and not even their Arab brothers and sisters – was going to put themselves out to help the Palestinians. In the end, if they were to get back what they had lost, they had to do it themselves. To achieve their goal they had to be just as ruthless, just as single-minded as the Zionists had been.

Impact of war

Conflicting nationalisms

Instability had been a hallmark of the Middle East since the collapse of the Ottoman Empire and the subsequent attempt to set up nation states in the region. After World War II, three developments undermined regional stability still further. The first we have already examined: the 1948–9 conflict and the emergence of the non-Arab, non-Muslim State of Israel. The second was a conflict of nationalisms, and the third the Cold War.

Arabs had been talking of 'Arab nationalism' for over a century. Although it had proved a useful stick with which to beat a common enemy – the Ottomans, British, French or Jews – it had rarely produced much in the way of cooperation. This was obvious after the appearance of Israel and the failure of the Arab forces to work together to crush the new state. Part of the problem was that most Arab countries were themselves new, insecure creations. In trying to forge feelings of national unity, their rulers had to overcome the rival pull of tribalism and regionalism. In these circumstances, calls for Pan-Arabism or Islamic unity were useful only when serving national rather than trans-national ends.

Cold War

The Cold War was the long period of superpower confrontation in which the Soviet Union, the champion of communism, stood toe-to-toe with the USA, the champion of democratic capitalism. It is generally said to have begun with Winston Churchill's famous statement, delivered at Fulton, Missouri, in March 1946, that an 'iron curtain' had fallen across Europe. The rivalry between the two sides of the curtain – communist East and capitalist West – fed wars, coups and terrorism all over the globe.

Two issues brought the Cold War to the Middle East. One was the falling of a second iron curtain across the Palestine region, dividing Jews from Arabs. Although both the US and the USSR had initially been favourable towards Israel, it was perhaps inevitable that before long they would try to use the regional stand-off to increase their local influence. The second issue was oil. The Middle East's share of world oil production was rising daily and was already crucial to the US.

The USSR generally had to play second fiddle to the US in the region. Its strongest cards were a traditional hostility to imperialism, a willingness to provide arms (often through an intermediary such as Czechoslovakia) and the popular appeal of socialism/communism in a region where wealth and privilege were often concentrated in a few hands. However, the Soviet Union was officially an atheist state with a history of persecuting its own Muslims. Nor did it have a tradition of involvement in the Middle East. Consequently, the Soviets found it difficult to take the initiative in a part of the world where Britain and, increasingly, the US were well established. Both of these powers knew, however, that the communists needed only half an invitation to move in.

Presidents Truman (1945–53) and Eisenhower (1953–61) were obliged to play a tricky balancing act: backing democratic Israel, which was strongly supported by the American people as well as certain powerful business and financial interests, while at the same time keeping in with the Arabs, particularly those of the oil-producing states. This resulted in the international politics of the Middle East becoming a contest of bluff and counter-bluff, deceit and counter-deceit that not even the players themselves were able to control.

Syria

When, under international pressure, the French withdrew from Syria in 1946, they left it with a shiny new democratic and republican constitution. Nevertheless, given the country's complicated religious, social and economic diversity, stability was unlikely. For the US State Department the tipping point came with the failure of Syria's corrupt Sunni government to triumph in the war with Israel. There was now a possibility, the US believed, that this vital link in the oil pipeline route from the Gulf to the Mediterranean would fall to the communists.

To pre-empt such an event, in March 1949, the CIA engineered a coup by Colonel Husni al Zaim. The plan did not achieve the desired results. Zaim soon fell and Syria entered upon a prolonged period of instability marked by several further coups. The corruption and chaos bred a new movement in Syrian politics: the Arab Socialist Renaissance (or Baath) Party. Fiercely anti-Western, its manifesto claimed all boundaries between Arab peoples to be merely imperialist devices.

Not surprisingly, Baathist sentiment was intractably hostile to Israel. The demilitarized zone between the two countries was already a source of friction. In 1953, tension in the region rose further when Syria strongly objected to Israel drawing irrigation water from the River Jordan as it flowed through the demilitarized zone. With no progress on turning the 1949 armistice into a permanent settlement, there was every chance that at some future date Israel and Syria would find themselves at war again.

Lebanon

Parliamentary democracy fared slightly better in Lebanon. The delicately balanced Muslim–Christian constitutional arrangement survived the war with Israel, prompting the leadership to declare that Lebanon was not really an Arab country and had never wanted to go to war in the first place. A Syrian-backed coup attempt was foiled. Thereafter, despite an assassinated prime minister, a president removed by a general strike and the destabilizing presence of large numbers of Palestinian refugees, Lebanon's Western-inclined political system survived more or less intact.

Jordan

King Abdullah of Jordan – condemned by his fellow Arabs as 'the dog who sold Palestine to the Zionists' – was the neighbour Ben-Gurion's government found it easiest to deal with. Both were realists. Given this trait in his personality, it is surprising Abdullah risked visiting the Al-Aqsa mosque in Jordanian-occupied Jerusalem. Here, on 20 July 1951, a Palestinian assassin shot him dead, claiming the King had betrayed the Palestinians and the entire Arab nation.

Two years later, Abdullah's schizophrenic son was declared unfit to rule. The crown passed to his 18-year-old son, Hussein, who had been beside his grandfather at the time of his death and had himself narrowly escaped being killed. The crown was scarcely less dangerous. With turbulent Palestinians inside his borders and ambitious Israelis just the other side, the young, English-educated King would need every one of the political skills he had inherited from his grandfather if he were to survive.

Iraq

Defeat of its small force by the Israelis did not bring about an immediate change of regime in Iraq, the only combatant country not to agree an armistice after the 1948–9 war. Regent Abdullah, helped by rising oil revenues and the behind-the-scenes power of the army, maintained a ragged version of democracy during the minority of King Faisal II. The overthrow of two prime ministers by popular uprisings and a period of martial law were not good omens, however, and a lot of hopes were pinned on the young Faisal. Alas! When he came of age in 1953, the anticipated reforms and crackdown on corruption failed to materialize. As would soon become apparent, the King's lack of charisma and political instinct (handicaps at the best of times) in post-war Iraq were fatal.

Egypt

The shaky constitutional monarchy that Britain had handed down to Egypt was disastrously undermined by the extraordinary figure of King Farouk, a bloated playboy monarch who dabbled in politics with dangerous ineptitude. His corrupt and inefficient government handled the conflict with Israel badly. It even scored a spectacular own goal when, in the middle of the war, an attempt to suppress the increasingly popular Muslim Brotherhood had led to the assassination of the prime minister and the subsequent killing of the Brotherhood's leader by government agents.

As well as disliking their own government and wanting revenge on Israel, Egyptians also harboured a strong dislike of the continued British presence in their country. Dating from a pre-war treaty, in the Suez Canal Zone Britain maintained and defended ten airfields and two naval dockyards. By the early 1950s, guerrilla attacks on these positions had become commonplace, provoking fierce retaliatory raids by the British. Egypt, the most populous and potentially most influential state in the Middle East, was ripe for revolution.

Farouk's fantasy reign ended with a near bloodless coup in July 1952. It was conducted, perhaps with CIA help, by a group of army personnel calling themselves the Free Officers. They were led by Colonel Gamal Abdul Nasser, a 32-year-old veteran of the Israeli war. For the time being, Nasser allowed attention to be focused on the higher-ranking General Mohammed Naguib, who became president of the Republic of Egypt.

Chaired by Nasser, a Revolutionary Command Council banned political parties, disbanded parliament and began reforming the country's grossly unequal system of landholding. Despite the new regime's undemocratic and socialist inclinations and its talk of uniting all Arabs into a single nation, several Western governments, including the US, gave it a qualified welcome. Israel was more sceptical, however, and it was not long before the US was coming round to a similar point of view.

In depth: Gaza Strip

Gaza had been the poorest district in the Palestinian mandate. The fighting of 1948–9 left the eastern section, the Negev, in Israeli hands and a tiny western section, the Gaza Strip, under Egyptian control. Almost overnight, this wretched parcel of land, some 45 kilometres long and eight kilometres wide, had become one the most densely populated and poorest areas in the world.

Around 80 per cent of Gaza's population lived in eight refugee camps hastily organized by the United Nations. Water was always scarce and electricity, where available, was unreliable. The sanitation often beggared belief. In these conditions, without sufficient arable land or irrigation, the traditional agricultural economy of orange groves and grain collapsed. There was no industry to replace it. The people of Gaza, whose average income was estimated to be around $80 US a year (£50), were almost totally dependent upon handouts of food and money from relief agencies. Only in the later 1950s, as trade opened up with Eastern Europe and better-off Egyptians used Gazan smugglers to by-pass Nasser's high tax regime, did the Strip's economy pick up somewhat.

The Gaza refugees lived in a political limbo. Unlike the West Bank, where Palestinian Arabs were offered Jordanian citizenship, Gazans were not invited to become Egyptians. Like those it replaced, the Nasser government feared an influx of poverty-stricken, revenge-seeking Palestinians and made it very difficult for Gazans even to visit Egypt. The only exceptions were small numbers of students gaining places at Egyptian universities. Within Gaza, political and other potentially inflammatory organizations were not permitted and the bands of *fedayeen* (meaning 'those prepared to sacrifice themselves') sent on raids into Israel were under strict Egyptian control (see p. 78).

Unwanted, stateless, poverty-stricken and traumatized, the Palestinians of the overcrowded Gaza Strip developed a unique camp society of their own. It was a curious mix of cold realism, despair and romantic yearning for a lost Palestinian paradise. Traditional tribal and extended family structures competed with new ones based around gangs and successful small-scale entrepreneurs. The soaring birth rate made the overpopulation rapidly worse. Where possible, those with skills moved out. They left behind a society shorn of educated leaders, where bickering and petty rivalries marred everyday life, and where cross-border and internecine violence was never far away.

The children and grandchildren raised in these hopeless circumstances are those who periodically burst upon our TV screens: given their tragic, desperate heritage, it is no wonder their lives are so torn by bloodshed and strife.

In depth: UNRWA

During the ethnic cleansing of Palestinians from Israel in 1948–9, streams of desperate, destitute refugees fled abroad. Some found their way into villages and towns, but the majority – several hundred thousand men, women and children – had nowhere to stay. Initially they sheltered as best they could, using such materials as they had brought with them or found – literally – lying around. Their suffering was immense and hundreds died.

Local individuals and services laboured selflessly to help. Before long they were being assisted by larger international agencies such as the Red Cross and Red Crescent. However, the scale of the problem demanded something special. Consequently, in December 1949, the United Nations General Assembly voted to set up UNRWA, the United Nations Relief and Works Agency for Palestine Refugees in the Near East. It began work the following May.

The first task of the Agency was to see those in its care given adequate shelter. At first this was mainly tents. By the mid-1950s, these were gradually being replaced by more substantial shelters of block and corrugated iron, large numbers of which remain in service today. Food and water were brought in daily. Communal standpipes and drains eventually followed, and shops and regular distribution centres were established. The larger roads were paved. Where possible the work was done, and still is, by members of the camps themselves. Payment was often in food.

In 1950, the medical situation was dire, with high infant mortality, widespread malnutrition and frequent deaths from communicable diseases like malaria, gastroenteritis and TB. Years of special diets, immunization and health education eventually brought the situation under control. Even then, adequate sanitation was still scarce.

UNRWA's education plan was its great triumph, providing the refugees with the most comprehensive primary education system in the Middle East. Girls, in particular, benefited. The programme's aim was to enable refugee children to find jobs and so end their families' cycle of deprivation. Sometimes this happened but despite UNRWA's efforts there are twice as many Palestinian refugees today as there were in 1950. Critics say that UNRWA is largely to blame for this. Its relief, they argue, has acted like a drug. By giving immediate respite without tackling the root causes of the malaise, it had produced a dependency culture that was difficult to quit.

06

the second round and its aftermath

This chapter will cover:
- border incidents between Palestinians and Israelis
- the Anglo–French–Israeli alliance and the Suez war, 1956
- Israel after the Suez war
- growing instability in the Arab world.

Israel and its neighbours

Security before peace

In 1948, as Israel was beginning its international war, the rest of the world was starting to recover from its second global conflict in 30 years. This had been caused partly by a failure of the victors of World War I. After defeating Germany and her allies, Britain and France had acted without either generosity or understanding. The legacy of humiliation and bitterness thus created had helped prepare the ground for Nazism and the outbreak in 1939 of a new and even more terrible European war. It is tragically ironic that this lesson – the need for magnanimity in victory – was lost on those who had suffered most as a consequence, the Jews.

Having won a startling and comprehensive victory by the middle of 1949, Israel failed to cement its position by reaching an accommodation with those it had overcome. Prime Minister Ben-Gurion's position was straightforward: after their embarrassing defeat in 1948–9, no Arab government would accept peaceful coexistence with Israel. The new state therefore was obliged to adopt a policy of 'aggressive defence' – responding to any threat, however small, with overwhelming retaliation and, if necessary, launching pre-emptive strikes. The policy persists to the present day, as those familiar with the news from Israel–Palestine will recognize.

Ben-Gurion also insisted that there was absolutely no question that Palestinian refugees, whatever their reasons for leaving, could be allowed back into Israel. Although by joining the United Nations in 1949 Israel had theoretically accepted a UN resolution insisting on the right of Palestinian return, Ben-Gurion had no intention of ever complying. He saw the refugees as an Arab problem, not an Israeli one: permitting their return would simply admit a gigantic and probably fatal fifth column.

Hawks and doves

To an outsider Ben-Gurion's stance might seem extreme, almost paranoid. That would be to ignore what he and like-minded Zionists saw as the bitter lessons of history. They argued that for almost 2,000 years, in much of the Middle East and Europe, the Jews had been a despised and persecuted race. This had culminated in the Nazis' deliberate attempt to wipe them out. Yet thanks to their remarkable resilience, intelligence, determination and, some believed, the protecting hand of God, they had survived and remained true to the ancient Jewish heritage.

Now at last, the hawks' argument ran, the Jews had a country of their own, a safe and secure haven where they would be free from persecution. It would be wicked folly to do anything, anything at all, that might threaten this new-found security. As the Arabs found at the barren Lausanne Peace Conference (1949), if there was to be lasting peace between Israel and her neighbours, it would be on Israel's terms. Until that time, it would wait, impervious behind its military superiority and continue to respond to any threat, real or perceived, with merciless force.

Not all Israelis signed up to the grim Ben-Gurion doctrine. Foremost among those who took a less hawkish line was the urbane, Ukrainian-born Moshe Sharett. One of the founders of Tel Aviv, the intellectual Sharett served as Israel's foreign minister in 1948–56. He played a key role in the armistices of 1949, in getting Israel accepted by the UN and in establishing his country's diplomatic network of embassies and consulates. Although accepting the prime importance of security, he believed that in the long term it could come only by reaching some permanent agreement with Israel's neighbours. This might at some future stage involve a land-for-peace deal.

The two positions – Ben-Gurion and Sharett, hawk and dove – have remained at the heart of Israeli politics from the moment of independence to the present day. Both are understandable. Yet neither addresses the view held by hundreds of thousands of Palestinians: that Israel was a state created on their stolen land.

Incursion and retaliation

The hostile rhetoric of Israel's Arab neighbours was not matched by significant military action. Evidence suggests that for several years Arab governments did not encourage commando-style raids on Israel. Their most successful measure was an economic boycott that included not just Israeli goods but those of companies trading with Israel. As oil wealth and population growth made the Middle East an increasingly important market for Western manufacturers, so the boycott came to bite deeper. A company like Land Rover, for example, because it traded with Israel, found itself excluded from the extremely lucrative Middle Eastern 4×4 market.

Only ten per cent of cross-border 'infiltrations' into Israel during 1950–5 were by military bands and they instigated only 25 major incidents. The bulk of the early border troubles were heart-breaking cases of desperate Palestinians sneaking back to collect possessions, harvest crops or even just set eyes on the homesteads they had lost. Sometimes the incursions were simply Bedouin tribesmen wandering across unmarked borders. Whatever the intruders' motives, the IDF responded with ferocity. Borders were mined and suspects shot on sight. The bodies of those slain were booby trapped to kill relatives coming to collect them. Over six years, perhaps as many as 5,000 Palestinians, most innocent civilians, were slain.

Fedayeen

Minor aggressive infiltration into Israel began in 1950. From then until 1956, the number of Israelis killed annually by Arab raiders rose from 19 to 54, and the wounded from 31 to 129. The first semi-military incursions were small-scale sorties by independent groups of Palestinian *fedayeen*. In 1953, with Egyptian backing, young Palestinians started launching regular, planned attacks on Israeli civilians. To counteract such activities and, if possible, wipe out these 'terrorists', the IDF set up Unit 101 under the ruthless Major Ariel Sharon. Opinion is divided over Unit 101's action. Critics say it provoked Palestinian anger and increased the chances of further attacks; defenders credit it with keeping Israel safer than it would otherwise have been. No one denies that its tactics were extremely fierce.

Within weeks of its creation, the non-uniformed Unit 101 was responsible for two incidents that the Palestinians were swift to label 'massacres'. The first occurred when Israeli forces, supposedly targeting an Egyptian *fedayeen* coordinator, were discovered inside the al-Bureij refugee camp in the Gaza Strip and fought their way out. Some 50 Palestinian civilians died. Two months later, Unit 101 responded to the *fedayeen* killing of an Israeli woman and her two children by destroying the Jordanian village of Qibya. Between 53 and 69 Palestinians were killed in the operation. Half of those who died were women and children.

Ben-Gurion lied that the atrocity had been carried out by local Jewish settlers provoked by Arab attacks. Few believed him and the US withheld aid worth $75 million. More significant for the future, the al-Bureij and Qibya attacks entered Palestinian

Suez

Nasser's honeymoon

The removal of the Egyptian monarchy by the Free Officers received a cautious welcome in the US (see pp. 71–2). Britain and Israel reserved judgement. Their fears were somewhat allayed when the Officers, despite a pledge to end colonialism, said they would not take sides in the East–West Cold War. The position was wisely pragmatic. Nasser, who assumed the presidency in 1954, needed all the economic and military aid he could lay his hands on. His stance was rewarded when the US and Britain offered $270 million to help Egypt build a high dam at Aswan to control the waters of the Nile.

Anglo-Egyptian talks on other matters went well, too. Britain agreed to give Sudan full independence and to withdraw from its bases in the Suez Canal zone by 1956, retaining the right to return if the zone were attacked by a third party. The deals brought howls of protest from the Muslim Brotherhood, Islamic fundamentalists who wanted union between Egypt and Sudan and Britain's immediate withdrawal from all Egyptian soil. When the Brotherhood sponsored an attempt on Nasser's life, he outlawed the movement and rounded up as many of its leaders as he could.

The Baghdad Pact

Meanwhile, with US backing, Britain was attempting to put together a NATO-style anti-communist alliance in the Middle East. Emerging in 1954, it was known as the Baghdad Pact. The first states to agree to work together against 'Soviet expansionism' were Turkey and Iraq, joined later by Britain, Iran and Pakistan. The key to the Pact's success, however, was getting Egypt on side.

To Britain's intense irritation, Nasser would have none of it. The Pact, he warned, was a 'festering crime' and an insult to the Arab nation. Egypt would not join. Moreover, he put pressure on Jordan not to sign up. It's important to remember that because of its size, population and history, Egypt was already the most influential Middle Eastern state. Nasser's flamboyant pronouncements on Arab unity and ending Western interference in the region enhanced this position.

Arms for sale

Size, population and rhetoric were all very well but, as Arabs recognized only too clearly after 1948–9, they needed to be supported by military force. Here Nasser had a problem. There was no difficulty with personnel – what he lacked were modern armaments in the form of tanks, artillery and aircraft. Britain and the US had provided him with some but their policy of balancing Israel's forces with those of its enemies meant he had far fewer than he wanted. Early in 1955, Israel proved his point for him. Responding to the killing of an Israeli cyclist by a Egyptian intelligence-gathering mission, the IDF launched a massive raid on Gaza that left 38 Egyptian soldiers dead.

Within weeks, prompted by a meeting with officials from communist China, Nasser had gone behind the US's back and struck a deal with the Soviet Union. In return for $300 million worth of cotton, the Soviets, using Czechoslovakia as an intermediary, would re-arm Egypt with 100 self-propelled guns, 200 armoured personnel carriers, 300 tanks, 200 MIG, 15 fighters and 50 bombers. Such a formidable battery of firepower would make Nasser a real force in the region and seriously threaten Israel's ability to defend itself in any future conflict.

The Soviets were not concerned that arming Egypt might harm Israel as their brief friendship with the Jewish homeland had already faded. By the mid-1950s they were much more interested in Syria, where their influence was growing markedly. Meanwhile, the Syrians' relations with Israel had deteriorated to the point of heavy border fighting.

Nasser, Israel and their allies

Egypt, the USSR's latest Middle East protégé, was also going through a difficult time in its relations with Israel. Even before the bloody Gaza raid (above), the Israeli secret services had been exposed as an international menace when an attempt to implicate Egypt in anti-Western terrorism – the Lavon affair – was badly bungled. In September 1955, Nasser raised the temperature several degrees by closing the Strait of Tiran, cutting access to the Red Sea from Israel's southern port of Eilat. Less than a year later, he made an even more dramatic gesture: he nationalized the Suez Canal.

The Canal was a vital international waterway. In the pre-supertanker age, two-thirds of Europe's oil, including one-third of Britain's, passed through it. It also provided Britain and France, major shareholders, with useful revenue. Nasser's offer of compensation was unacceptable because of the one-sided way he had acted and because neither of the European powers wanted such a key strategic link in the hands of someone they did not trust. Talks aimed at reaching a compromise got nowhere, nor did efforts by the French, British and Israeli secret services to eliminate Nasser.

Franco-Israeli cooperation was already an established fact. Paris detested Nasser for the support he was giving to the FLN independence fighters in the French colony of Algeria. France had supplied Israel with the technology to build a nuclear power plant, and therefore possibly a nuclear bomb. The French had also become Israel's major arms supplier, providing sophisticated Mystère jets and tanks in larger quantities than was announced officially. It was no great surprise, therefore, to find Israel and France plotting together against Egypt.

A combined Anglo-Israeli operation was much more of a surprise. It was, after all, only eight years since Jewish gangs had been killing British soldiers and civil servants in the mandate territory, and Britain's traditional friendships were with their ex-colonies and protectorates in the Arab world. Nevertheless, Nasser's opposition to the Baghdad Pact and high-handed action regarding the Canal had so angered Prime Minister Anthony Eden that he was prepared to risk his career to bring down the man he now termed 'the Muslim Mussolini'.

The secret plan was as simple as it was crude. Using recent *fedayeen* incursions as an excuse, the IDF would drive across the Sinai to the Suez Canal. Britain and France, pretending to act as mediators, would demand that Egypt and Israel withdraw their forces from the war zone. When Nasser refused to remove Egyptian troops from Egyptian territory – as he surely would – the Europeans would invade, Nasser would fall... and all would be well with the world once more.

The Suez campaign

The first part of the coalition plan went like clockwork. Israel's one-eyed Chief of Staff, Moshe Dayan, eager to get to grips with Egypt before their Soviet rearmament was complete, swept into Gaza and the Sinai on 29 October 1956. Within a week the IDF was at the Canal. When Nasser rejected the Anglo-French ultimatum, European fighter-bombers smashed Egyptian military installations and destroyed almost all its air force's new hardware. The Canal was blocked accidentally by a bombed ship and deliberately by concrete-filled Egyptian hulks. British and French marine and airborne troops landed nearby – and there the stop-Nasser campaign fell apart.

To begin with it had been poorly planned. Neither Britain nor France had consulted with potential supporters, nor had they got the media on side with careful briefing. The time that elapsed between the air bombardment and invasion had been too long, allowing public opinion to turn against the venture before it had properly begun. A blocked Suez Canal necessitated fuel rationing in Britain, which was already close to bankruptcy. The situation worsened when Syria, hearing that Iraq had given the attack a tentative welcome, cut the pipeline that conveyed Iraqi oil to the Mediterranean.

Far more serious than all this was the response of the superpowers. The Soviets threatened missile attacks on Israel, France and Britain unless the fighting stopped immediately. US President Eisenhower was not only furious at his allies' lack of consultation, but he was simultaneously in the middle of conducting an election campaign on a peace manifesto and trying to handle the crisis caused by the Soviet invasion of Hungary. He absolutely refused to toe the anti-Egyptian line. Israel dared not go against so powerful a paymaster, while Britain had neither the heart nor strength to countermand the leader of the West. Therefore, when the US took the matter to the UN and an immediate ceasefire was demanded, Israel and Britain obliged. This forced France to do the same.

Anglo-French forces were home by Christmas 1956. The Israelis lingered longer, refusing to give back their conquests until they had received assurances about open seaways, *fedayeen* raids and a UN peace-keeping force (UNEF) in Sinai. When these were given, they too went home. President Nasser, having outfaced two major imperial powers and kept Sinai and his nationalized Canal, was the undisputed hero of the Arab world.

Israel after Suez

Ill at ease

The Suez War changed for ever the way Israel was seen in the world. Despite its small size, it was now perceived in the West as an important power rather than simply a collection of valiant homesteaders. Outbreaks of violent behaviour had damaged its reputation, too. In April 1956, an artillery bombardment of Gaza City had left 59 dead. Just before the fighting broke out, at Kafr Qasim, 47 Israeli Palestinian agricultural workers were unnecessarily shot and killed for being out after a curfew about which they had not been told. It was estimated that during the war a further 1,000 Palestinians died, many of them civilians.

Israel was also less at ease with itself. Ben-Gurion, the elderly godfather of the state who by now could do no wrong in his people's eyes, remained prime minister until his resignation in 1963. The Suez setback had ended any lingering hopes he may once have had of Israel living at peace with its neighbours within secure frontiers. He considered further conquest unwise, however, urging instead that Israel remain ready to meet any threat the Arabs might pose. This involved massive military spending, which by the 1960s accounted for one-third of the country's Gross National Product (GNP).

Prosperity and change

Israel's economy continued to grow, the GNP doubling between 1952 and 1965. However, by 1963 inflation stood at 18 per cent and the trade deficit at over $500 million a year. Solvency was possible only with massive help from overseas. This came from the US, where first Democratic Senate leader L.B. Johnson and then Democratic President J.F. Kennedy looked more favourably on Israel than Eisenhower had done. The other major donor was West Germany, whose reparation payments met a quarter of Israel's budget.

Israeli society was changing too. Fresh waves of immigration and a high birth rate drove up the population to around 2.2 million by 1961. Not long after this, the Sephardi element outnumbered Ashkenazi for the first time. The distribution of power did not change, however, with Ashkenazi (the 'First Israel') dominating almost all important positions in politics, the military, academia and employment. The result was resentment from the Sephardi (the 'Second Israel') that in 1959 led to riots in the slum Wadi Salib suburb of Haifa.

Such incidents, coupled with the continued third-class status of Israeli Arabs and the dreadful misery experienced by their fellow Palestinians in the camps, led to painful heart-searching among more liberal-minded Israelis. Was there a possibility, some wondered, that the people who throughout history had suffered more than others from racial discrimination were now themselves guilty of the same injustice? Might the Ashkenazis' treatment of the Sephardis and the Jews' treatment of the Arabs be almost a form of apartheid?

The 11-year peace

Israel and the world

The Suez campaign bought Israel 11 years of peace and only a slightly shorter period free from cross-border *fedayeen* attacks. For the Palestinians who hoped of one day establishing their own state, it was a time of increasing hopelessness and desperation. Israel was untouchable, powerfully backed by France, Germany and, increasingly, the US. The USSR was prepared to make the appropriate anti-Israeli noises to attract Arab opinion but to take no action. The same, it seemed, applied to President Nasser.

With several Arab states moving to the left (see p. 86), the Western-backed Israel found itself isolated from the affections of much of the Third World. It used two tactics to get round this. The first was to act as a conduit for clandestine US support for anti-Soviet regimes, such as those in Uganda and Ethiopia. The second was to befriend states, like Iran and Turkey, that were hostile to Egypt. On occasion Israeli agents were even believed to have warned Nasser's enemies of assassination plots.

Dwight Eisenhower was US president until 1961, during which time he maintained his policy of not showing undue favour towards Israel over its Arab neighbours. In 1957, for example, in the 'Eisenhower Doctrine' he declared the US willing to support any Middle Eastern state exposed to the 'possibility of communist aggression'. During the two years the policy was current, the US strongly backed Jordan and Lebanon, states that had fought to prevent the emergence of Israel in 1948–9.

Eisenhower was less than impressed when his spy planes revealed that Israel's industrial complex at Dimona was not a textile factory, as advertised, but a secret plant using French technology for the development of a nuclear weapon. President JF Kennedy (1961–3), on the other hand, was prepared to value Israel as a key piece in his Cold War jigsaw. The Hawk surface-to-air missiles he sent to Israel, for example, were that country's first official arms provision from the US.

Palestinians sidelined

President Nasser's pro-Palestinian stance went no further than setting up a Voice of Palestine radio station, a Palestinian newspaper and getting the first Arab summit to create the Palestine Liberation Organization (PLO, 1964) and, two years later, the Palestine Liberation Army (PLA). Nasser selected Ahmad Shukayri to lead the PLO. The blustering lawyer from Acre did so with some proficiency, exerting his supremacy over the elderly but still active Haj Amin al-Husseini (see pp. 41–2). Nevertheless, Shukayri, the PLO and the PLA were all creatures of the Arab states that had set them up. It was their masters' will they were obliged to follow, not that of the Palestinian people.

The PLO had been established as a response to Israel's completion of the National Water Carrier scheme, a canal ('Beit Netopha') that took water from Lake Tiberias to the Negev Desert. Understandably, the development infuriated Syria and, on several occasions, disputes between the two countries over the use of water from the River Jordan flared into serious border conflicts. In 1963, Syria had actually called for all-out war with Israel; Nasser refused to go along with the idea.

Meanwhile, a far more significant event in the history of Israeli–Palestinian relations had taken place. Despairing of ever getting their Arab brethren to take meaningful action on their behalf, in 1959 a group of Palestinian exiles living in Kuwait had formed a nationalist organization of their own (see p. 87). Its name was Fatah and among its leaders was a man who more than any other would determine the nature of the Palestinian struggle: Yasser Arafat.

Times of troubles

The years that followed the Suez War saw growing political turmoil in the Arab world. This revolved around three basic issues: East–West alignment in the Cold War, Arab nationalism (were the Arabs one nation or many?) and the regional leadership of Egypt's President Nasser. These coincided in 1958 when, to the surprise of many, Egypt and Syria joined together to form the United Arab Republic (UAR).

Officially non-aligned in the Cold War, the UAR designated Egypt the 'Southern Province' and Syria the 'Northern Province'. The military were under Egyptian command and Nasser was the head of state. It was heralded, somewhat optimistically, as the first step towards full Arab unity. The move delighted most Palestinians, who believed that their best hope of being restored to their homeland lay in all Arabs uniting in a single state. Such hopes were soon dashed. The UAR collapsed in a couple of years when the Syrians decided they wanted to be a bit more than just a province.

Playing his political cards well, Nasser replaced US funding for the Aswan Dam with loans from the Soviet Union, which also leant money to extend Egypt's programme of nationalization. Further indications of the progress of the left in the Middle East came when the Iraqi monarchy was overthrown in a socialist-inclined army coup. Seriously worried that events in Iraq might spark coups in Jordan and Lebanon – both more or less pro-Western and reasonably favourably inclined towards Israel – the US sent troops into Lebanon and British paratroops went to shore up the authority of the young King Hussein of Jordan.

The interventions had the desired effect, although Hussein's position remained precarious. In 1960, for example, his prime minister was assassinated by Palestinians whom the King believed had Syrian backing. Only US pressure persuaded Hussein not to take matters into his own hands and invade his northern neighbour. More coups in Syria and Iraq saw the Baath Party come to power in both states. These were followed in 1963 by further talk of Arab unification, this time with the aim of bringing Iraq, Syria and Egypt together in a left-leaning federation similar to the defunct UAR. Once again Palestinian hopes were raised, only to be dashed when the talks broke down.

In conclusion, although the Suez War had not been followed by another international conflict, by 1963 the situation in the Middle East remained dangerously volatile. The Palestinians, exiled or under occupation, were bitter and frustrated. Iraq, Syria and Egypt had still not made peace with Israel, and their governments, many highly unstable, were prone to histrionic outbursts against the Jewish state. Jordan was less hostile but in no position to act unilaterally. In such circumstances, further armed confrontation was a distinct possibility. The only reasonable certainty was that, as on the two previous occasions, war would solve almost nothing.

In depth: Fatah

Founded in Kuwait in the late 1950s, Fatah's name, which means 'conquest', was a reverse acronym, in Arabic, of the Palestinian National Liberation Movement. Its founders, Yasser Arafat prominent among them, had become fed up with the failure of their fellow Arabs to help the Palestinians. Consequently, at first Fatah rejected the Palestine Liberation Organization (PLO) as just another empty gesture by the Arab states.

Fatah's claim was that by force of arms the Israelis had created a state that had no right to exist. Its aim was to destroy this state and replace it with a single, secular Arab–Jewish Palestine. Its platform, therefore, was both destructive and constructive. Unfortunately for its image, it was the former that attracted the most attention. However justified its cause, Fatah's violent tactics alienated a broad spectrum of world opinion. Attacks, bombings and hijackings carried out in the name of Fatah or one of its factions became a fact of life in the late 1960s and early 1970s (see pp. 91–4). The weaponry and explosives were communist-supplied and Syria was identified as the state most likely to shelter Fatah's fighters. The movement was less well received elsewhere in the Arab world. Its leadership was forcibly expelled from Jordan in 1970–1 and from Lebanon ten years later (see p. 114).

Arafat led the Fatah-dominated PLO from 1968, and during his lifetime the two organizations were often indistinguishable. From 1982 to 1993, for instance, while Arafat was taking refuge in Tunis, the Fatah and PLO leadership and administration were there with him. The Oslo Accords, which required the Palestinian leadership to renounce terrorism and led to the formation of the Palestinian Authority, obliged Fatah to consider more constructive policies and strategies (see pp. 178–82). It did not find the change easy for three reasons. First, it was essentially a guerrilla organization, attracting warrior types with little interest in administration and peaceful politics. Second, it was basically inefficient, even corrupt, and faction-ridden, unsuited to the task of government. Finally, Fatah was very much the creation of one man, Yasser Arafat. His energy and charisma held it together. When he died in 2004, Fatah found itself in trouble.

The Fatah veteran Mahmoud Abbas (see p. 209) was elected president of the Palestinian Authority in 2005, but in the 2006 elections to the Palestinian parliament, Fatah was trounced by the better-organized, more focused Hamas. There followed a period of trauma and strife marked by in-fighting, sometimes violent, between Fatah and Hamas, and between different factions within Fatah itself (see pp. 213–16).

In depth: President Gamal Abdul Nasser (1918–70)

Born the son of a village postmaster near Alexandria, Nasser showed a strong interest in politics from an early age. He graduated as an infantry officer in 1938 and was posted to the Sudan. Here his anti-colonial sentiments led him to plan an anti-British coup with Axis agents. Fortunately for him, the idea never got off the ground.

After World War II, Nasser worked at the Military Academy where he helped form the Free Officers Association, the group that engineered the 1952 coup (see pp. 71–2). Two years later, already the commanding figure on the all-powerful Revolutionary Command Council, he became head of state. He was made president in 1956 and held the position until his death. His offer of resignation after the humiliating 1967 war was rejected by popular acclaim (see pp. 96–101).

A number of developments helped secure Nasser's place in Egyptians' affections. He took much credit for the long-needed agricultural reform instituted after the fall of Farouk. His brave reaction to a (possibly staged) assassination attempt in 1954 gave him heroic status. British withdrawal from the Suez Canal zone, and the subsequent failure of Israel, France and Britain to hold on to the gains they had made in the 1956 war, enhanced Nasser's prestige still further and made him the darling of anti-imperialists everywhere.

Over the next 13 years, a series of misjudgements and policy failures ensured that Nasser's legacy was at best mixed, although his popular status remains undiminished. To maintain his position, he made Egypt a police state. This drew him into conflict with Muslim extremists, liberal democrats and the judiciary. Closer relations with the Soviet Union brought welcome funding, particularly for the Aswan Dam (completed 1970), but took the Egyptian economy down the path of inefficient nationalization and state control.

Nasser's political and military errors were even more harmful. The plan for a United Arab Republic got no further than a temporary and half-hearted union with Syria (see p. 86). Egypt's armed intervention in Yemen was a military and economic disaster. Worse still was the posturing that provoked Israel into launching the Six-Day War of 1967, with consequential humiliation, loss of life and destruction of Egypt's military (see p. 98). Finally, more than perhaps any other Arab leader, Nasser was prepared to use the Palestinian issue as a rallying cry while doing nothing practical to help the exiles. This merely fed Palestinian extremism and made any settlement of the Israeli–Palestinian situation even harder to achieve.

the Six-Day War

07

This chapter will cover:
- Palestinians in the mid-1960s
- the build-up to war, 1963–7
- the Six-Day War, 1967
- the aftermath of the Six-Day War.

Palestinian dead end

Pan-Arabism

As we saw in the last chapter, the Suez War did nothing to help the Palestinian cause. Those Palestinians living within Israel – whom the authorities registered as Arabs, never as Palestinians – remained largely at the lower end of the economic spectrum and outside the political process. The only party that would accept them was the Israeli Communist Party, known as Maki, and under its auspices they were able to express limited anti-Zionist Pan-Arab sentiments. This was hardly political power or influence, and not until the 1990s were the votes of Arab members of the Knesset used to sustain a government (Rabin's: see p. 171).

Outside Israel, the Palestinians of the Gaza Strip had returned to Egyptian governorship after a brief period of Israeli military rule. Life in the overcrowded enclave remained as forlorn as before. Developments on the Jordanian-controlled West Bank were somewhat more interesting. Here, despite the best efforts of the royal government to integrate them into Jordan, the Palestinians obstinately retained their separateness. The well-intentioned work of UNRWA in the camps helped maintain the occupants' refugee status. Elsewhere, despite the official suppression of all expressions of Palestinian nationalism, the more numerous, better-educated and generally more prosperous immigrants remained unwilling to shed their separate identity.

After the establishment of Israel, as noted above, most politically-minded Palestinians had looked to Pan-Arabism as their most likely saviour, arguing that there was no way Israel would be able to resist the demands of a single, mighty Arab state. Consequently, the majority had given Pan-Arabism priority over their own, Palestinian activism. The collapse of the Egypt–Syria–Iraq unification talks in 1963 shook this standpoint severely and the heavy Arab defeat in the Six-Day War would finish it off completely. Before then, however, a replacement had already emerged.

Fatah

At the time of its formation, Fatah was just one of numerous Palestinian nationalist groups. Under the energetic leadership of Yasser Arafat, ably backed by the superior organizational skills of Khalid al-Hassan and Khalil al-Wazir (aka Abu Jihad), it found a distinctive voice based upon three principles: (1) the Palestinians alone were responsible for their own fate; (2) the liberation of Palestine took priority over Arab unity; (3) the only effective tactic to achieve the desired goal was armed struggle.

If these seem somewhat naïve, we should remember that at this time revolution was in the air the world over. From Greece to China, Algeria to Kenya, Cuba and Vietnam, armed struggle was the watchword. Fatah saw itself as not just anti-Israeli but part of a global struggle against all forms of Western imperialism. For several years, therefore, Arafat had found himself swimming against the prevailing Pan-Arabist tide. Indeed, he might even have sunk had not President Nasser persuaded his fellow Arab heads of state to establish the PLO (see p. 85).

Assifa

The formation of the PLO and the Palestine Liberation Army (PLA) seriously worried the Fatah leadership. Both were clearly an attempt to bring the various Palestinian groups under centralized control and prevent them from provoking Israel into war before the surrounding Arab states – united or not – were confident of victory. Arafat boycotted the first PLO convention, held in East Jerusalem, which drew up a Palestine National Covenant condemning Israel as an illegal, colonialist and racist state. Attracted by the publicity and the prospect of joining a Palestinian army, Fatah supporters deserted for the PLA. To save their movement, Arafat and his colleagues urgently needed to do something to divert the spotlight of publicity away from the PLO and draw it on to themselves.

What happened next is a remarkable example of the unpredictability of history. Amid a flurry of advance publicity and attempts by the Arab authorities to prevent it happening, a Fatah battle group named Assifa (the Storm) sneaked into Israel from Lebanon and planted an explosive charge on the National Water Carrier canal. To give the saboteurs time to get away, they set the detonator's timer for an extra long delay – so long, in fact, that Israeli security forces found the device and defused it before it could go off. That should have been the end of that: total failure for Fatah. Instead, the Israelis gave the attack huge publicity in an attempt to show the world the sort of ruthless 'terrorists' they were up against. This had the unexpected effect of making Fatah overnight heroes in Palestinian eyes and

Arafat, who had been briefly arrested in Syria during the debacle, was suddenly a figure of international importance.

At last, after 15 years of waiting, the exiled Palestinians had a figure around whom they could rally, a fighter, a man prepared to die for the Palestinian cause. Nasser and other Arab leaders took fright and denied Assifa's existence, saying it was a creation of Western intelligence and the National Water Carrier incident had been dreamed up to push the Arabs into a war they did not want. Too late. Shukayri and his PLO had been eclipsed and thousands of young Palestinians flocked to join Assifa, which became Fatah's official military wing.

Over the next 18 months, Fatah launched a further 100 attacks into Israel, killing 11 and wounding 62. When Israel precipitated the Six-Day War, it listed the cross-border raids as a major provocation. Later, after the Israeli victory had confirmed the failure of Pan-Arabism, Arafat's Fatah was more than ready to replace it as the focus of Palestinian hopes.

The path to war

Hawks and doves

During the mid-1960s, opinions on both sides were divided over the advisability of another major Arab–Israeli conflict. Within Israel, Prime Minister Eshkol, who had replaced Ben-Gurion in 1963, was until the last minute wary of a war that would be costly, possibly even disastrous, and which was not strictly necessary for security purposes.

Other Israelis, including the ex-guerrilla fighters Menachem Begin and Moshe Dayan, a founder of the Haganah and chief of staff during the Suez War, were openly hawkish. Their message was simple: only by responding ferociously to Arab threats could Israel's security be guaranteed. Besides, the country would be easier to defend if its frontiers were expanded to include the water-rich Golan Heights on the border with Syria, the West Bank and the Sinai as far as the Suez Canal. Eshkol brought Begin and Dayan into his cabinet just before the outbreak of hostilities.

The Palestinians, with the Fatah faction to the fore, certainly wanted war. It was, after all, their only chance of getting their land back. The Lebanese and Jordanian leadership, on the other hand, were against further conflict. Syria, which experienced yet another change of regime in 1966, had earlier called for war over Israel's exploitation of Lake Galilee. The new government was strongly pro-Palestinian, too. However, it could fight only if supported by other Arab nations. Iraq, where a Sunni regime based on the clans around the northern town of Tikrit was establishing itself, was in a similar position.

The key player in all this was Egypt's President Nasser. He talked aggression. At an Arab summit in September 1965, for example, he agreed a three-year plan to build up Arab armies for a fresh assault on Israel. The next year he backed the formation of the PLA with the same intention. He spoke of the very existence of Israel being an 'aggression'. Yet in private he dreaded a war that he knew very well would probably end in humiliating defeat. In short, he was trapped. Leadership of the Arab world demanded striking rhetoric and gestures. Viewed from inside Israel, such behaviour was extremely worrying and played into the hands of the hawks. The end result was a war Nasser did not want.

Cross-border conflicts

As early as 1963, the UN had been called in to settle a dispute between Israel and Syria over the former's use of the waters of the upper Jordan and Lake Galilee. Two years later there was more fierce fighting as the Israelis smashed Syrian dams intended to divert the headwaters of the River Jordan. There were clashes again in early 1967 when an Israeli tractor ploughing land within the demilitarized zone was fired upon and an artillery duel began. Syrian Soviet-built MIGs and Israeli French-built Mirages soon appeared overhead, a dogfight took place and four MIGs were downed. Two more were shot down within sight of the Syrian capital, Damascus, which the Israeli planes then buzzed. It was provocative action by any standard.

Meanwhile, Fatah and other groups had been stepping up provocation of their own. As early as 1965, their cross-border raids had drawn fierce Israeli reprisals. The following year, despite efforts by King Hussein to prevent attacks on Israel from Jordan because he was worried about their consequences and about his ability to control the guerrillas, members of Fatah, the PLA and the Arab Nationalist Movement (ANM, another militant group) raided Israel several times from southern Lebanon.

In November 1966, there were attacks in Jerusalem and Hebron, the latter destroying an Israeli military vehicle, killing three soldiers and injuring a further four. The IDF's response was unprecedented. In broad daylight, protected by aircraft, a large force of tanks descended on the West Bank village of Samu. Reports vary, but perhaps 5,000 villagers lost their homes, their clinic, school and mosque. Several were killed and injured. Jordanian forces rushing to investigate were ambushed and more than 50 were killed and wounded. A Royal Jordanian Air Force plane was shot down.

The Samu raid had long-lasting consequences. In the rioting that followed, Hussein was almost overthrown for his failure to protect the Palestinians under his care. He was personally angered by the raid, too, which had taken place on his birthday and caused the death of a friend. Of all Israel's neighbours, Jordan had hitherto been the one it felt closest to. No longer. The raid angered world opinion and led to calls for revenge in Arab states that wondered where the Israelis would strike next.

False report

For several years the Arab–Israeli conflict had been closely tied into the Cold War. As mentioned, for some time Israel had been in receipt of French weapons: the Mirage fighters that buzzed Damascus, for example. In 1965, following a mutual recognition agreement, the IDF was given West German armaments, too. In the same year, Democrat US President Johnson showed his willingness to maintain Kennedy's pro-Israeli policy by delivering a consignment of 210 US tanks and 48 Skyhawk bombers to his number one Middle-Eastern ally. The Soviets, already on quite good terms with Nasser, got on even better with the new regime in Syria. Their next move was to improve relations between the two states, which had been at a somewhat low ebb since the failure of the United Arab Republic in 1961. The result was a Soviet-brokered Egypt–Syria defence pact, which Nasser agreed to in November 1966 in the hope of steering the more aggressive Syria away from open conflict with Israel. The plan backfired, with appalling consequences for both Egypt and Syria.

At this point, shortly after the artillery and air battle on the Israeli–Syrian border, Anwar Sadat, the senior Egyptian aide in Moscow, was handed some alarming information from Soviet intelligence. Israeli forces were massing on the border with

Syria. Their intention was clear: invasion. The information was false, and to this day no one is really sure why it was issued. Explanations range from the influence of alcohol (not as fanciful as it might seem in Russia) to a wish to precipitate a war in order to embarrass the Americans. Although he soon ascertained for himself that the Israelis were not preparing an attack, Nasser felt obliged to act in order to keep in with his Soviet paymasters and to avoid losing face among his fellow Arabs. So Egyptian forces would be free to attack Israel from the south if it invaded Syria, Nasser asked Secretary-General U Thant to withdraw the UN observers (UNEF) from a section of Egypt's Sinai border with Israel.

War

Alarmed, U Thant talked to the Israelis and Egyptians and eventually decided to call Nasser's bluff by pulling UNEF back from all its positions in Sinai, Gaza and Sharm al-Sheikh (at the entrance to the Strait of Tiran). Contrary to the Secretary-General's expectations, Nasser made the grand gesture of occupying Sharm al-Sheikh and shortly afterwards closing the Strait of Tiran to Israeli ships and those of other nations carrying military supplies to Eilat. To Israel such action was tantamount to a declaration of war, particularly as Nasser accompanied it with another round of flamboyant anti-Israeli speechifying. Intended to make Arab hearts swell with pride rather than with the spirit of war, the aggressive rhetoric was just the excuse for combat that Israel's hawks had wanted.

For a couple of weeks, as the two sides eyed each other up with mounting suspicion, there was a flurry of diplomatic activity. The Soviets warned of dire consequences if Egypt were attacked. The Americans, reluctantly, stood by their ally while at the same time urging restraint. King Hussein, forced to come off the fence, flew to Cairo and made a defensive pact with Nasser. Other Arab nations made appropriate noises of solidarity. In Israel the mood was edgy. Frightened by Nasser's clumsy manoeuvring and expecting to be attacked at any moment, the Jewish population rallied behind their government. Behind the scenes the war cabinet planned a devastating 'anticipatory counter-offensive' – doublespeak for an attack.

figure 7 the 1967 War

The Six-Day War

Unequal contest?

As in 1948, it is easy by simply looking at the map (Figure 7) to see the 1967 War as another David vs. Goliath contest in which the little boy overcame the threatening giant. Certainly the combined populations of Israel's Arab neighbours vastly outnumbered that of Israel and, correspondingly, the potential number of troops they could have put into the field was also much greater. But that, and the fact that geography might enable them to attack Israel on several fronts at the same time, was where their advantage ended.

Israel was a state built by war. Defence, including aggressive defence, had always been its top priority. Each war it fought was, literally, a struggle for survival – military defeat might well mean the end of the Zionist dream. To avoid this, its defence forces were highly trained and extremely efficient. The pilots that began the assault early on the morning of Monday 5 June, for instance, had practised their attacks so often that they were able to fly in complete radio silence. Israel's tanks, artillery and aircraft were superior to those of their enemy and they knew how to use them more effectively. Above all, they had the supreme advantage of surprise, launching the war when and how they chose.

In contrast, Israel's Arab enemies – essentially Egypt, Jordan, Syria and Iraq, although others sent token contingents and provided some funding – were ill-coordinated, often poorly trained and were furnished with equipment, much of it made by the Soviet Union and its allies, that frequently proved less effective than that produced by the competitive capitalist armaments industries of France, Germany and the United States. Jordan, having made a defence pact with Egypt only at the very last minute, was a reluctant combatant. Fearing a repetition of 1948–9 and 1956, Nasser did not want war either. Iraq had no border with Israel while the new regime in Syria had only a tenuous hold on the affections of its people. A more inauspicious set of circumstances would be hard to imagine.

Air strike

Moshe Dayan and his commanders knew that a swift, decisive strike was essential. If a war in which the Arabs were being defeated dragged on beyond a week or two, there was a very real chance that either the Soviets would become involved in some way or the US would come down heavily on Israel to prevent escalation. A quick victory necessitated blitzkrieg tactics as employed by the German armies in 1940.

Unlike Korea and Vietnam (the two theatres of major conflict since 1945) the terrain beyond Israel's borders was ideally suited to a war of rapid movement – upon one condition: control of the air. Just as the Germans in 1940 would not risk exposing their forces upon the open sea between Britain and France before they had control of the air space above, so the Israelis could not risk exposing their armour and artillery in the open desert without first winning mastery of the skies. Again, the parallel with the Battle of Britain (1940) is instructive. The Luftwaffe came closest to victory not when it tackled the RAF in the air but when it struck at its airfields and planes on the ground. Indeed, had Goering persevered with his attack on British airfields and not diverted his aircraft to attacking London, he might well have won control of the skies and enabled the German armies to invade Britain. This vital lesson was not lost on the Israelis.

At 7.45 a.m. on Monday 5 June 1967, the Israelis put into operation a plan they had been hatching for five years. It began with a devastating attack by almost the entire Israeli air force on Egypt's air bases, radar sites and communications installations. The strike was unannounced and followed no declaration of war. The Israelis later lied that it had been provoked by large numbers of Egyptian troops moving towards Israel's southern border. A little over two hours and 500 sorties later, 309 of Egypt's 340 serviceable aircraft had been destroyed, including all its long-range bombers. With total control of the air and Egypt's communications in complete disorder, Israel was now able to drive across Sinai to the Suez Canal and south to link up with a naval force that had taken Sharm al-Sheikh. Thousands of Egyptian troops lost their lives in a merciless rain of high explosives and napalm. Beside their often unrecognizable bodies, the bleak desert was strewn with the burned-out hulks of around 700 tanks and countless guns, trucks and other debris of Israel's ruthless advance.

Unaware of what was going on to the south – Nasser actually told King Hussein on the phone that the Israeli air force had suffered heavy losses – planes from Jordan, Syria and Iraq made a few hesitant darts at Israeli targets. Within hours these air forces had suffered the same fate as Egypt's. Jordan's was wiped out completely, Syria's reduced to one-third of its original strength and Iraq's irreparably damaged. By nightfall at the end of the first day, victory was already Israel's.

Expansion

Over the next five days the amount of land under Israeli control tripled and the US and the Soviet Union came close to armed confrontation. Nasser, his reputation in tatters, accepted the ceasefire supposed to come into effect around midnight on 7 June. Jordan's King Hussein had offered a cessation of hostilities the moment he learned of the loss of his air force. Despite US pressure, the Israeli cabinet rejected this offer. Their minimum target was East Jerusalem, with its old Jewish quarter and holy sites. While warplanes mercilessly harried the poorly coordinated Jordanian and Palestinian soldiers from the air, the IDF advanced steadily through the streets of Jerusalem and more quickly across the hills of the West Bank to the River Jordan. When they had reached all their objectives, they accepted the ceasefire. King Hussein followed suit, thereby also ending Iraq's ability to influence the conflict.

Since the destruction of its air force, Syria had done little but shell Israel across the border. Such inactivity was a good example of the Arab nations' failure to coordinate their military efforts. A Syrian offensive into northern Israel while Israeli troops were occupied elsewhere would probably not have altered the outcome of the war, but it would have made Israel's triumph considerably more difficult. As it was, the Israelis were able to leave the Syrian front until their hands were free. By then the continuation of the war was getting difficult.

The ceasefire of Wednesday 7 June, supposed to cover all fronts, had been accepted by Syria as well as Israel. It was with consternation and annoyance, therefore, that the following day President Johnson heard the Israelis were blitzing Syrian positions on the Golan Heights overlooking northern Israel. This action was particularly dangerous because of Syria's alliance with the Soviet Union. Johnson, who already had his hands full with the war, insisted that Israel abandon its action immediately and abide by the ceasefire.

At this point one of the most controversial acts of the war occurred. The US was monitoring Israeli communications via a clearly-marked intelligence-gathering vessel, *USS Liberty*, that was patrolling off the coast of Gaza. Saying they believed this ship was Egyptian, Israeli planes attacked it repeatedly. Although it did not sink, 205 of its crew were killed or wounded and its communications systems were smashed. Many Americans now believe the attack was deliberate, masterminded by Dayan himself. On the other hand, the Israelis still insist, as they have done all along, that the attack was a ghastly mistake. Deeply embarrassed, Johnson hushed the incident up. Temporarily free from US oversight, the Israeli high command was free to launch the final part of its battle plan, the assault on the hills that fed the River Jordan.

The IDF attacked on the morning of Friday 9 June, claiming it was responding to provocative Syrian shelling. Although they resisted bravely, the Syrians were driven back until it was thought the Israelis might push on to Damascus itself. The recently-opened hotline between Moscow and Washington glowed red as Soviet Premier Alexei Kosygin threatened dire retribution unless the attack on his ally was stopped. President Johnson, unwilling to be seen to bend to Soviet threats, ordered the US Sixth Fleet to hold a course that brought it into the path of a large fleet of Soviet warships... An even greater disaster was averted only when the Israelis, now in full possession of the Golan Heights, ceased hostilities on the evening of Saturday 10 June.

The war had lasted just five-and-a-half days.

After the war

The cost

The casualties reflected the fighting. The Israelis lost only 779 soldiers and little equipment. The Arab casualties were around 20 times higher. Perhaps 11,500 Egyptians died with over twice that number wounded. Jordan lost about 6,500, including many Palestinians, and suffered approximately the same number of wounded as Egypt. 2,500 Syrians died and 5,000 were wounded. Iraqi casualties were negligible. The Arabs' loss of equipment was catastrophic, especially the destruction of virtually all their air forces. The combatant Egyptian land forces lost some 80 per cent of their equipment. The Jordanian and Syrian armies suffered equally severely.

In under six days of fighting, the IDF had captured the entire West Bank, Gaza, Sinai (closing the Suez Canal again) and the

Golan Heights. This almost tripled the amount of territory under its control. It did not increase the size of Israel itself by much because, of the land it had captured, only East Jerusalem and a few surrounding areas were officially assimilated. The rest was simply occupied. Contrary to international law and convention but in accord with its long-standing declared intention, Jerusalem was made Israel's capital city. To make way for Israeli development, scores of Palestinian homes were bulldozed and hundreds of families made homeless. For 'strategic' reasons, other Arab villages were flattened elsewhere in the West Bank.

There were two reasons for Israel's unwillingness formally to incorporate all the captured territory. First, by keeping the West Bank and the Gaza Strip as zones of military occupation that might be returned, the possibility of a future 'peace for land' deal was left open. Second, if all conquered land had been absorbed into Israel, its large Palestinian populations would have become Israeli citizens and therefore entitled to vote. Given Israel's proportional electoral system, they would have had enough influence in the Knesset to destabilize the state. On the other hand, to have made them Israeli citizens without the right to vote would have been clear apartheid.

Role reversal

As in the previous armed confrontations between Israel and the Arab world, it was the Palestinians who suffered most. The war created an estimated 323,000 new refugees, the majority from the West Bank, over 100,000 from the Golan Heights and 38,000 from Sinai. There were reports of Israeli police and army units actively encouraging Palestinians to flee, wrongly warning them that their houses were about to be shelled and shepherding them across the murky waters of the Jordan. By the end of 1967, over 1 million men, women and children who regarded themselves as Palestinians were living outside the land they knew as Palestine but which most of the rest of the world called Israel.

Cruelly, however, the 1967 War had helped the Palestinian cause by bringing together around 1 million Israeli, Gaza, Golan and West Bank Palestinians under the same administration. Although communications and travel were always difficult, the ironic consequence of Israeli military success was a greater sense of Palestinian cohesion and unity. This was fostered by Arafat's Fatah and the PLO, which it soon came to dominate. The war had finally revealed Pan-Arabism to be no more than a chimera born of a romantic reading of history. In its place Palestinians espoused Arafat's new, uncompromisingly aggressive and nationalistic leadership. Its unashamed acceptance of violence, within the Middle East and way beyond, would shock the entire world.

Israel had shocked the world, too. The war confirmed that it was a regional power, and one that even the West could not assume would automatically tread the moral high ground. No longer a mere survivor, it had shown itself to be a ruthless conqueror and a cruel master. In contrast, very gradually, and often despite their bloodthirsty actions, it was the turn of the Palestinians to attract significant international sympathy and attention. In short, they would change from being simply the sorry victims of war to a specific 'problem' that needed international attention.

Resolution 242

There was much talk before, during and after the 1967 War about resolving the Arab–Israeli problem peacefully. Very roughly, Prime Minister Eshkol, King Hussein and President Nasser represented schools of thought that believed in a possible compromise involving the return of captured land in exchange for guarantees of peace. Hard-liners on both sides – the Syrians and Menachem Begin, for instance – would have none of it. Begin and his right-wing Zionist ilk were in favour of gradually colonizing and absorbing all conquered territory into Israel. Syria opposed any talk of peace with Israel and managed to get this incorporated in a 'three-noes' resolution – no recognition, no negotiation, no peace – at an Arab summit in September 1967.

Meanwhile, the UN Security Council was searching for a peace formula of its own. The result was the British-worded compromise Resolution 242 of November 1967. This spoke of the illegality of conquest by force of arms, called for a 'just settlement of the refugee problem' and demanded that Israel return 'territories occupied' in exchange for peace. The word 'territories' was chosen, without a preceding 'all' or 'the', as deliberately ambiguous. Versions in other languages – French and Russian, for example – were more specific. The Israelis took the original text to mean 'some territories' while the Arabs believed it meant 'all'. It was three years before Israel accepted the Resolution, which became the basis of its future peace treaties with Arab states. Among the Arab governments, Syria was bitterly hostile to the Resolution.

The Palestinian leadership, as represented by Arafat, rejected Resolution 242 out of hand. The reference to the 'refugee problem' they condemned as feeble and insulting. And the concept of peace for land was to them preposterous. As in their eyes *all* Israel was stolen territory, they argued that it was morally reprehensible to talk of returning some of these conquests in exchange for peace and recognition of the others. To do so would mean accepting that ultimately might was right, contradicting the Resolution's statement on conquest.

In many ways, therefore, the 1967 War and its aftermath fundamentally altered the Israel–Palestine situation. A formula now existed that eventually enabled Israel and all but one of its neighbours to make peace. In the end, a number of Palestinians would come round to the land for peace position, too. But that was still a very long way off, and the compromise would never be agreed by all. The way ahead remained long, bitter and bloody.

In depth: Yasser Arafat (1929–2004)

No figure in the Israeli–Palestinian conflict was more controversial than the man popularly known as Yasser Arafat. From his uncertain progeny and birthplace to his death from an undiagnosed blood disorder, the first chairman of the PLO and first president of the PNA lived a life of charismatic complexity. Born to middle-class Palestinian parents in Cairo (or Gaza or Jerusalem, depending on which version of autobiography one chooses to follow), Arafat trained as an engineer. He was also attracted to politics and signed up to fight for the Arab cause against Israel in 1948–9. He flirted with the Muslim Brotherhood and served in the Egyptian army before going to work in the British protectorate of Kuwait. Here, with a group of Palestinian exiles, he helped set up Fatah in about 1959.

Fatah was slow to get off the ground and did not launch its first guerrilla attacks on Israel until 1965. Arafat soon became well-known for his determination and bravery, as well as for his quick temper and equivocation. Fatah's reputation climbed rapidly after the Six-Day War and in 1969 Arafat was elected chairman of the recently-founded PLO.

The PLO was now based in Jordan, where it came into conflict with the government of King Hussein. The rivalry came to a head in 1970 when, following a mini civil war, the PLO was forcibly expelled from the Hashemite kingdom. Arafat and his supporters fled to Lebanon where once again they set about creating a Palestinian state in exile. Guerrilla warfare, seen by most as naked terrorism (a good example being the attack on the Munich Olympics) raised the profile of Arafat, Fatah and the PLO to the point where, in 1974, he was invited to address the UN General Assembly.

Eight years later the Israeli army invaded Lebanon and Arafat was once again obliged to flee, this time to Tunisia. Here he and the PLO continued to launch *fedayeen* attacks, but found themselves increasingly out of touch with what was happening on the ground among their fellow Palestinians. Undaunted, Arafat recaptured the initiative in 1988 by renouncing terrorism and proclaiming the entire area of the British mandate to be the independent state of Palestine. Despite the blunder of backing Saddam Hussein in 1990–1, Arafat was gradually accepted as a genuine seeker after peace. Complex negotiations led to the Oslo Accords of 1993 and the formation of the Palestinian National Authority of which he was elected president in 1996.

From this time onwards, Arafat appeared to lose control of events, descending into a confusion of contradictions and possibly lies. It appears that he re-espoused violence as a way of counteracting the Islamist threat. As a result he was virtually imprisoned by the Israelis in a rubble-strewn compound in Ramallah from where he was finally airlifted to Paris to die.

In depth: the Israel Labour Party (also Mapai and the Alignment)

Israel's proportional electoral system produces a far more fluid party structure than is found in most other democracies. Discipline is weak and parties emerge and dissolve quite regularly. This makes generalization a tricky business, never more so than when dealing with the left-wing/social democrat grouping that here is generally simplified as 'Labour'. In fact, we are talking about at least three parties: Mapai (1930s–1965), Alignment (1965–1992) and Labour (1992 onwards).

Mapai, a Hebrew acronym for the Land of Israel Workers' Party, emerged during the mandate era as a socialist-Zionist coalition led by David Ben-Gurion. As the guiding force behind victory in the War of Independence (1948–9), it was rewarded with 35.7 per cent of the popular vote in the state's first elections. With 46 of the Knesset's seats, it formed the core of the coalition government and remained the dominant force in Israeli politics until merging with Labour Unity to form the Labour Alignment.

Technically speaking, Alignment was really a combined list of candidates for electoral purposes rather than a true party, so it is customary to talk of Labour remaining in power through the Six-Day War and the October 1973 War until losing control of the Knesset in 1977.

Since its inception, Labour had made security its number one issue (as it was in all Israeli politics) and its economic and social policies were not all that different from those of similar centre-leaning parties. By the 1980s, after the initial setback of the October War and the shock of subsequent electoral defeat, Labour was generally more willing than its main rival, Likud, to seek some form of permanent settlement with the Palestinians. It was Yitzhak Rabin, a Labour prime minister, who signed the Oslo Accords and another, Ehud Barak, who tried to take the process further in the late 1990s.

Having joined Sharon's Unity Government in 2001, Labour left it in 2003. However, it went on to support Sharon's unilateral Disengagement Strategy of 2004–5 and, after coming second to Kadima in the elections of March 2006, joined Olmert's coalition. As minister of defence, Labour leader Amir Peretz was heavily criticized for the handling of the 2006 War with Hezbollah.

08

Arafat and the PLO

This chapter will cover:
- Israel after the 1967 War
- how the Palestinian *fedayeen* attracted the world's attention
- ongoing conflict between Israel and its Arab neighbours after 1967
- the Yom Kippur War, 1973.

Where now?

A divided nation

Israel did not find it easy to come to terms with its position and status after the 1967 War. The communist Rakah Party, which with the support of most Arab voters had won three Knesset seats in 1965, called for immediate withdrawal from what the Israelis called the 'administered territories' of the West Bank and Gaza. Interestingly, this position was also that of ex-Prime Minister Ben-Gurion, who believed the conquered land would become a millstone round Israel's neck.

Perhaps a majority of Israelis thought and even hoped, however vaguely, that one day, when peace had been made with surrounding Arab states, the occupied land would be handed back either to those who lived there or to its previous rulers. A third group, the Zionist right, condemned such thinking as tantamount to treachery. Some of them argued that the 1967 frontiers, stretching to the physical boundaries of the Golan Heights, the River Jordan and the Suez Canal, would always be essential for Israel's future security.

More extreme in their views were Orthodox and Ultra-Orthodox Jews, many of whom regarded the 1967 triumph as a God-given opportunity for the Jewish people to return to the land given to them by the Almighty in Biblical times. Now the land was under Israeli control, it was their duty to settle it. In June 1968, by sneaking into a hotel in the West Bank city of Hebron disguised as Swedish tourists, a determined group of Jewish families outwitted Eshkol's uncertain government and established the first Jewish settlement in the Occupied Territories. Many, many more were to follow. The settlement issue split Israel's Labour movement from the Zionists, thereby breaking up the partnership that had masterminded the formation of the state. From this time forwards, a settlement of the Israeli–Palestinian situation became infinitely more difficult.

Carrot...

Israel's policy towards the Arab land it was occupying has been described as a classic case of 'carrot and stick'. The 'carrot' arose out of an understanding that it was much easier to manage an occupation if those affected were content. To this end, the people of Gaza and of the West Bank were given a high degree of self-government. The 1970s saw two rounds of municipal elections. The first returned largely conservative, Jordan-orientated candidates, but the second saw gains for the PLO. Education and most local affairs were left in Palestinian hands and in 1972 the first Palestinian University, Bir Zeit, opened. There were two more by the end of the decade.

Economically, the Palestinians under Israeli occupation fared much better than they had under Egyptian and Jordanian rule. Again, the West Bank, a more viable entity than the Gaza Strip, gained most. The frontier with Israel was kept open, as was that with Jordan. This enabled goods to pass relatively freely and 'West Bankers' (as they tended to identify themselves at this stage, rather than as 'Palestinians') flocked in their thousands to work in Israel. Movement was helped by the network of roads the Israelis constructed for military purposes. By 1973 one-third of the West Bank workforce was employed in Israel – albeit in what were generally low-paid jobs – mostly in agriculture. Electrification spread and health care improved. Many benefited from the money sent back from better-paid family members who had left to work abroad, especially in the Gulf.

Of course, there remained tensions and the occasional violent flare-ups between the West Bank's original inhabitants and the refugees. Moreover, there was always the presence of the Israeli military and police, sometimes just patrolling but also engaging in harassment or heavy-handed retribution for deeds committed by the *fedayeen*. On the whole though (and this not saying very much), the 15 years after the 1967 War were some of the least stressful experienced by the nationless Palestinians.

...and stick

As before the 1967 War, Israel continued its policy of counteracting the Palestinian *fedayeen* with overwhelming and often ruthless force. This, coupled with the drawn-out military activity in the south, put a huge strain on the economy. The ongoing Arab boycott of any nation that traded with Israel was to some extent alleviated by the addition of Palestinian consumers who became the second largest external market for Israeli produce. Even so, Israel grew ever more dependent upon US aid.

Israel's security forces used a range of tactics when dealing with real or suspected *fedayeen* violence. These escalated dramatically during the later 1960s. In 1969–70 alone, for example, Israel reported some 560 incidents on its border with Lebanon. Curfews were imposed, institutions closed and suspects held without trial. Sterner measures included bulldozing houses and undertaking retaliatory or pre-emptive raids into neighbouring states.

Several incidents attracted a great deal of attention. The first, in March 1968, saw a powerful Israeli strike force cross into Jordan about 16 kilometres north of the Dead Sea and make for the sizeable village of Karama (often spelt 'Karamah'). The Jordanian Army, the PLA and Fatah, which had set up a base in the village, managed to ambush the invaders and inflict quite heavy casualties on them before superior Israeli firepower, coordination and training became overwhelming. Although they lost over 170 men, the Palestinians and Jordanians hailed the temporary rebuff to the IDF, the killing of 28 of its soldiers and the destruction of some of its equipment as a victory. The Israelis were no longer invincible, they crowed, and recruitment to the various Palestinian armed factions increased sharply. Undaunted, the IDF continued to push Palestinians from the Jordan Valley, driving up to 100,000 from their homes.

In terms of simply putting an end to attacks on Israel, the most successful operation was conducted by Ariel Sharon in Gaza in 1971. Entering the Strip with colossal force, he organized the destruction of houses and other buildings, the shooting (if they resisted) or arrest of numerous *fedayeen*, the detention of many suspects in specially-built camps in Sinai, and the closure of the organs of Palestinian self-government. Attacks on Israel from Gaza were stopped for many years, but a legacy of suspicion and hatred was established that lasted even deeper.

Longer-range Israeli strikes included two in 1973. The first hit Palestinian camps in southern Lebanon, killing around 40; the second targeted the Fatah headquarters in Beirut, killing three of the movement's leaders. The Israeli security services also waged a worldwide campaign of assassination of *fedayeen* leaders. Bombs – letter or less discrete – were the favoured weapon and several prominent Palestinians were slain in this way.

Self-reliance

The Six-Day War brought to an end any realistic idea of Israel's neighbours 'liberating' the Palestinians. It was now obvious that, in the short-to-medium term at least, the Arab states were simply not militarily strong enough to tackle Israel. Activist Palestinians, therefore, had little choice but to accept what Yasser Arafat had been saying all along: there was no point in waiting for someone else to restore their land for them; they had to do it themselves. It was a similar mindset to that of the Jewish leaders who had established Israel in 1948.

The defeat of the Arabs, including his PLA, made Shukayri's position as head of the PLO untenable. Within two years, Fatah dominated the organization and Arafat was its leader and head of its executive committee. His style of leadership was charismatic but controversial: his energy, his determination, his bravery were never in doubt, and no one did more to bring the plight of the Palestinians before the international audience, but his political and administrative skills were often called into question. Some say the ramshackle, inefficient and corrupt nature of the PLO's structure and the constant divisions within the broader Palestinian movement were not his business. He was the figurehead, the inspiration, but never the manager. Critics, on the other hand, accuse him of inflexibility, organizational incompetence and political ham-fistedness. It will be a very long time before anything like an historical consensus materializes.

Under Arafat's leadership, the post-1967 Palestinian movement evolved towards three policies. One was the proposed replacement of Israel and the Occupied Territories with a single state that harked back to the days of the British mandate: a secular, multi-racial and democratic Palestine in which Jew and Arab could live side-by-side. It was an attractive idea but one that had been impractical in the 1930s, let alone after 20 years of bloody conflict.

The second strand was building up the idea of a Palestinian nation in Gaza and the West Bank. There were also efforts at creating a separate Palestinian identity in Jordan and Lebanon, with disastrous results (see p. 112). Nation-building, helped by elected organs of local government, was further developed by Fatah-prompted trade unions, schools, clinics, training centres and a range of other institutions and movements, including the Boy Scouts. One of the more difficult tasks was settling differences between the original West Bankers – those whose families had lived there before 1948 – and the refugee settlers in camps and elsewhere who had arrived subsequently and put pressure on the region's scanty resources.

Palestinian nation-building was equally vigorous outside the Occupied Territories. The arrival in Lebanon of the PLO leadership and administrative apparatus in 1970 led to the emergence of a state within a state. Lebanon's 235,000 Palestinians, many within cramped camps, paid Palestinian taxes, listened to Palestinian radio, were tried in Palestinian courts, went to schools where the curriculum was specifically Palestinian, and were treated in Palestinian clinics and hospitals. By the mid-1970s, the PLO employed an estimated 8,000 of its own civil servants. Not surprisingly, the effect on Lebanon – already a highly insecure state – was seriously destabilizing and a major reason why it plunged into a horrific civil war (see pp. 139–40). Beforehand, precisely because he had seen that this might happen in Jordan, King Hussein had expelled the PLO from his country.

'External operations'

The third prong of Palestinian policy was armed action against any target that might, however vaguely, be Israeli or pro-Israeli. The operational *fedayeen* and their sympathizers referred to the assaults as 'external operations'. To Israel and the West they were simply terrorism.

At this point the story of Palestinian resistance becomes almost unbelievably complicated. The reason is that beneath the PLO umbrella there appeared an impossibly large number of *fedayeen* groups: in 1970 there were perhaps 30 operating in Jordan alone. Some were independent; most were backed by an Arab state or a communist power, primarily the USSR and China. Many were infiltrated by the Israelis, the CIA or both. There were groups founded for a single mission and others with perhaps no more than two or three members. There was little or no coordination between them. Small wonder, then, that after an attack it was quite common for more than one group to claim responsibility.

The largest *fedayeen* organization was Arafat's Fatah, operating mainly out of Syria, Lebanon and Jordan (until 1970). Relatively small before the Six-Day War, its reputation was greatly enhanced by the Battle of Karama (see p. 110). Its best-known operation outside the Middle East, said to have been organized because Arafat was jealous of the high-profile actions of other groups, especially the Popular Front for the Liberation of Palestine (PFLP, see opposite), came at the 1972 Munich

Olympics. In a poorly planned and ill-executed operation, Palestinian 'Black September' *fedayeen* tried to take hostage the Israeli athletic team. In the subsequent chaos and bloodshed, 11 Israeli athletes, five *fedayeen* and a German policeman were killed. The IDF responded with heavy bombing of Fatah positions in Southern Lebanon and Syria, leaving between 200 and 300 dead. Around half of those who died were civilians. Neither side came out of the episode with their reputation enhanced.

The PFLP, founded by the Marxist George Habash in 1968, had its roots among the students of the American University of Beirut. It combined its campaign against Israeli ('that lap dog of capitalist imperialists') with an assault on the capitalist world in general. The following year saw the emergence of the Democratic Front for the Liberation of Palestine (DFLP), whose stance was even further left than that of the PFLP. Of the two, the PFLP, which specialized in hijacking aircraft, attracted the most attention.

The world beyond the Middle East had became directly involved in the Israel–Palestine confrontation in July 1968, when the PFLP hijacked an El Al (the Israeli airline) airliner en route to Rome from Algeria. The passengers were allowed to go free after the release of Palestinian prisoners. Following an attack by the same group on another El Al plane in December, Israeli commandos retaliated by destroying 13 Arab aircraft at Beirut airport. The violence escalated in 1969, with further hijackings, one of an American TWA airliner, and bomb attacks in Jerusalem and London. *Fedayeen* strikes, bombings and hijackings continued over the next few years, many provoking ferocious Israeli reprisals. None of this brought the Israeli–Palestinian problem any nearer solution; if anything, it had the opposite effect. Nevertheless, whatever the morality of the violence, it had managed to keep the situation in the Promised Land on the front pages.

'Black September'

The most dramatic development among militant Palestinians took place in Jordan. Here, as in Egypt and most of the other Arab states, the *fedayeen* were regarded with suspicion because of their independent, anarchic ways, extreme tactics and links to the far left. Jordan's King Hussein did not approve, either, of their absolute refusal even to contemplate acknowledging Israel's existence. More immediately, he objected to the lawless behaviour of the PLO and its associates within the Hashemite kingdom. Many behaved as if they were above Jordanian law, terrorizing the locals with theft, extortion, beatings and even murder and rape. To the PFLP the King was no more than a puppet of the West and clashes between his troops and the *fedayeen* were frequent and bloody.

Things came to a head in 1970. In the first half of the year, Hussein made two moves to solve the problem. First, with tacit Israeli support, he stepped up attacks on the *fedayeen*; second, he offered Yasser Arafat the post of prime minister within a Jordanian government. Shocked and a bit non-plussed by the idea of secure respectability, the PLO leader said no. Finally, after two further attempts on the King's life, the gloves came off.

In September, following a PFLP hijacking of four Western airliners, three of which were destroyed at Aman airport, Hussein declared martial law, clamped down on freedom of expression and sent in the army to tackle the militant Palestinians. Arafat responded by calling for the King to be deposed and urging his fellow Palestinians to lead the revolution. The pattern of subsequent events, in which Jordan descended into a brief civil war, was extremely complex. Estimates of the numbers killed vary hugely, from 1,500 to 30,000. The true figure was probably at the lower end – perhaps around 3,000. Iraq sent support for Hussein while Syria backed the Palestinians. Only the threat of US–Israeli intervention prevented Syrian forces from participating openly in the Jordanian mayhem.

By the end of a month the *fedayeen* would remember as 'Black September', forces loyal to King Hussein had got the upper hand and large numbers of Palestinian fighters had fled the country. Their chosen refuge was Lebanon, most making their way there via Syria while a few risked passing through Israeli-occupied territory. Hussein had survived and would live long enough to see his country at peace with Israel. The 'Palestinian problem', however, had merely been moved on – as the Lebanese would shortly discover to their cost (see Chapter 10).

The War of Attrition

If the Israelis thought their overwhelming victory in the Six-Day War would bring about a cessation of hostilities, they were wrong. As we have seen, *fedayeen* attacks escalated after 1967. Nor was Nasser, who had been deeply humiliated by his military's failures, content to let things rest where they were. Not surprisingly, therefore, US Secretary of State William Rogers' early attempts at brokering a post-war peace deal came to nothing. Back on the front line along the Suez Canal, things were hotting up. By June 1968 the Egyptians were quite regularly bombarding Israeli positions along the Bar Lev, a massive defensive line they had constructed beside the Canal. The Israelis responded with shelling and air raids. By the following year the conflict, now even more ferocious, was becoming known as the War of Attrition.

Rogers arranged a ceasefire in July 1970, by which time the War of Attrition had taken a heavy toll. Israel had lost about 1,000 soldiers and the Egyptians many more. The fighting, which had included unwise Israeli air raids far beyond the battle zone, had caused 1.5 million Egyptians to flee their homes. Even more alarming, the war had brought the US and the USSR closer to their respective allies. In particular, the Soviets had poured weaponry, including sophisticated SAM-3 anti-aircraft missiles, into Egypt. Soviet pilots had even flown Egyptian aircraft over the Canal battle zone.

Nasser and Sadat

The political geography of the Middle East changed dramatically just after the ending of the War of Attrition when President Nasser died of a heart attack and was replaced by the hitherto unspectacular Anwar Sadat. Egypt's new president was a realist and a pragmatist. His wish was to do whatever was best for Egypt and thus, inevitably, for his reputation. If this meant playing off the US against the USSR or side-stepping the plight of the Palestinians, so be it. War with Israel, he believed, was a costly and dangerous mistake that could bring the people of Egypt only suffering, economic hardship and political instability. Sadat's primary aims, therefore, were the restoration of his country's economy and a secure peace with Israel.

It did not take Sadat long to realize that his two objectives were inextricably linked. Slowly unpicking Nasser's state-centred socialism brought little if any quick economic benefit to the mass of the people, and poverty, unemployment and discontent remained rife. Only a cut in military expenditure and a redirection of funds and energies into peaceful productive enterprises could revive Egypt, Sadat determined. And that meant peace. But when he approached Prime Minister Golda Meir and her cabinet with a peace offer based on UN Resolution 242 (peace for land – see pp. 103–4), they flatly turned him down.

The Egyptian premier had to think again. Because of Israel's overwhelming military might and confidence, he realized, it had no need of peace because it had nothing to fear from war. What if that were to change? What if Sadat managed, somehow, to prove the equal of the Israelis in battle? Might that not induce a change of heart in them? Musing along these lines, Sadat began to contemplate a most cunning and desperate plan.

Towards war

In the early 1970s, eager for Jewish votes, US President Richard Nixon significantly increased his country's military aid to Israel, including production technology as well as actual arms. In little over one year, the total value of US aid to Israel rose from $93 million to $634 million, of which $545 million was military aid. Simultaneously, National Security Advisor Henry Kissinger reached an agreement with the USSR to maintain the status quo in the Middle East. This infuriated Sadat as it implied Soviet acceptance of Israeli occupation of Arab lands, including the Egyptian Sinai. Sadat responded in July 1972 by expelling thousands of Soviet military advisors. The US rejoiced, believing it had scored a major diplomatic victory over its communist adversary and had made yet another Middle East war distinctly less likely.

American assumptions were wildly optimistic. Although for a moment taken aback, the Soviets responded to Sadat's snub by making Syria their principal arms recipient in the region. Syria was now in the hands of its hard-nosed ex-minister of defence, Hafiz Assad, who had engineered his own election as president in 1971. His goal was simple: the expansion of Syrian power and the enhancement of his own glory. The destruction of Israel would suit his needs perfectly. As that was unrealistic, at least in the short term, the recapture of the Golan Heights would do –

nothing would boost the prestige of the new and still vulnerable dictator more than a short, sharp victory.

Assad and Sadat began planning in late 1972. The following January their forces were put under joint overall command. Both wanted a swift triumph, but for different reasons. The former sought prestige, the latter hoped to force Israel to make peace. (Israel rejected an Egyptian peace offer as late as February 1973.) After recent re-arming, the two Arab countries' forces were now significant: Syria had more tanks on the Golan Heights than Israel and Egypt's sophisticated anti-aircraft defences now extended 16 kilometres beyond the Suez Canal. Beneath that protective umbrella, its ground forces would be able to face the Israelis on equal terms. Convinced they could reverse the Arab fortunes of the three previous wars, the two presidents sought only one last piece to make their jigsaw complete: surprise.

Yom Kippur War

Surprise

The Arab attack began on 6 October 1973. They chose their moment well. Many Israelis were at home celebrating the Jewish Yom Kippur (Day of Atonement) festival with their families. Although the intelligence services had reported a build up of forces in Egypt and Syria, the reserves had not been mobilized and the danger of an Arab pre-emptive strike, 1967-style, had been rejected. Golda Meir's government had simply not taken the threat seriously. On the ground, the routine maintenance of some tanks and other vehicles had been let slip. In short, the Israeli war machine, previously the epitome of ruthless efficiency, had grown over-confident and slack.

Thousands of kilometres to the west, Israel's principal succour and support, the US, was enmeshed in the final stages of the Vietnam conflict, as well as the navel-gazing complexities of Watergate and the tax affairs of Vice-President Spiro T. Agnew. Sadat and Assad could hardly have chosen a more opportune moment to strike.

Three-phase war

The brief war (6–24 October) may be outlined in three phases. Phase one was marked by striking Arab advances on the Golan

Heights and across the Suez Canal. Reinforced by Jordanian and Iraqi tanks and token forces from Kuwait and Saudi Arabia, the Syrians drove the Israelis back towards the steep western escarpment of the Heights, destroying many tanks and inflicting heavy casualties. In the south, the Egyptians and their Algerian and Moroccan allies crossed the Suez Canal by blasting through the Bar Lev barrier of sand, steel and concrete with high-pressure hoses and blocking pipes designed to flood the Canal with burning oil. Overhead, Soviet-built SAM-3 missiles kept the soldiers free from attacks by Israeli aircraft.

After three days Israel had lost about 50 planes and around 500 tanks. Defence minister Dayan told his prime minister that he believed they were 'heading for a catastrophe'. The myth of Israeli invincibility had been destroyed and Arab military prestige restored. For the first time, Arab forces had inflicted a major defeat upon the Israelis. His point proved, Sadat would have been happy to end the war there and then. Assad had other ideas – he had not yet managed to recapture all the Golan Heights, the territory seized by Israel when he had been Syria's defence minister.

Phase two saw the Arab offensive grind to a halt. The US had organized a massive and immediate airlift to Israel of $2.2 billion worth of military equipment of every kind except nuclear. Nixon, like all US presidents, was determined to enable Israel to survive without having to resort to the ultimate weapon. Re-equipped and now fully mobilized, the IDF was able to stop the Arab advance and plan one of its own. In Sinai, as the front moved beyond the narrow defensive screen offered by the SAM-3s, the Egyptians lost dozens of aircraft to superior Israeli planes.

Phase three was the Israeli offensive. Despite fresh Soviet armaments worth even more than those provided to their enemies, by the second week of the war the Arab armies were being driven back on all fronts. A breakthrough on the Golan Heights was prevented from becoming a drive to Damascus only by heroic Syrian defence. In the south, after being delayed while a 400-tonne temporary bridge was laid over the Suez Canal, General Sharon crossed into Africa and encircled the Egyptian Third Army. With the Soviets threatening to send in troops to save the Egyptians and both the superpowers on alert, a ceasefire was finally agreed by all the belligerent states apart from Iraq.

Aftermath

Technically speaking, the Yom Kippur War was another Israeli victory: they had beaten off Arab attacks and were advancing beyond the 1967 frontiers at the time of the ceasefire. Their casualties, although high at 2,700 killed, were less than those of the Arabs (8,500 killed). However, from a political point of view it was the Arabs who had come out on top. Sadat – now the 'hero of the crossing' – claimed victory in the first part of the war and said that the subsequent reverse had occurred only because Egypt could not compete with the combined strength of Israel and the US. The outcome was just what he had wanted: Israel had to take Egypt and its peace proposals seriously.

The war had troubled Israel domestically, too. Its self-confidence had been badly shaken and the traditional ruling Labour élite discredited. Prime Minister Meir resigned in 1974, making way for Yitzhak Rabin. The Israeli economy was in turmoil and more dependent than ever upon US aid. This was partly because its enemies had seriously deployed the 'oil weapon' for the first time. The Organization of Arab Oil-Producing Countries (OAPEC) imposed a boycott of crude oil sales to the US and the Netherlands, and cut overall production by 25 per cent. World oil prices soared from $3US to over $11US a barrel. Israel was hit harder than most by the major world recession instigated by OAPEC's action.

Because the war had yet again threatened to spark a superpower confrontation and because of the recession caused by OAPEC, it was now in almost everyone's interest to get Israel and her Arab neighbours to make peace. The exception, as so often in the past, was the Palestinians. As members of the PLA and smaller bands, they had fought and died beside their fellow Arabs. Yet in the aftermath of the war – UN Resolution 338 that harked back to Resolution 242, and a peace conference that met in Geneva, Switzerland – the Palestinian issue was very much secondary. Despite all the protests, the cries, the reasoned arguments and the bombings, the Palestinians were being shifted further and further from the centre of the stage.

In depth: West Bank

The term 'West Bank', meaning 5,880 sq kilometres (2,270 sq miles) of rugged land to the west of the River Jordan, was coined by the Jordanians in 1948. It is now in general use, although 'Palestine' and the older 'Judea and Samaria' are also employed. Rising to 1,022 metres (3,353 ft) at Tall Asur on the central mountainous spine and falling to 409 metres (1,341 ft) below sea level at the Dead Sea, this much-coveted territory is hardly the most agreeable place to live. Less than 40 per cent is used for agriculture, its only natural resource; the rest is barren scrub or human habitation. Water is scarce and getting scarcer; sewage disposal is a serious problem.

By 2006, the West Bank's population was reckoned to include around 2.5 million Palestinians and, if the population of East Jerusalem was included, approaching 500,000 Israelis. The holy city of Jerusalem, Israel's capital, is by far the largest city in the region. Technically speaking, only the east of the city lies within the West Bank. The surrounding area teems with places of deep significance to Christianity, Islam and Judaism. Hebron, Bethlehem, Jericho and Nazareth are among the better known.

Before the establishment of Israel, it was generally agreed by all parties, including the Jewish Agency, that the area now called the West Bank should be part of an Arab state. Amid the turmoil of 1948–9, it was seized by Jordan. Israel then overran it in the war of 1967 and administered it as Occupied Territory. Jordan gave up its claim to the West Bank in 1988 and seven years later Israel and the Palestinians agreed a new administration. The West Bank was divided into three sectors. One (the smallest in area) was fully administered by a Palestinian National Authority; another was wholly Israeli-administered; and the third was under joint administration. Israel kept control of all borders, roads, airspace and, crucially, water. In international law the West Bank still belongs to no one.

Talks on allowing the West Bank to form the basis of a Palestinian state have been seriously hampered by the growing number of Israeli settlements there, most controversially along the Jordan Valley. In recent years, the region's bleak, camp-like status (some 30 per cent of the Palestinian population are refugees from Israel) has been enhanced by the massive 'security fence' that Israel has constructed along much of the border between itself and Palestinian-occupied areas.

In depth: Golan Heights

A raised plateau of dark stone and soil, the Golan Heights are bordered by Syria, Lebanon, Israel and Jordan. Rivers mark its limits on three sides, while the indistinct eastern edge merges with the broad Syrian plain. Although only around 520 metres (1,700 ft) above sea level at its highest point, the steep escarpment on the Golan's western side commands spectacular views over northern Israel. The slopes of Mount Hermon, to the north of the Golan, are Israel's only ski resort. The region is punctuated by underground springs and receives more annual rainfall than the surrounding areas. The fertile plateau's plentiful water supply and strategic importance have ensured that ownership of the Golan has been the subject of international dispute for many years.

Because of the comparative richness of the soil, until the fighting of the mid-twentieth century the Golan Heights were relatively densely populated. Today the region is home to only about 40,000 people, about half of whom are Druze. Muslims number not more than a couple of thousand.

After some argument, the Golan became part of the French mandate of Syria in 1923. The formation of Israel led to further conflict in the area, especially about water. In the Six-Day War of 1967, Israel captured the Golan after fierce fighting, during which around 100,000 locals fled. They have yet to be allowed to return. Over the following 40 years some 20,000 Israelis established themselves in new settlements, and the Knesset's Golan Heights Law of 1981 made the region virtually part of Israel.

Ownership of the Golan is not a straightforward Israel–Syria issue. Lebanon also has a claim on a small area in the north known as the Shebaa Farms. Both Israel and Syria say the farms are theirs. Indeed, Syria states unequivocally that it is legally entitled to ownership of the entire Golan Heights and insists that their return is a prerequisite to peace with Israel. The Israelis are extremely wary of handing back all the Golan to a potential enemy because of the way the western escarpment dominates north-east Israel. Israel's critics, on the other hand, say that it hangs on to the Golan less for strategic reasons than for the district's rich soil and plentiful water.

09

peace and war

This chapter will cover:
- the aftermath of the 1973 October War
- the advance of Israel's right wing
- seeking peace, 1976 onwards
- Camp David and its immediate consequences.

Nearer yet further apart

Like the 1967 Arab–Israeli War, the conflict of 1973 made a long-term solution to the Israel–Palestine conflict easier to envisage yet harder to bring about. Optimism stemmed from the fact that, based on their first creditable military performance, the Palestinians' Arab backers now had some political authority. The willingness of the PLO to accept a compromise settlement was also encouraging for the peace process. At the same time, the mid- and late 1970s saw major developments that made a settlement much harder to achieve: the rise of the uncompromising right in Israel; the isolation of Egypt within the Arab world; open armed confrontation between Israel and the PLO in a war-torn Lebanon; and ominous signs of a further fragmentation within the Arab world with the rise of Islamic fundamentalism.

Possibilities for peace

Shuttle diplomacy

Although the post-war Geneva conference fizzed out almost before it had started, it was not in the interests of the major players to let the peace process die. The Nixon administration in the US, although beset with domestic difficulties that would eventually bring it down (Watergate), was keen to keep Middle East negotiations going. The task fell to ex-academic Henry Kissinger, who was both Assistant to the President for National Security Affairs and, from 1973, Secretary of State.

Kissinger saw the Middle East situation as part of the Cold War. His view was essentially this: with the US backing Israel, there was a tendency for Israel's enemies also to be hostile towards the US and therefore obvious targets for Soviet blandishments. Consequently, peace in the Middle East was needed to undermine the power of the USSR. To this end, employing his famous 'shuttle diplomacy' and 'step-by-step' approach, Kissinger flew back and forth between Jerusalem, Cairo and Damascus. The result was two significant agreements known as Sinai I and Sinai II (1974 and 1975). By their terms the Israeli and Egyptian armies disengaged, a UN force was installed between them, and the IDF withdrew to a significant distance east of the Suez Canal. Both sides also agreed publicly that the conflict between them should henceforth be resolved by peaceful means.

Negotiations with Syria were trickier because President Assad, who had ambitions to take over Nasser's mantle of leader of the Arab world, was loath to be seen to back down. Eventually, a disengagement agreement was reached in May 1974 that separated the two forces on the Golan Heights, imposed UN observers between them, and allowed only limited armaments on either side of a demilitarized buffer zone.

Stagnation

After Sinai II the peace movement lost momentum. Kissinger and President Gerald Ford, who had replaced the disgraced Nixon, blamed the new Israeli Prime Minister Rabin for intransigence. In fact, neither the Israelis nor the Egyptians were ready at this stage to commit themselves publicly to one-on-one treaty negotiations. The premiers of both countries feared domestic hostility and Sadat was worried about leaving his Arab partners behind.

Therefore, though impressive, the Kissinger settlements went nowhere near the heart of the Arab–Israeli problem. Israeli–Egyptian relations had definitely improved and Egypt had been brought closer to the US sphere of influence. Syria, on the other hand, had done no more than grudgingly accept reality. In addition, nothing had been done for Palestinians. Indeed, Kissinger had told Rabin that the US would not even talk to the PLO until it accepted UN Security Council Resolution 242.

Fedayeen and terrorists

Arafat and the PLO had kept a low profile during the 1973 War. Such relatively quiescent tactics cut no ice with Kissinger, who smartly rebuffed Arafat's tentative approaches for talks. As far as the US secretary of state was concerned, Arafat was a close friend of the Kremlin and many of his fellow Palestinian activists were unashamedly communist. Moreover, Kissinger saw the PLO and all its official and unofficial *fedayeen* offshoots as tarred with the same evil brush of terrorism.

As if to support Kissinger's thesis, in April 1974 a small band of PFLP-General Command *fedayeen* descended on the northern Israeli village of Qiryat Shemona. Here 18 Israelis died, many of them children, before the intruders were themselves shot dead. The next month 21 Israeli schoolchildren perished when security forces attacked a school in which *fedayeen* of the Democratic Front for the Liberation of Palestine (DFLP) were holding over 100 children hostage. Israel responded with a ferocious strike into southern Lebanon, from where the attacks had come, killing at least 60 civilians.

A major problem for those Palestinians seeking a settlement with Israel was that their movement was so fragmented. The PLO and Fatah offered a degree of leadership, but Arafat lacked that indefinable presidential quality that might have persuaded all parties to coalesce around him. Consequently, he was torn between trying to exert his authority over breakaway groups and giving them coded or half-hearted praise when their actions won the applause of his fellow Palestinians.

We need to remember that deeds dismissed as despicable terrorism in the West were seen by many Palestinians as heroic. *Fedayeen* who died in 'battle' were hailed as martyrs for the Palestinian cause and quickly became the stuff of song, poem and legend. This was not because the Palestinians were particularly insensitive or bloodthirsty. Like the Catholic supporters of the IRA in Northern Ireland, they were desperate people who believed they were being oppressed by a cruel and overbearing tyrant. In such dire circumstances, they declared, any tactic was permissible.

'Two state solution'

An Arab summit in Algiers shortly after the end of the 1973 War made a number of secret yet highly significant decisions. Two were especially important. First, the PLO was the sole representative of the Palestinian people. Second, for Israel to live at peace with the Arabs it had first to surrender the lands it had conquered in 1967. This was a decidedly more realistic aim than persuading Israel either to return to the UN partition arrangement of 1947 or to accept the PLO idea of a single secular state of Palestine.

These two decisions put the PLO in a very strong position – as long as it was prepared to alter its aim of one Palestine for Jews and Arabs. If it would accept the implied 'two state solution' – Israel separate from a Palestine based on the West Bank and Gaza Strip – then it would get the backing of major Arab governments and, very likely, the majority of other world powers too. At a meeting in the summer of 1974, the PLO hinted that it was moving towards the proposed compromise.

The new Palestine, it declared, would begin in 'liberated' Palestinian territory. Needless to say, this idea was not accepted by all Palestinians. A number of hard-liners, led by George Habash of the PFLP, rejected the compromise. Not long afterwards, this 'Rejectionist Front' left the PLO. Such internal bickering only added to the Palestinians' difficulty of being taken seriously on the international stage.

It should be noted that Arafat, leader of the PLO, continued to tread his equivocal path between aggression and peace-seeking. He would not openly condemn 'terrorist' acts and in public he still promised audiences the eventual 'destruction' of Israel. Such uncompromising rhetoric ensured that in Israel he and his supporters continued to be seen as a murderous threat.

'Olive branch and gun'

Moderate talk of a two-state solution bore rich fruit in November 1974 when Arafat was invited to speak to the General Assembly of the United Nations. Israel and the US had resolutely opposed the invitation, which proved to be a major diplomatic rebuff to them both. With a pistol ostentatiously showing, Arafat said he dreamed and hoped that one day there would be a single secular Palestine. However, he also intimated, with talk of peace, that there might be a compromise: 'Today I have come bearing an olive branch and a freedom fighter's gun. Do not let the olive branch fall from my hand.'

It was dramatic stuff and well received around the world. Not long afterwards, the PLO was given 'observer' status at the UN – this was tantamount to official recognition that Palestine was a nation-in-waiting. A year later the US finally accepted the inevitable and admitted that the Palestinians were more than just 'refugees' (as they had been described in UN Resolution 242). It was done in a low-key manner when Deputy Assistant Secretary of State Harold H. Saunders declared that in a general Middle East settlement, 'the legitimate interests of the Palestinian Arabs must be taken into account.' It was also suggested that the US might help the Palestinians if they accepted Resolution 242 and recognized Israel's right to exist.

It was a very small step on a very long journey, but at least it was movement.

Labour's difficulties

The nature of the 1973 October War had been a shock to Israelis. The greatest power in the region had been taken by surprise and brought perilously close to defeat. It had been saved not just by its own steadfastness but also by the US. For the first time since 1948, Israel's citizens had seen just how vulnerable their little state was.

The war left Israel even more dependent upon the US for diplomatic and military help, as well as more general aid. The conflict also undermined national confidence. This had two effects. One was a widening of the rift that was already a marked feature of Israeli political life: conservatives and traditionalists moved further to the right, while moderates and those on the left showed a greater willingness to compromise for peace. The second was mounting dissatisfaction with the Labour-based coalition that had been in power ever since the country's formation.

Golda Meir found it difficult to form a government and resigned in the spring of 1974. After a fiercely-contested vote, she was replaced as head of Labour by Yitzhak Rabin, the first locally-born politician to head the country's government. A native of Jerusalem, he had fought with the Haganah against the Palestinians and, latterly, had served as Israel's ambassador to the US. Elected to the Knesset only in 1973, his lack of political experience was compounded by an awkward manner.

Things went badly for Rabin and his Labour-led administration. When the troubles in Lebanon finally flared into civil war in 1975, for a while there was a very real fear that Israel's northern neighbour might fall into the hands of the PLO. To prevent this happening, Israel felt obliged to intervene actively in the Lebanese conflagration (see p. 145). This put still further strain on an overstretched economy.

Nearer home, the government submitted to constant pressure from extremist Zionists and accepted the first Israeli settlements in the occupied West Bank. Constructed contrary to international law, the new Jewish outposts worried moderates and infuriated the Palestinians. In the longer term, they would make it considerably more difficult for future Israeli administrations to find a compromise peace deal acceptable within Israel and with the PLO. From November 1975 onwards there was serious protest against the new settlements and against a plan to grant 'civil administration' (limited autonomy) to residents of the Occupied Territories. The latter was interpreted as simply a way of preparing the Palestinians for permanent occupation.

The world's press, once sympathetic towards 'plucky little Israel', was now increasingly likely to label Israel a bully state. This change of mood was reflected in a resolution passed by the General Assembly of the United Nations in November 1975: 'Zionism is a form of racism and racial discrimination.' Israel's sense of international isolation grew still more painful.

Palestinian identity

1976 was even grimmer for the Israeli government than 1975 had been. As the slaughter in Lebanon intensified, so Israel's commitment there grew (see p. 145). In March the Arabs living within Israel called for protests and a general strike to show disapproval of the government policy of appropriating land in Galilee for Jewish settlers. Six Arabs died when troops fired on a demonstration and the date – 30 March – became 'Land Day', an annual day of Palestinian protest.

From inside Israel, the commemoration of Land Day spread to the Occupied Territories. Here it became part of a swelling sense of Palestinian nationalism and identity. It was fostered by students, especially those of the new Palestine National University at Ramallah, by expanding trade unions and by women's groups. It expressed itself in protests, in art and literature. As we have seen, the *fedayeen* provided an endless stream of folk heroes (see p. 79). Poets, able and otherwise, immortalized their legendary qualities and exploits. Songs, such as *Biladi, Biladi!* ('My Country, My Country!'), sung to an Egyptian tune, roused the spirits of a people that for generations had found little to smile about or feel proud of.

The stirring of the national consciousness expressed itself in the Occupied Territories' municipal elections of April 1976. Although Israel had deported many community leaders, the turnout was high and the PLO and nationalist candidates swept the board. Two years later, the new mayors of Nablus, Ramallah and other large towns formed themselves into a National Guidance Committee. Thus slowly, almost imperceptibly at

Enter Likud

Harassed from abroad and unsure at home, Rabin's cabinet found little to quicken the pulse. Its one relief came in the summer of 1976, when Israeli commandos made a daring and successful raid on Entebbe airport, Uganda, to rescue 98 Israeli and Jewish passengers who had been on board an Air France plane hijacked by the PFLP. Less than a year later, Rabin resigned over accusations of an illegal overseas bank account. The following month, following a sharp electoral turn-around, the Labour party failed to gain sufficient Knesset seats to set up a new coalition. Consequently, for the first time since its formation, Israel had a right-wing government. This illustrated the division within Israeli society about the very nature of the new country. Profoundly harmful to the peace process, the rift remains to this day.

Likud had been formed four years earlier. At its core were the old Liberal and Herat ('Freedom') Parties, the heirs of Irgun and Lehi, and its principal electoral support came from the growing number of Sephardi who felt shabbily treated by successive Labour administrations. Intellectually and practically, Likud was hard-line: Israelis had a religious duty to take back and settle all the lands given to them by God in Old Testament times; He had allowed them to conquer the West Bank ('Judea and Samaria'), Gaza and the Golan Heights – now it was up to them to go and live there; as for the Palestinians, they were not a nation but simply Arabs who had been living in the province of Palestine; if they needed a homeland, then they had one in Jordan; there was nothing to be gained by negotiating with them, especially as they were led by *fedayeen*.

Such views were hardly conducive to the long-term peace of the Middle East. Coupled with the Palestinians' growing nationalism, their sense of outrage at the continued neglect of their plight, the ongoing *fedayeen* campaign, and the bitter fighting in Lebanon, the outlook was decidedly gloomy.

The new prime minister was Menachem Begin, a man against whom Ben-Gurion had warned several years before. Having lost family members in the Holocaust, been detained by the Soviets, fought with the Polish and with Irgun, he was a tough, suspicious, hard-headed individual. He saw anti-Semitism in all opposition to Israel, no matter how reasonable, and he believed that to survive in the sea of enemies that surrounded it, Israel had to stand firm behind an iron wall.

Begin's cabinet contained, somewhat surprisingly, the Labour Foreign Minister Moshe Dayan, Ezer Weizmann in charge of defence and Ariel Sharon as Minister of Agriculture. This last post encompassed settlement – what the right-wing called 'facts on the ground'. Within 25 years there were 220,000 Israeli settlers living in 'Judea and Samaria' and Gaza, another 200,000 in and around East Jerusalem and a further 15,000 on the Golan. 80 per cent of the West Bank's precious water was piped to Israeli settlements or to Israel itself.

The quest for peace

Jimmy Carter

Before Israel's elections had signalled a move to the right, the US had slipped towards the centre of the political spectrum with the 1976 election of Democratic President Jimmy Carter. Whereas Nixon and Ford had been pragmatists, focusing on the immediate problems of the Cold War, Carter was a 'big picture' man. Deeply religious, scrupulously honest and perhaps at first a little naive, he thought in terms of universal peace and moral justice, especially for the developing world. He was the first US president openly to acknowledge the sufferings of the Palestinians, declaring shortly after taking office that he believed they should have a 'homeland'. Later, when Israeli settlements in the Occupied Territories were declared technically illegal according to international law, the US State Department called on Israel to withdraw from the land it had seized in 1967. The European Community echoed the same request and by the end of 1977 there was talk of re-starting the Geneva Peace Conference.

It is now clear – as it was to many at the time – that the chances of getting all parties involved in the Israel–Palestine problem – not just Israel and the PLO, but Syria, Egypt, Jordan and Lebanon as well as the US and the USSR – round the same table, let alone talking constructively to each other, was negligible. There was hope, however, if the scale was reduced and the targets simplified.

At the end of the 1973 October War, the Egyptian Chief of Staff had observed to his Israeli deputy counterpart, 'Look... a war between us has ended in equality... From here we can negotiate.' From such sentiments had stemmed Sinai I and II before the process had ground to a halt (see p. 124). Sadat was keen for it to continue. Egypt's economy was suffering badly and in early 1977 there had been food riots in Cairo. As Carter was prepared to offer aid for peace, talks with the US were clearly to Sadat's advantage. A few hundred kilometres to the north, Prime Minister Begin was having similar thoughts. His prime concern was to secure his southern frontier so that the IDF could concentrate fully on the threat from the PLO in Lebanon. In other words, both Sadat and Begin wanted peace for their own very limited and practical reasons – and the Palestinians did not feature prominently in the thinking of either of them.

Deadlock

The autumn of 1977 saw a flurry of diplomatic activity in which Morocco's King Hassan II acted as a sophisticated go-between. Despite his best efforts, though, by November negotiations appeared to be grinding to a halt again. Sadat could not be seen openly to abandon the Palestinians while Begin could not accept any formula that accommodated them. On 9 November 1977, Sadat broke the impasse in the most dramatic manner possible. Speaking before the Egyptian National Assembly, he declared himself prepared to go 'to the ends of the earth' to find peace, even 'to the Knesset itself'. Astonished, the world awaited Begin's response. He dared not refuse the challenge and the Egyptian president was duly invited to Israel and asked to address the Knesset.

Sadat's speech was broad-ranging, talking of a general peace in the region, self-determination for the Palestinians and a return of the Occupied Territories. Deeply suspicious, Begin replied that certainly there could be talks, but with no pre-conditions. He did not once mention the Palestinians.

As if to emphasize Begin's uncompromising position, not long after Sadat's momentous initiative, new Israeli settlements were authorized in the Occupied Territories and further help was given to Christian militia fighting the PLO in Lebanon (see p. 145). Meanwhile, the Arab world had roundly condemned Sadat for breaking ranks. Israeli–Egyptian talks, begun in Ismailia in December 1977, meandered on into 1978. The atmosphere was not helped by the reuniting of the PFLP and PLO, the assassination of PLO leaders who had talked of reconciliation with Israel, and the murder of a Ramallah politician accused of collaborating with the Israelis.

In March 1978, Fatah *fedayeen* attacked a bus near Haifa in northern Israel. The ensuing slaughter saw 37 Israelis and six hijackers killed. Apparently, the aim of the attack had been to demonstrate that, to be meaningful, any talks about peace had to include the PLO. The raid had the opposite effect: the chances of the PLO now being involved in any formal discussions with the Israelis were non-existent. Begin likened Arafat to Adolf Hitler.

Camp David

Shangri-La

Jimmy Carter saved the day. In a move almost as startling as Sadat's visit to Jerusalem, he invited Sadat and Begin to discuss their differences at the presidential country retreat of Camp David, Maryland. Neither leader dared refuse. Originally named Shangri-La, Camp David was an excellent choice of venue. Its atmosphere was informal, relaxed even; there was sufficient suitable accommodation for each delegation to have its own separate building; above all, it was remote. This had two advantages: there was not a press microphone, TV camera or journalist's notebook for miles, and it was a very difficult place to leave. One could not simply storm out of Camp David because access was by helicopter and there was nowhere in the immediate vicinity to storm to. Begin even described it as an 'elegant jail'. Once Carter had got the two leaders inside the perimeter fence, he was determined not to let them go until they had reached an agreement.

The three heads of state were accompanied by extensive retinues that included, on the American side, Secretary of State Cyrus Vance, National Security Advisor Zbigniew Brzezinski and, towards the end, Vice-President Walter Mondale; the Israeli contingent contained Foreign Minister Moshe Dayan, Defence Minister Ezer Weizmann and Attorney General Aharon Barak; among President Sadat's advisors were the minister Muhammad Ibrahim Kamil and the Senior Presidential Advisor Osama El-Baz.

Consequently, although the Egyptian and Israeli premiers clearly disliked each other, there were sufficient wise men present for a number of mutual understandings to develop. For 14 days, Carter and his aides shuttled back and forth between the two sides, cajoling, suggesting and even threatening. Eventually agreement was reached and everyone was allowed to go home.

Accord

The Camp David Accords, which were formalized in a peace treaty the following March, were essentially under two heads. Israel and Egypt were at peace. Egypt received about $1 billion a year for much of the 1980s and Israel withdrew from the Sinai, dismantling its settlements and bases there. The US compensated their losses with a $3 billion loan. Relations between Israel and Egypt were restored to normality, with an exchange of ambassadors, air links and so forth.

The second part of the agreement – a 'Framework for Peace in the Middle East' – was a good deal less concrete. Israel accepted the 'legitimate rights' of the Palestinians, whatever that might mean, and agreed to their having 'full autonomy' after a transitional period – another equally vague phrase. Nothing was said about Jerusalem or Israeli withdrawal, although Begin had at least recognized that the Palestinians existed. In practical terms, though, he had committed to nothing, and he did nothing. Like Sadat, he had got what he wanted. The IDF now had a free hand to tackle the PLO in the north.

The aftermath

Begin and Sadat were both awarded Nobel Peace Prizes, although President Carter probably deserved one more than either of them. In 1981 Sadat paid for his with his life when he was assassinated by Muslim fanatics. By this time Egypt had been ejected from the Arab League and subjected to sanctions from other Arab states. Significantly, still keen to get on the right side of the US, Arafat maintained secret links with the Egyptian government.

Begin was criticized by Zionist extremists who called for the agreement with Egypt to be scrapped. They were to some extent mollified when it became clear that Begin planned to do nothing about Palestinian 'autonomy', which he defined as a purely personal matter, and when Israelis were allowed to make private purchases of land in the West Bank. After Camp David, despite an Israeli High Court ruling that settlements made for political purposes were illegal (1979), the number of Jewish villages in the West Bank doubled and the total number of Israelis living within the Occupied Territories rose fivefold. In protest, Moshe Dayan resigned from the government in 1979 and Ezer Weizmann followed him a year later.

And the Palestinians? When post-Camp David talks for a wider peace in the Middle East collapsed in 1979, their worst fears were confirmed: in the last instance, their fellow Arabs would always put national and self interest before that of the wider Arab world. Palestinian condemnation of the Camp David Accords was almost universal and there were violent attacks on those who showed any inclination to support them. Yet the Egyptian 'sell-out' brought a wave of Arab sympathy for the Palestinians and Gulf funding for the PLO increased. Furthermore, an Israeli government had at least mentioned Palestinian autonomy. That, at the very least, was a start.

A start it might have been, but there it would rest for a long time. The Camp David Accords were not the only dramatic change taking place in the region. Civil war still flared in Lebanon and the PLO and Israelis were both heavily involved. Even more significant, at the beginning of 1979 the Shah of Iran was overthrown and his country became an Islamic republic. The age of militant Islam was dawning, bringing a new spirit of fiery intolerance to the already intractable Israeli–Palestinian confrontation.

In depth: Gush Emunim

Gush Emunim was the most prominent of several extreme Zionist religious groups that led the settlement of lands occupied by Israeli forces during the Six-Day War of 1967. Its work infuriated the Palestinians and made any long-term solution to the problem of the Occupied Territories much harder to achieve.

The fervent Zionist Rabbi Zvi Yehuda Kook (1891–1982) taught that in returning to the land of Israel, given to them by God in Biblical times, the Jews had hastened the coming of the Messiah (Saviour). The remarkable conquests of 1967, he believed, had instigated the Messianic Age, which would be crowned by the Saviour's arrival. Therefore it was the duty of all those of Jewish faith to settle (or re-settle, as they saw it) the land that God had placed in their hands.

Gush Emunim ('Block of the Faithful', also known as 'Those Who Are Faithful to the Land of Israel') was established to see Rabbi Kook's teaching put into practice. In 1968, led by Rabbi Moshe Levinger, a small band of Gush Emunim fanatics established a presence at Kiyat Arba, just outside Hebron. They were returning, they said, to where Jews had lived before the 1929 massacre. The site comprised no more than temporary shelters until 1971, when more permanent structures were begun on an abandoned army base. By 2005 the population of the settlement and surrounding homesteads was over 9,000.

Even more significant was the offshoot of Gush Emunim that attempted to settle at Elon Moreh, a kilometre or so north of the Palestinian town of Nablus. Israeli troops forced them to leave seven times before Prime Minister Rabin, pressured by Ariel Sharon, relented and let the settlers stay. The permission, temporary at first, soon became permanent. Thereafter, Israeli settlements on the Occupied Territories mushroomed. To his dying day Rabin bitterly regretted having given way to Gush Emunim, a movement that he believed was a threat to Israel's democracy. Whether it was or not, its band of dedicated followers had altered the course of the country's history and with it the history of the whole region.

In depth: PFLP

Nowadays the Marxist-Leninist Popular Front for the Liberation of Palestine (PFLP) appears rather old-fashioned, although it retains a surprisingly large following among better-educated Palestinians, especially students. The movement was founded in 1967 by George Habash, a Palestinian Christian whose family the Israelis had forced into exile in 1948. In keeping with its founder's far-left, secularist views, the Front called for Palestinians to join an armed pan-Arab, anti-capitalist movement to crush Israel and all other reactionary and West-favouring regimes in the Middle East. A confusing array of splinter groups, such as the Popular Front for the Liberation of Palestine – General Command (PFLP-GC), the Maoist Democratic Front for the Liberation of Palestine (DFLP) and the Popular Revolutionary Front for the Liberation of Palestine (PRFLP) all broke away from the PFLP during the 1960s and early 1970s.

The Front, which was second in size only to Fatah within the PLO, first came to public attention with its attacks on aircraft and airports. It was bitterly opposed to the Camp David Agreement and the Oslo Accords but found the rise of Islamist groups, which shared many of its political aims, a difficult challenge to meet. Regarding itself as scientific and modern, the Front held that a return to beliefs and practices of former times would in the long run do nothing to help the cause of Palestinians and the working-class in general. This was an awkward stance because the bulk of the Islamists' support came from the very people – the poor and ill-educated – for whom the Front professed to be fighting.

The PFLP boycotted the 1996 Palestinian elections but backed Marwhan Barghouti in the 2004 vote to replace Arafat. It then contested the 2006 elections to the Palestinian legislature, winning 4.2 per cent of the vote and gaining three seats. Such moderate success may have been due to the way it had resumed its guerrilla campaign with fresh energy at the onset of the Second Intifada, claiming the lives of over 20 Israelis.

10

Lebanon

This chapter will cover:
- Lebanon, the PLO and civil war
- Israel and the Occupied Territories, 1979–87
- Israel's invasion of Lebanon
- further international attempts at peace making.

The compromise state

Uneasy stability

The modern state of Lebanon was created by the French after World War I. Within its boundaries lived a diverse and potentially explosive collection of peoples and faiths that may be simplified as Palestinians, Christians, Druze, Sunnis and Shia. Tragically, by the 1970s, the conditions that enabled the subtle power-sharing constitution to hold the country together were rapidly breaking down.

The Christian minority, not more than 40 per cent of the population, had always been the wealthiest sector and had traditionally cornered the most influential positions, including the presidency. Among the Christians, the Maronites, numbering perhaps a quarter of all Lebanese, were particularly prominent. As the population grew, the proportion of comparatively poor rural Muslims also increased. Beirut, the capital, had expanded to the point where almost one half of all Lebanese lived within or close to its perimeters. It had also grown into a divided and increasingly wary city in which the different ethnic and religious communities inhabited distinct and discrete quarters.

Lebanon's refusal to join with the other Arab nations in their wars with Israel in 1967 and 1973 angered many Lebanese Muslims. There was also the problem of Palestinian refugees. Since 1948, around 270,000 of them had found shelter in Lebanon, some doing well (Lebanon's largest construction company was Palestinian-owned) but the vast majority remaining poor and landless. Like the majority of Lebanon's Muslims, the Palestinians felt their interests were ignored by the ruling class.

Enter the PLO

Into this dangerous mix came the PLO. Driven from Jordan at the end of 1970, they arrived in Lebanon with their weapons, their separate organization and, above all, with their independent, aggressive attitude. Many Lebanese, especially the Christians and the more intellectual, better-educated Palestinians, regarded them as little more than bandits who levied taxes, set up road blocks and generally behaved as if they owned the place. The PLO was tainted by corruption, too, and

It was rumoured that some of its bureaucrats earned a private income by selling arms to the Lebanese Christians. To add to the frustration of the PLO's opponents, Palestinian cross-border sallies against Israel drew disproportionately violent and destructive reprisals.

That, however, is only part of the story. To many of the refugees the PLO was, almost literally, a godsend. It had money and confidence, commodities a generation of camp-dwellers singularly lacked. The Palestine National Fund which the PLO had at its disposal, most of it Gulf money, reached about $233 million a year by the late 1980s. Long before that, its members had infiltrated themselves into all aspects of camp life, making and mending roads, providing electricity, running schools, clinics, hospitals and even their own revolutionary courts. Equally significant, they fostered a sense of Palestinian nationalism, flying the Palestinian flag at every available opportunity, teaching nationalistic songs, publishing nationalistic stories and poetry. The young, especially, were fostered for the cause: for the boys there was the *Ashbal* (Lion Cub) movement, for the girls the *Zahrat* (Flowers).

Much of the PLO's work was crude, ignorant and bullying. There was corruption and internecine squabbling that on occasion became violent. Yet overall the effect was to build up a sense of steely purpose and hope among a downtrodden people. Small wonder Menachem Begin had signed the Camp David Accords in the belief that they would free him to turn north and obliterate the PLO's state within a state.

Civil war

One more piece of the Lebanese collage remains to be explained: the paramilitary Phalange. This was a right-wing, Christian, military-political organization whose 10,000-stong militia was as ruthless as it was well-armed. With a neo-fascist motto that proclaimed 'God, the Fatherland, and the Family', they believed themselves to be descended from the ancient Phoenicians, not the Arabs; they rejected Pan-Arabism and hated the PLO.

In 1975, Lebanon slid into civil war: the fishermen of Sidon went on strike; clashes with the authorities turned violent; a prominent Muslim was assassinated; shots were fired in a church; the Phalange ambushed a busload of PFLP supporters... and by May the country was tearing itself apart. Central government collapsed and local warbands imposed what order they could. Arms, ranging from sophisticated rocket launchers to simple rifles and grenades, flooded into the country, particularly from Syria, Iraq and Israel. Planeloads of Lebanese fled the mayhem, destruction and slaughter. Of those who could not get away, some 70,000 lost their lives. Most were innocent civilians.

Lebanon's neighbours and others, all with their separate agendas, inevitably kept a close eye on the situation. Initially Syria helped the PLO against the Christian militias, who were backed by Israel. However, when by mid-1976 it looked as if the Christians might be wholly defeated and Lebanon fall into the hands of the PLO and its Muslim allies, the Syrians made common cause with the Israelis to prevent this happening. President Assad had long regarded Lebanon with covetous eyes and had no wish to see his prosperous neighbour become a left-wing Palestinian stronghold. Therefore, in the most Machiavellian of moves, a secret deal was brokered by the US in which Syrian forces entered Lebanon, ostensibly as peacekeepers but really to fight alongside the Christian Tiger and Phalange militias. That summer the Palestinian losses were horrific.

Impasse

A ceasefire agreed in October 1976 reduced the violence but did not stop it. Broadly speaking, the Syrians remained in control of the east and north of the country – the Christian bases were north of Beirut – while the PLO had strengthened its positions in the south. Despite the warfare, Arafat was trying to present the PLO as a reasonable organization willing to come to terms with Israel. This may have been true, but there were many under the PLO umbrella (the 'Rejectionists') to whom accord with the enemy was impossible, and from 1977 Israel had a prime minister who considered accord with the PLO unthinkable. The old cliché was painfully relevant: Arafat was between a rock and a hard place.

The autumn of 1977 saw a number of bloody incidents on the Israel–Lebanon border. On one occasion the IDF advanced towards the Litani River, only to be recalled when an irate President Carter learned that the Israelis were deploying US equipment provided for strictly defensive purposes. The following March, the IDF again drove into what it called 'Fatahland', this time reaching the Litani. Perhaps 1,000 Palestinians and Lebanese were killed, including 75 when an air strike hit a mosque. A ceasefire was quickly called, accepted by Fatah and policed by the

UN The Rejectionists turned it down and attacked the UN peacekeepers. In the far south, Israel established a 'good fence' policy, providing Lebanese Christians just across the border with aid of every kind, including weaponry, in return for help against the PLO. This led to the formation of the Christian, Israeli-backed South Lebanese Army (SLA).

That, more or less, was where things stood as Begin signed his Accords with President Sadat. Likud and its right-wing backers in the Knesset wanted the PLO eliminated and a pro-Israeli Christian government firmly established in Beirut – at almost any cost. Moderate-minded Israelis were worried at their country's new aggressive posture and the more militant of them had joined a growing Peace Now movement. Arafat, boosted by understanding noises coming out of the Carter White House, seemed genuinely keen to find a peaceful solution to his people's difficulties. He was increasingly isolated from the sentiments of the Occupied Territories, however, where Palestinian nationalism was becoming more anti-Israeli (see p. 155); he was also unable to control or convert the more hard-line Palestinian factions, who were pledged to settle for nothing less than the destruction of Israel. In the short term, it seemed, diplomatic solutions were out of the question. It was down to sheer brute force.

Israel, Likud and the Occupied Territories

Divided Israel

This is essentially the story of two competing nationalisms, two peoples contesting ownership of the same piece of land. During the 1920s and 1930s it was hoped the two could live together in the same state. When that was clearly impossible, partition was suggested. This was rejected by those who owned the great bulk of the land, the Palestinians. In the fighting that followed over the next 25 years, the Palestinians lost control over all their land and found themselves either in exile or under foreign domination. They had never been a self-governing nation and now, in the 1980s, they were a scattered and divided people.

This is roughly how the Jews had been before 1948. Since then, although bound together by a distinctive religion, a common language and ancient heritage, they had found nation-building a difficult process. Israel of the mid-1980s was a mini-United Nations: under 20 per cent of the population were Israeli-born; slightly more were of Asian (largely Russian) or African origin, and just under 40 per cent came from Europe or the US. Each sector bought with it distinctive customs and attitudes.

Broadly speaking, Sephardi Israelis (see p. 62) were conservative, less well educated and inclined to be less tolerant than their Ashkenazi counterparts. Many had come from cultures where life for Jews had been hard – and cheap. They had had to fight to survive. When aligned with the religious zealots who came to Israel from all parts of the globe determined to fulfil what they believed were holy Biblical prophesies and commands, they created a powerful and illiberal bloc that democratic politicians ignored to their cost. Under its influence, Israel followed aggressive policies that the state's founding fathers would never have considered. Much of the remaining international sympathy for Israel drained away, and across the country the deep and grievous socio-political divide widened.

Likud returns

The elections of the summer of 1981 gave Likud one more Knesset seat than Labour and enabled Begin to remain as prime minister. The opposition had been hampered by squabbling between its two senior men, Yitzhak Rabin and Shimon Peres, and by votes going to Peace Now. In contrast, at the last minute Begin had used a daring display of military machismo to pick up the votes of wavering right-wingers who disapproved of the Camp David Accords: three weeks before the elections, Israeli bombers had penetrated Iraqi air space and destroyed a reactor said to be capable of producing nuclear warheads.

Secure in the cabinet, Prime Minister Begin, Foreign Minister Shamir and Defence Minister Sharon were free to pursue their policies of confrontation and containment of the Palestinians. The emotional and economic strain these put on Israel was enormous. Over 600 soldiers were killed, international opprobrium soared, and the economy came close to collapse as unemployment rose and inflation topped a staggering 400 per cent per annum. The strain on Begin was great too, and, depressed by the death of his wife, he broke. After resigning in August 1983, he had some sort of collapse and disappeared from public life.

Shamir took over as prime minister in October and invited Labour to join a government of national unity to sort out the mess. Unpopular economic austerity measures were one reason why Likud won less seats than Labour at the 1984 elections. More significant in terms of the way Israeli society was now divided, Shamir lost votes to the crypto-fascist ultranationalists. Nevertheless, Labour did not have enough support to form a cabinet of its own and so a unique power-sharing device was organized. A unity government would be headed by Labour's Peres for two years, then Shamir would take over for the next two years. Rabin was Minister of Defence under both. The new administration took the necessary steps to restore the economy but did nothing to placate the rising sense of furious frustration in the Occupied Territories.

Settlement

Before 1981, the man with the most influence in the Occupied Territories was Agriculture Minister Ariel Sharon. His policy was simple: settle the West Bank and Gaza with Israelis, making the future establishment of a purely Palestinian state there impossible; clamp down on Palestinian nationalism; and, where practicable, encourage Palestinians to emigrate to other parts of the Arab world. Though pleasing to Israel's hard-right, such as the influential National Religious Party, in the long run these tough measures proved painfully counter-productive.

The 'creeping annexation' of Gaza and 'Judea and Samaria' was speeded up by giving financial incentives, such as cheap mortgages, to those willing to go and live there. Sharon's policy took over eight per cent of Israel's budget. Its consequences were dramatic: the proportion of the West Bank under direct Israeli control, either through ownership or by military order, rose from about one-third in 1983 to almost nine-tenths by 1988.

Settlements on open hilltops were less controversial than those in or very close to large Palestinian conurbations, such as Hebron, the 'City of the Patriarchs' holy to Jews, Muslims and Christians. A decision to restore the centre of old Hebron in 1983, for instance, and maintain an Israeli presence there was highly contentious. Even more so was the Basic Law (equivalent to a constitutional amendment) of July 1980 that annexed all Jerusalem to the State of Israel, although maintaining open access to believers of all faiths. The extension of Israeli law to the Golan region the following year provoked a furious reaction from the local Druze. Their strikes and other protests drew fierce repression.

'Iron fist'

To counter the influence of the PLO and rising Palestinian nationalism, in 1978 the Israeli government appointed a secular governor of the West Bank and sought to establish pro-Israeli 'Village Leagues'. The experiment was a complete flop and abandoned in 1981. Instead, the occupiers came to rely on a repressive policy known as the 'iron fist'. From a purely practical point of view, the policy made sense: if the Israelis let Palestinian nationalism grow unchecked, they would quickly find the Occupied Territories slipping from their grasp. However, they soon discovered that harshness only increased the sentiments they were trying to crush.

'Iron fist' measures included cancelling municipal elections in the West Bank, banning all contact with the PLO, censorship, curfews, the use of live ammunition when quelling riots, bulldozing or blowing up the houses of those taking part in or suspected of taking part in anti-Israeli activities, and banning display of the Palestinian flag. In 1982 the National Guidance Committee of elected mayors was outlawed and several mayors sacked and replaced by appointed Israeli officials. The clamp down became even tighter in the mid-1980s, with detention of suspects without trial and deliberate breaking of the bones of those detained.

When two Palestinian *fedayeen* were taken alive after a failed hijack in 1984, it was announced shortly afterwards that they had died of their gunshot injuries. Since many had testified to the men being uninjured at the time of their capture, suspicions were raised. A committee of investigation found that members of Shin Bet, the Israeli internal security agency, had killed the prisoners while they were held in custody. Ten years later it was revealed that their skulls had been crushed between massive stones, apparently a common Shin Bet practice.

In contrast to the heavy-handed treatment of the Palestinians, Israeli military and legal officials tended to treat lightly settlers who perpetrated violence. Even so, in 1984 they did foil an attempt by the Jewish 'Terror Against Terror' group to blow up Jerusalem's Al-Aqsa mosque. Less impressive was the way Israeli troops stood by when, in 1980, militant Islamists burned down the Gaza offices of those associated with the secular Fatah.

At this point it should be emphasized that in no way did Israel have a monopoly of violence or cruelty. Indeed, it may be argued that in striking indiscriminately at civilian Israelis – woman and children as well as men – the *fedayeen* were the more reprehensible. Moreover, they were accountable to no one. Israel was at least a democracy where the rule of law was supposed to run. But it was a democracy permanently at war, and in those circumstances normal decent and humane standards are invariably lowered. We may also add in defence of Israel that, however unpleasant its policies and tactics, outside the Occupied Territories the freedom of the press was not curtailed and the people were allowed to protest at what their government was doing. And many surely did, loud and long.

Israel remained a free enough society for army reserve officers to make a public protest in 1982 against what they were being asked to do in the West Bank. Acting with 'violence and brutality' against crying women and stone-throwing children, they complained, 'we are losing our humanity'. One cannot imagine such public statements being allowed in any other Middle Eastern state at the time, let alone in an area controlled by the PLO. On 2 March 1986, the PFLP assassinated the Israeli-appointed but PLO-approved mayor of Nablus, Zafir al-Masri. His crime? Building links between West Bank leaders and Jordan with a view to a possible confederation of the two. Certainly, the Palestinians had no more reason to be proud of their behaviour than had the Israelis.

Invasion of Lebanon

Ceasefire and breach

When Ariel Sharon was installed as Israeli Defence Minister in mid-1981, Prime Minister Begin had a man after his own heart in the key position for a final push against the PLO. Despite Arafat having said privately that he would recognize Israel in return for Israel recognizing a Palestine in the West Bank, Begin was convinced that the PLO was a 'terrorist organization' dedicated to the 'destruction of the Jewish state'. To a Jew of his generation, with such people there could be no compromise.

Israel had recently been active in Lebanon before Sharon took over. In April 1981, Israeli jets supporting the Christian militia shot down two Syrian helicopters. In July, following attacks with Soviet-made Katyusha rockets into Galilee, the IDF bombarded Southern Lebanon and launched an air attack that obliterated the PLO headquarters in Beirut. The US then brokered a ceasefire that Arafat was intent on keeping. Eager for a peace deal, he was desperate to prove himself a man of his word. It was later revealed that the PLO and the US were actually holding secret peace talks at the time. For the moment, therefore, Begin and Sharon were stymied.

The Israeli cabinet was buoyed by the recent election of Ronald Reagan. The Republican president had already expressed a strong dislike of all things left of centre, including the PLO, and of any organization that smacked of terrorism, which also included the PLO. Moreover, his unsophisticated secretary of state, Alexander Haig, regarded Israel as a 'strategic asset' in America's Cold War. Begin was sure that, in public at least, his actions would be supported by the White House.

Nevertheless, although all the world knew Israel was bursting to move into Lebanon, a viable pretext for invasion was still required. Despite provocation, it took a while. In October 1981 a car bomb wrecked a PLO base in Beirut. The following spring Israel twice attacked PLO strongholds in Lebanon and at one stage shot down two Syrian MIGs. But still the PLO abided by the ceasefire. Eventually, Begin and Sharon got what they needed from an ex-Fatah fighter by the name of Abu Nidal. Rejected by mainstream Palestinians, this near-psychopathic killer was pursuing his own trail of murder and on 21 April shot the Israeli ambassador in London. The man survived. To Begin and Sharon this was irrelevant, however, as was the fact that Abu Nidal had been thrown out of the PLO for attempting to assassinate Arafat himself. Declaring 'they're all PLO', Begin ordered the IDF into Lebanon.

Peace for Galilee

Announcing they were advancing 40 kilometres into Lebanon to make the 63 settlements in northern Israel safe from PLO attacks, Israel launched Operation Peace for Galilee with overwhelming force: 80,000 troops, 1,240 tanks, 1,520 armoured personnel carriers and hundreds of artillery pieces. Reaching the 40 kilometre mark in a matter of hours, Sharon commanded the IDF to press on. By 13 June they had surrounded Beirut. Most of the PLO and thousands of civilians were trapped inside the city. On the road, the Syrians had been pushed back to the east and the PLO crushed.

Before it happened, the invasion idea had general approval within Israel. Now it had clearly gone further than many expected, support began to waver. Abroad, condemnation of blatant aggression against a sovereign state was almost universal. The major exception was the US. While saying the Israeli action was 'deplorable' and banning the shipment to Israel of certain exotically cruel weapons such as cluster bombs, President Reagan vetoed the Security Council resolution excoriating his ally's behaviour. And it was US funds that permitted Begin and Sharon to continue their $1 million-a-day campaign.

Beirut and to a lesser extent Tyre and Sidon were besieged, bombed and shelled for two months. To add to the misery, water and electricity supplies were cut. Lebanon's capital, once the proud 'Paris of the Middle East', was reduced to a scarred and stinking ghost town of rubble, pock-marked concrete and dark, sinister voids. Around 33,000 died, mostly civilians, and at least 100,000 were made homeless. As the conflict was conducted before the world's TV cameras, Israel's international reputation reached its nadir.

Mission failure

The added tragedy of operation 'Peace for Galilee' was that it failed. First, the Lebanese Christian leader, Bashir Jemayel, refused to play the part the Israelis had assigned to him. He would not send his men into Beirut to drive out the remains of the PLO. Neither, later, would he make peace when Begin wanted him to. Sharon's dream of a compliant puppet state on Israel's northern border remained unfulfilled.

Nor was the PLO destroyed. In mid-August, to prevent what he termed another Holocaust, President Reagan finally called the Israelis off. After one last day of horrendous bombardment, Sharon silenced his guns and the PLO, which had fought with remarkable courage and bravery, were allowed to leave by sea. Taking their small arms with them, most made their way to Tripoli, where Arafat established a new headquarters. By destroying the PLO, Sharon had hoped to cut Palestinian nationalism off at the root. Instead, the PLO had survived and Palestinian nationalism, boosted by 1,000 new martyrs and stories of legendary heroism, was stronger than ever.

Massacre

Lebanon's tale of horror was far from over. Before the arrival of an international peace-keeping force of largely American, French and Italian troops, the Israelis made themselves masters of much of the south and west of the country by occupying Beirut. The previous day, Bashir Jemayel, now president elect of Lebanon, had been killed by a bomb that blew up his party headquarters. The Syrians were implicated, and the outraged Phalange thirsted for revenge.

In West Beirut, four kilometres north of the airport, lay the two large Palestinian refugee camps of Sabra and Shatila. They were filled not only with their normal incumbents but with Muslim refugees – including Palestinians – who had fled there during the recent fighting. Among them were some PLO and other *fedayeen*. The day after the Israelis took charge of the area, heavily armed Christian militia entered the camps to weed out the guerrillas. They did so with Israeli consent and approval. At night fall the Israelis even lit the scene to assist their allies.

As soon became obvious from the pandemonium within the camps, the militia had not gone in simply to hunt down a few paramilitaries but to indulge in wholesale slaughter, rape, mutilation and other ghastly crimes. Men, women and children all suffered. No one knows how many died. The Lebanese Army said the figure was 474, including 16 children, 14 women and 21 Iranians. The IDF's figure was 700–800 dead. Other sources, talking of mass graves, said the number was between 1,800 and 3,000.

Whatever the true figure, the slaughter was an inexcusable and horrific crime. It provoked massive protest rallies in Israel and universal worldwide condemnation. Bowing to public pressure, Begin's government announced a full-scale enquiry. The Kahan Commission found that although Sharon and the IDF could not be held directly responsible for the Sabra–Shatila massacre, the Israeli forces could have done more to prevent it. Sharon stepped down as Minister of Defence (1983) but remained within the cabinet.

The slaughter goes on

Following the Sabra and Shatila massacres, Israel negotiated an armistice with President Amin Gemayel, brother of the assassinated Bashir. It lasted, on and off, for about a year and involved the IDF falling back to a line south of Beirut. Eventually, in the spring of 1985, Israel's unity government, headed by Prime Minister Peres, ordered the IDF back towards the frontier with Israel. Its last elements finally pulled out of southern Lebanon in 2000.

In the meantime, the tit-for-tat fighting with various types of *fedayeen* continued. In 1983, open warfare broke out between Fatah groups hostile to and supporting Yasser Arafat. At the end of the year, a bomb destroyed the Israeli headquarters in Tyre, killing 60. Shortly afterwards six civilians were killed by a PLO bomb on a bus in Jerusalem and, two months later, Katyusha rockets were again falling on Galilee. 1985 saw Israeli/CIA attacks on a new, Iranian-backed force in the region, Hezbollah (see p. 152). There was also more Fatah in-fighting, an Israeli air force attack on the PLO headquarters in Tunis (from which Arafat amazingly emerged unscathed), and a *fedayeen* hijacking of the cruise liner *Achille Lauro* in which a disabled Jewish-American passenger was killed. At the end of the year, Abu Nidal grabbed the headlines again by bombing Rome and Vienna airports, killing 20 and wounding over 100.

Lebanon's complex and ever-shifting civil war dragged on to the end of the decade, concluding only when the Syrian Army was in a position to impose a ceasefire. This was something the international peacekeepers had singularly failed to do. By the spring of 1983, Americans, Italians and French were being picked off by another, Syrian-based *fedayeen* group, Islamic Jihad (see pp. 189–90). When one of its suicide bombers drove a truck laden with explosives into the American Embassy in Beirut and blew away the central section of the building, human remains were found floating in the Mediterranean. The attack prompted the US into an ineffective offensive against the Evil Empire of the red flag and its sympathizers. Nothing symbolized the operation's inappropriately heavy-handed impotence more than the USS *New Jersey* lobbing 40-centimetre (16-inch) shells inland in the general direction of Druze positions. Stung into even more determined resistance, in October 1983, suicide bombers slew over 300 American and French peacekeepers in their bases. Within a year, the international forces had gone home.

Searching for peace

The bitter fruits of war

Intended to end the Israel–Palestine problem, Israel's intervention in the long-drawn-out Lebanese civil war had only made things worse. As we have seen, one effect of the October 1973 War had been to strengthen Israel's political right (see p. 127). This gave political power and influence to hard-line religious Zionists who had little time for compromise. The Lebanese escapade had now brought hard-line fanatical Muslims into the equation on the Palestinian side. The emergence of Hezbollah ('the Party of God'), for instance, appeared to stem directly from the IDF's attacks on Shia communities that had hitherto been neutral. Backed by the theocratic regime in Iran, such zealots barely understood the meaning of compromise.

By the mid-1980s, therefore, it was even more difficult for moderates on both sides – and there were times now when even Arafat was starting to look like a moderate – to find a deal acceptable to all their constituents. This became abundantly clear when a whole series of proposed compromise deals proved stillborn or died in their infancy.

Peace talks

Early in 1981, the Soviet leader Leonid Brezhnev put forward a Middle East peace plan based upon Resolution 242. He hoped to re-fashion his country's image in the Middle East and take back the diplomatic initiative from the US now that the memories of Camp David were fading and the Americans had been humiliated by the Iranian Revolution. The Soviet plan proved barren. The US's secret talks with the PLO ended the following year with no agreement. Before that, Crown Prince Fahad of Saudi Arabia had thrown his hat (or rather *gutra*) into the ring by offering an eight-point peace plan of his own. It was rejected by Israel and later, under pressure from Syria and others, by Arafat. Eventually, even Syria came up with a peace-for-land deal. The chances of Begin accepting anything put forward by Assad without US backing were non-existent.

In September 1982, just after the PLO had been forced from Lebanon, President Reagan came up with a new and quite feasible peace proposal. It featured three ideas. First, the Palestinians should have their own self-governing entity, based on the West Bank and Gaza but linked to Jordan. Second, Israel should freeze settlement-building in the Occupied Territories. Third, the future of Jerusalem should be left for negotiations at a later date. For the first time the Americans were formally including the Palestinians in their plans and Arafat gave the proposal a cautious welcome. The Israeli Labour party liked it, too, but not Likud. Begin's immediate response was to approve still more West Bank settlements. Although accepting a settlement freeze would have deprived him of the support of the far right, his reaction was singularly provocative.

Five days after the launching of the Reagan Plan, the Arab Summit meeting in Fez came up with yet another set of proposals. Some believe that if the Americans had leaned a little harder on Israel at this stage, the combined Reagan and Fez initiatives might have got somewhere. Sadly, though, it did not happen. Talks, open and secret, continued over the next two years. Arafat was keen to compromise. The negotiations were serious enough for Abu Nidal to assassinate an important figure in the PLO team and for the PFLP and several similar splinter groups to form a 'Democratic Alliance' against what was happening. This split the Palestinian leadership three ways, between Arafat's compromise-seeking Fatah, the new anti-negotiation left-wing Alliance, and the religious hard-liners who were equally unwilling to talk to Israel.

The closest the negotiators came to agreement was in 1985, when Arafat and King Hussein produced an Aman Accord for a confederacy between Jordan and the Occupied Territories. Although not acceptable to the PFLP and its associates, Prime Minister Peres of Israel at first reacted to the proposal with a degree of flexibility. The optimism was short-lived. Arafat would not accept Resolution 242 as it did not mention Palestinian self-determination and Peres agreed to the bombing of the Tunis headquarters of the PLO in retaliation for the murder of three Israelis in Cyprus. This 'Israeli state terrorism', as the PLO put it, badly soured relations again. Finally, an agreement between Peres and King Hussein, made in October 1986, drowned in a sea of acrimony when it was revealed to Yitzhak Shamir, who had just replaced Peres as prime minister under the terms of their 1984 post-election pact.

If all this seems complicated, tortuous to the point of irritation and ultimately deeply frustrating, it was. Particularly to the pawns in the middle of it all, those whom all the fighting and talking were about: the ordinary Palestinian men, women and children of the West Bank and Gaza Strip. In the end, tired of being ignored, fought over and bullied, they decided to take matters into their own hands. The result was one of the most extraordinary demonstrations of people power since World War II – the Intifada.

In depth: Hezbollah

Hezbollah – the 'Party of God' – emerged in 1982 out of a group of around 2,000 Iranian revolutionary guards sent to Lebanon to fight the Israelis. A band of leading Shia clerics acted as midwives for the birth. The movement's original aim was to help drive the invader from Lebanon. After that it grew into a huge military, religious, socio-economic and political force within that country. It won 14 seats in the Lebanese Parliament in 2005 and was rewarded with two ministerial portfolios.

Within Israel and the West, Hezbollah was known as a terrorist organization dedicated to carrying Iran's Islamist revolution across the face of the globe by whatever means it deemed necessary. This included the use of extreme violence in the form of guerrilla warfare and suicide bombings. Hezbollah operated primarily in Lebanon with support from Syria and Iran. Western security services also believed it had managed to establish cells in Europe and the Americas. Among its notable operations were the spate of kidnappings of Westerners in Lebanon in the 1980s, the truck bombing of a US marine barracks in Beirut in 1983, attacks on Israeli–Jewish targets in Argentina in 1992 and 1994, and the capture of two Israeli soldiers in the summer of 2006 which led to the Israeli bombardment and invasion of Lebanon.

By the 1990s, Hezbollah was a potent force in Lebanese politics. Its support was strongest among exiled Palestinians and native Lebanese from the impoverished Shia community. Adherents were attracted by the group's programme of social welfare, providing help with schools, houses, mosques, medical centres and other such facilities. There was evidence that those not wedded to Hezbollah's extreme religious views were prepared to pay lip service to them (wearing 'seemly' dress, for instance) in order to receive assistance.

Hezbollah showed itself capable of acting independently of Tehran and Damascus. Indeed, its relationship with the secular Syrian regime was complex, revealing a degree of pragmatism among its leaders that hinted at the possibility of a compromise peace with Israel one day.

In depth: the Herut and Likud parties

Founded by Menachem Begin in 1948, Herut or 'Freedom' was one of Israel's earliest right-wing parties. Its roots lay in the Irgun paramilitary group that had fought the British before Israel's independence, and all its life Herut maintained an uncompromising attitude towards anyone or anything that might imperil the State of Israel. Its right-wing mix of nationalism, Zionism and racism so worried some prominent American Jews that in 1948 they openly condemned the party as neo-fascist.

Throughout Labour's long dominance of Israeli politics, Herut controlled around 10–20 Knesset seats and hounded successive governments with assiduity. For example, it helped bring down the ruling coalitions in 1954 and 1961. Herut's support came mainly from Sephardi and blue-collar workers resentful at the perceived dominance of a wealthy, liberal-minded Ashkenazi élite. In the 1970s, Herut merged with other right-wing parties to form first the Likud coalition, then a distinctive Likud Party.

Likud ('Consolidation'), led by Begin, formed Israel's first right-wing government in 1977. Not until 1988, however, was it formally instituted as a single political party. Its policies were anti-socialist and, in matters of security, largely against any compromise with the Palestinians. Three of its four leaders – Menachem Begin (1973–1982), Yitzhak Shamir (1983–1992) and Ariel Sharon (1999–2005) – were robust military men who had seen action first hand. Together with Benjamin Netanyahu (leader 1993–1999, 2005 onwards), they openly opposed the establishment of a Palestinian state and were highly reluctant to surrender any of the Golan Heights, Gaza Strip or West Bank.

That said, it was Likud's Menachem Begin who signed the Camp David Accords with Egypt and Yitzhak Shamir who agreed to meet with the Palestinians (but not the PLO) at the 1991 Madrid Conference. Moreover, Sharon's controversial acceptance in 2004 of unilateral Israeli withdrawal from some of the Occupied Territories (the Disengagement Plan) sent shivers of horror through Likud ranks. The party was thrown into further disarray when Sharon left to form Kadima at the end of 2005.

The 2006 Knesset elections gave Likud only 12 seats, its lowest ever total. At the time some said this was the end of Likud and of a major right-wing power bloc in Israeli politics. Others were less sure and Benjamin Netanyahu, leading the party for a second time, vowed to restore its fortunes.

11

despair and hope, 1986–93

This chapter will cover:
- the causes of the Palestinian uprising ('Intifada')
- the nature of the First Intifada and its effects
- the impact of the end of the Cold War and the First Gulf War, 1991
- the Madrid peace process, 1991–3.

The forgotten people

Depression

By the end of 1967, the original Arab population of Britain's Palestinian mandate had been divided four ways. Slightly over 150,000 had remained in Israel, some eventually accepting Israeli citizenship, others remaining what the government enigmatically called 'present absentees'. By the end of the century, the total Palestinian community within Israel had risen to about 1 million. A larger number of Palestinians, fed by emigration of around 20,000 a year from the Occupied Territories, during the 1970s, lived in neighbouring states. The remainder were divided between the Occupied Territories: the tiny Gaza Strip and the larger West Bank. In 1986, the former contained around half a million native Gazans and a slightly smaller number of refugees, half of whom still lived in camps. Of the West Bank's 372,000 remaining refugees, some 100,000 were still camp-dwellers. Since about 1980, the mood within the Occupied Territories had become one of mounting despair.

For all their fine talk about solidarity, neighbouring Arab states appeared to be unwilling to exert themselves to help the Palestinians. Nothing had epitomized this apparent betrayal more than Egypt's separate peace with Israel and its vague, swiftly evaporating talk of sorting out the problem of Palestine. The Palestinian leadership, the PLO, had been driven first from Jordan then from Lebanon and was now in remote, impecunious and largely impotent exile in Tunisia. The Palestinians of the Occupied Territories felt trapped in a political cul-de-sac.

The economic situation had deteriorated, too. After the oil-price boom of the 1970s, remittances sent home by Palestinians working abroad had fallen. Unemployment rose fourfold between 1980 and 1985, fed by Jordan's economic problems and the growing tide of Soviet immigrants (not all of whom were Jews) looking for work in Israel. Some sources say that the unemployment rate in the Gaza Strip reached 50 per cent. Rising poverty brought with it the usual portmanteau of difficulties: crime, depression, drugs, deteriorating health and so forth.

figure 8 facts on the ground – Israeli settlements in the West Bank, 2007

Changing attitudes

At the same time, Israel's attitude towards the Occupied
Territories had shifted, mirroring changes within Israel itself.
The State of Israel had been founded on European secular,
liberal principles dating back at least to the eighteenth century
Enlightenment. Although at times these had been seriously
compromised, they remained more or less intact. By the 1980s,
however, they were coming under pressure from a massive
influx of Sephardi and Soviet Jews largely alien to the essentially
open-minded ideas of Western Europe. One consequence was
the Likud-led coalition, a more religious, intolerant and hard-
hearted administration than most of its predecessors. This
reflected a broader change in attitude towards Palestinians in
general: racism was on the rise.

New Jewish settlements in 'Judea and Samaria' proliferated and
the settlement population trebled between 1982 and 1986, by
which time half the land within the West Bank was under direct
Israeli control. Some settlements were provocatively close to
established areas of Palestinian habitation. New Israeli roads,
regularly patrolled by the army, cut off Palestinian areas from
each other. The aim, sometimes known as the 'Drobles Plan',
seemed to be to squeeze the Palestinian settlements, like
toothpaste in a tube, until those who lived there either became
totally submissive or emigrated in despair. To make matters
worse, Israel was still taking 80 per cent of the West Bank's
water for its own use. In fact, the area provided Israel with one-
third of all its water. This was reason enough to explain its
extreme reluctance to lose control there.

Taking no more

In the 1980s, as we have seen (pp. 144–5), Israel had begun its
'iron fist' policy towards the Palestinians within the Occupied
Territories. The foremost exponent of the approach was a
Labour politician, Yitzhak Rabin, Defence Minister within the
unity administration. His approach was to substitute the stick
for the carrot whenever feasible.

Israel proper remained a state in which the rule of law was
paramount, but the Occupied Territories, under military
command, did not come under the same jurisdiction. On
occasion the judiciary seemed to turn a blind eye, or at least to
act with unwarranted lenience when confronted with
unacceptable behaviour. Deportations (illegal according to the

terms of the Geneva Convention), press censorship, demolition of their homes, closure of facilities like schools and colleges, curfews, road blocks, searches, petty cruelties and humiliations – all these and more became part of everyday life for many Palestinians.

In the end, unloved, ignored and downtrodden, the Palestinians of the Occupied Territories spontaneously decided they would take no more. Spectacularly taking matters into their own hands, they rose up against their perceived persecutors. There had always been acts of violence against the forces of occupation, averaging 350 recorded incidents a year between 1968 and 1976. This had risen to 700 a year over the next seven years, then to around 3,000 a year in the early 1980s. These figures were nothing compared with what happened next. In the first six months of 1987, the IDF reported no less than 42,355 cases of active hostility towards it. The rebellion had begun.

Intifada

Rumour and riot

On 6 December 1987, an Israeli trader was stabbed to death in a Gaza market. This was not unusual. However, the next day an Israeli tank transporter collided with two vans carrying Palestinian workers back to their homes in Gaza's Jabaliya refugee camp. Four workers were killed, seven seriously injured. Rumour – always wickedly at work in such situations – said that the collision had not been an accident but was a planned revenge for the stabbing. Riots broke out at the funerals held that evening and an Israeli guard post was stoned. Tensions rose sharply.

Three days later, another resident of the Jabaliya camp died – shot dead by Israeli soldiers chasing stone-throwing youths. Hundreds of Palestinians took to the streets in protest. The security forces were reinforced. More stone-throwing, more firing. The conflagration soon spread to the West Bank and within two weeks the situation had flared out of Israel's control. The Palestinians called their extraordinary uprising – similar in some ways to what was to happen in parts of Eastern Europe two years later – the *Intifada* or 'Shaking Off'.

Sticks and stones

The Intifada was a widespread, long-drawn-out campaign of civil disobedience and constant harassment of the occupying forces. It lasted until around 1992, by which time its nature had changed. At first spontaneous and leaderless, it soon came under the loose direction of the United National Leadership of the Uprising (UNLU). Comprising second-rank, local officials of existing groups such as Fatah, it put forward a 14-point plan for Palestinian self-determination. Its principal instrument was the clandestinely-printed letter carrying instructions, suggestions and exhortations. Letter 40, for example, urged Palestinians to kill an Israeli soldier or settler for every Palestinian slain in the Intifada. The Israeli media, of course, described such action as 'terrorism', while Palestinians claimed simply to be responding to Israel's 'terrorist' act of stealing their country.

When the PLO leadership in Tunis realized that the uprising was more than just another bout of rioting, it became more closely involved. Iraq and Iran provided funds totalling an estimated $40 million US, while Baghdad Radio gave the movement a source of information and propaganda beyond Israeli control. Most significantly, within a year, a new-style, Islamist leadership had emerged in the form of Hamas and Islamic Jihad (see pp. 189–90). Over time the nature of the Intifada changed, too. The heavy economic and personal toll of gestures such as strikes, boycotting Israeli goods and refusal to work in Israel were self-defeating. Greater emphasis was placed on acts of aggressive defiance such as knifings, arson and kidnap.

The hallmark of the uprising was the stone-throwing youth or child. Often adorned with the distinctive kafiya head-dress and frequently egged on by their elders, the young emerged in their thousands to taunt the occupying forces with sharp words and stones. Stone-throwing was a traditional Islamic practice to ward off evil spirits. One of the remarkable features of the Palestinian experience after 1967 had been the emergence of a 'literature of resistance'. A key image in much of this work was the martyred stone-throwing child.

The children of the Intifada were a desperate generation that had grown up amid violence and cruelty. Lacking any concept of a better future on earth, they were fearless. Fleet of foot and knowing the terrain far better than their enemy, they made an impossible target. When the panicking Israeli conscripts employed excessive force – live ammunition was increasingly used against stone-throwers – they appeared before the world's media as child murderers. The only Israeli alternative was to hand back the streets, alleyways and markets to the Palestinian mob – an admission of failure. Practically, the Intifada gave the Israelis an insoluble problem: unless they resorted to genocide on a Holocaust scale, there was no way 3.5 million of them could hold down 1.5 million Palestinians determined to resist. For the first time, Israel was in a battle it could not win.

Bullets and broken bones

Shamir's government responded to the Intifada in the usual no-nonsense manner. Reservists were called up and the security presence within the Occupied Territories increased significantly. Schools, colleges and other places where crowds might gather were closed down. The uprooting of 120,000 precious fruit trees deprived many Palestinians in rural communities of their living. The bulldozing of their houses left them homeless. All forms of media were heavily censored. Ringleaders were identified, rounded up and detained without trial. Crowds were broken up with tear gas, rubber bullets and, sometimes, live ammunition. Deportation was also used, although it flouted international law. Suspected bases of the insurgency's leadership were bulldozed or blown up, even when they were private houses lived in by women and children. Upon Rabin's instruction, the limbs and fingers of stone-throwers were deliberately broken to prevent them continuing their assaults.

The Israelis were not above employing their own form of 'state terrorism' in the battle, too. Although there is no definitive proof of Israeli participation, it is widely agreed that Abu Jihad, the PLO mastermind organizing the Intifada, was taken out in Tunis by Mossad-led commandos. The operation, launched in April 1988, was supervised by Ehud Barak, a future prime minister of Israel. The piercing of Abu Jihad's body with 150 bullets before the terrified gaze of his wife and child ensured that the act was widely condemned, even in the US, and guaranteed the Palestinians yet another martyr.

The Intifada accounted for 396 Palestinian deaths in the first year and over 1,200 by 1992. It is essential to bear in mind that only slightly over half of these were at the hands of the Israelis. Intra-Palestinian bloodletting was also escalating alarmingly (pp. 163–4). The most serious single Israeli-on-Palestinian incident was the shooting dead of 21 Palestinian protestors and the wounding of 150 others when an Israeli extremist group calling itself the Temple Mount Faithful tried to lay the foundation stone of a new Jewish temple on Temple Mount (1990). Yet again the world condemned what it saw as Israeli over-reaction. As well as the shootings, some 40,000 Palestinians were detained during the first two years of the insurrection. Thereafter they were joined by tens of thousands of others.

Israeli dislocation

The Intifada hit Israelis and Palestinians alike. In the long run it was probably the latter who came off worst. Nevertheless, Israel's international reputation struck an all-time low. At the end of 1987, even the US was not prepared to veto a Security Council resolution condemning Israeli violence against protesters. The economy was badly dented, too. Security costs soared. The call-up, Palestinian boycotts and frequent border closures deprived Israeli businesses of labour. The country's total national wealth fell by an estimated 1.4 per cent. As a consequence, the opinion of many Israelis about the Occupied Territories began to change. Originally seen as essential to the country's security, they were now more likely to be regarded as a liability, actually weakening the country and its economy.

Equally serious was the divisive effect of the Intifada on Israeli society which, as we have seen, was already riven by a painful left–right schism (p. 142). Those of a liberal persuasion, including President Herzog (re-elected in 1988), believed that the measures taken to control the Occupied Territories were undermining the country's democracy and its key virtue of tolerance. Others went further, saying that Israel's tactics were horribly reminiscent of those employed by the Nazis. Several Israeli groups were formed – such as Hotline – with the specific intention of assisting distressed Palestinians. The Israeli right, on the other hand, horrified by Palestinian killings and lawlessness, urged still sterner measures to restore law and order and protect the burgeoning Jewish settlements in 'Judea and Samaria'.

The two contradictory currents were reflected at election time. The 1988 vote gave Likud 40 Knesset seats and Labour 39. By allying with a number of small, right-wing religious parties, Shamir was able to install another unity government. This time, however, the premiership was not for rotation. The election also saw a rise in the number of seats for religious parties, and the emergence of Shas, a party of Orthodox Sephardi. Predominantly Arab parties won six seats, and after the election a Labour Knesset member, Abdel Wahab Darawashe, left Labour to form the Arab Democratic Party. This was the Knesset's first purely Arab party. Another post-election development was the creation of Meretz, a coalition of left-leaning peace parties.

The stresses of the Intifada and US pressure for peace talks gradually pulled the unity government apart (p. 150). Shamir lost a vote of confidence in 1990 but, after much political wrangling, managed to remain in power at the head of a Likud-led right-wing government. This survived until 1992, when Labour, led by 'iron fisted' Yitzhak Rabin, won 44 Knesset seats. Joining with Meretz and the Arab Democratic Party, a new administration was formed intent on hammering out some form of peace deal with the Palestinians.

Palestinian problems

If Israel was shaken up by the Intifada, the Palestinians were even more so. Its internal effects were essentially fourfold:

1 As we have already seen, individuals and families suffered serious physical and emotional hardship (pp. 160–1).
2 The economies of the Occupied Territories were shattered and Palestinian wealth dropped sharply. The GNP of the Gaza Strip and the West Bank fell an estimated 30 per cent in three years. Retailers' turnover fell by 80 per cent. There was an increase in economic self-reliance, the West Bank producing four-fifths of its dairy needs, for instance, but this was scant compensation. Ominous for the future was the closure of many schools and colleges for weeks on end, thereby depriving the next generation of key skills and training.
3 The sudden violent upsurge of desperate feeling within the Occupied Territories drew the world's attention to these 'forgotten people' and forced the PLO to reconsider its position on a number of issues in order to retain the support of fellow Palestinians. Most importantly, it had to listen to the

message coming from Gaza and the West Bank: the people had had enough of suffering. The PLO's refusal to recognize Israel was all very well as a political gesture but in practical terms it made no sense at all. Palestinians worked in Israel, traded with Israel and in many cases had relatives living in Israel, some as Israeli citizens. Like it or not, the Jewish state was a very real fact of their lives. The armed struggle had failed. From such thinking came a major strand of what came to be known as the 'peace process' (see p. 167).

In June 1988, the PLO representative at the Arab summit in Algiers demanded a two-state solution to the Israeli–Palestinian problem. That was the closest it had yet come to recognizing Israel. A few weeks later, King Hussein renounced all claim to lands beyond the River Jordan, allowing the PLO to say it was formally taking control of the West Bank and Gaza. The most significant move came on 15 November, at a meeting of the Palestine National Council. Here, speaking to an astounded world, Arafat announced that henceforth Palestine was an independent state with East Jerusalem as its capital. Much more dramatic was the ex-*fedayeen*'s renunciation of all forms of terror, his acceptance of UN Security Council Resolution 242 as the basis for talks, and the recognition of Israel within the pre-1967 borders. Before long, 100 states had formally accepted Palestine as an independent country. After all those dark years, the first rays of peace were finally peeping over the horizon.

4 The Intifada proved fertile ground for Islamists. Their rapid advance, advocating principles very different from those of the essentially secular PLO, meant that Arafat's change of heart may have come too late for an all-embracing peace.

To understand the significance of what was going on, we need to stand back and take in the broader context.

During the second half of the twentieth century, militant Islam emerged as a radical alternative to both communism and liberal capitalism. Its appeal was particularly strong in those cultures whose social customs, academic norms and entrepreneurial achievement seemed at odds with the world of the late twentieth century, engendering a feeling of unease, even inferiority. Unable to compete with the modern, rational world on its own terms – unlike many Asian cultures – whole segments of the Middle East turned to the past for solace and meaning.

The first important manifestation of the new movement (or, rather, the revival of a very old one) was the Iranian Revolution of 1979. Next came the emergence of Hezbollah in Lebanon (see p. 152). Palestine's turn came with the appearance of the Hamas Islamic Brotherhood in 1988. The more militant Islamic Jihad emerged slightly later. By the time Arafat was making his dramatic gestures, these contrary but equally revolutionary forces had reached the Occupied Territories and were taking root within Palestinian society. The Islamists challenged the PLO at every point. They rejected its secular stance, its left-leaning politics, its nationalism, its local corruption, the self-seeking of some of its leaders, and its Western views on matters such as female emancipation.

As an alternative to the PLO way, the Islamists offered the idea that Palestine was part of a larger Islamic Trust (*waqf*) that would be held by the faithful until the Day of Judgement. To this end, nation-states, especially infidel ones like Israel, had to be cleared away. On this sacred duty there could be no compromise. While many Palestinians, especially women whose lives it threatened to ruin, remained sceptical or even hostile to the Islamists' religious teaching, the new movement rapidly gained support. Its strengths were grass-roots knowledge, energy, less corruption (initially, at least) and laudable programmes of practical assistance funded by Iranian money. It opposed strikes as a weapon against Israel, for example, because they hit the strikers harder than those they targeted.

Fighting between the Islamists and the PLO had already broken out in Lebanon and it was not long before it spread to Palestine. As each side sought to dominate the other in the battle for hearts and minds, killings, maimings and blackmailings rose. The Israelis, who first saw the Islamists as a useful ally against the PLO, soon realized the danger they posed. After the first Hamas *fedayeen*-style action in April 1989, the kidnapping and killing of two Israeli soldiers, membership of Hamas was outlawed and 300 of its activists arrested. Their number included Sheikh Yassin, one of the movement's founders.

Cold war and hot war

End of the Cold War

The emergence of militant Islam was not the only change sweeping the globe during the last quarter of the twentieth century. Even more significant, in the short term at least, was the collapse of Soviet communism and the end of the Cold War. This had a massive impact on the Arab–Israeli confrontation. Previously, with the US standing unflinchingly behind Israel, the Palestinians and many Arab states had turned to the Soviet Union for arms and aid. The PLO had been formed as a left-wing organization – Arafat had been a guest of Moscow – and the whole panoply of offshoot *fedayeen* groups were similarly socialist-orientated.

All this now changed. Socialism and talk of revolution and the people's armed struggle was replaced by praise for market forces, liberal democracy and diversity. There was now only one superpower, too. For a short time, until the Islamists became a global nuisance, US presidents no longer felt obliged to support Israel as an unshakeable ally in a world threatened by communism. They could now lean on Israeli administrations as never before, threatening a variety of economic sanctions safe in the knowledge that there was no one else the Israelis could turn to. The result was the 'peace dividend' that emerged in the late 1980s.

The First Gulf War

By 1990, attempts to cajole the Shamir government and the PLO into finding at least some common ground between them had ended in deadlock. This was broken, somewhat surprisingly, by the Iraqi dictator Saddam Hussein.

For a series of reasons, none of which make sound political or military sense to the outsider, in the summer of 1990 Hussein sent his well-trained and well-organized army into Kuwait. Within hours he was master of the small but oil-rich sheikhdom. When this blatant aggression was condemned by just about every country in the world, including the wealthy oil-producing Arab states, he offered to pull out if Syria left Lebanon and Israel returned to its pre-1967 borders. This unsubtle attempt to link his conquest to others' was a failure, and a mighty coalition began assembling under the auspices of the UN to drive him out.

All this while, the PLO, the PFLP and the Palestinian people in general had remained steadfastly behind the Iraqi president. In a way this was wholly understandable and even laudable: Hussein was one of the few world leaders who had openly declared his support for the Palestinian cause – and backed up his words with arms and money. In practical terms, however, support for Iraq was an act of Palestinian political suicide. Not only was Hussein reviled almost universally, but his cause was hopeless.

The US-led coalition attacked in January 1991 and within days the Iraqis had been driven from Kuwait and were in headlong retreat towards Baghdad. Desperate to destroy his enemy's solidarity, Hussein bombarded Israeli cities with Scud missiles. What he wanted, of course, was for Israel to retaliate, thereby presenting the coalition Arabs with the unenviable choice of siding with Israel against an Arab state or changing sides and joining him against the traditional enemy. As it was, although 4,000 Israeli flats were destroyed (but only one person killed), the Shamir government resisted the calls of warmongers like Ariel Sharon to retaliate. Israel's planes remained on their runways and its tanks behind its borders. Hussein's gambit had failed.

Iraq was crushed and Arafat and the PLO, having made considerable headway over the previous few years, were utterly discredited. The PLO was financially bankrupt, too. Arafat's decision to back Hussein was probably the worst he had ever made. By the summer of 1991, impecunious and impotent, he had no option but to swallow his pride and return to the negotiating table.

The peace process

Arafat's initiative

Back in November 1988, Arafat had won international acclaim for declaring Palestine an independent state, denouncing terrorism outside Israel and calling for peace talks based on Security Council Resolution 242 (see p. 163). Even so, the climb-down had cut no ice with the US and Israel, both of whom still insisted that the PLO was a terrorist organization and therefore not one with which talks could be held.

In December, Arafat made the US–Israeli position even more awkward. Speaking before the UN, temporarily transferred to Geneva as the US would not allow him into New York, he spoke of the 'State of Israel', called for a comprehensive Middle East peace conference, openly accepted Resolutions 242 and 338, and again condemned terror. At a news conference held afterwards, replying to questioners who asked how far he was prepared to go to meet US demands, he made his famous reply, 'Enough! Do you want me to do a striptease?'

Shortly afterwards Arafat did clarify a little by declaring the original PLO charter, calling for the destruction of Israel, null and void. By now the UN General Assembly had accepted Palestine's declaration of independence. Within weeks, finally convinced of Arafat's good intentions, the US began indirect, preliminary talks with representatives of the PLO. After decades of impasse, this was indeed a momentous move.

Prime Minister Shamir, on the other hand, still would not budge. Then Labour's hard-handed Defence Minister Yitzhak Rabin, realizing perhaps that settling the Intifada required something other than just brute force, suggested that they might at least try talking to some Palestinians. Shamir played for time. He talked vaguely of granting Palestinian 'autonomy' – but only after the Intifada had been called off – and ruled out the possibility of direct negotiations with the PLO. Meanwhile he pressed ahead with yet more settlements in the Occupied Territories. As immigration from the former USSR was now approaching an average of 100,000 a year, he argued, new living space was essential. Privately he believed 'facts on the ground' would eventually make return of the conquered land impossible. (See Figure 8, p. 156.)

In the autumn, US Secretary of State James Baker came up with various peace plans. Shamir stalled before rejecting them in March 1990. In the ensuing chaos, all talk of resolving the half-century dispute came close to collapse. First, a deranged Israeli reservist deliberately shot dead seven Palestinian workers. Ten days later Israeli security forces killed an entire Palestine Liberation Front (PLF) *fedayeen* group attempting an attack on Tel Aviv. Two weeks after that James Baker stormed out of talks with the Israelis, infuriated by their lack of flexibility. When the PLO failed to condemn the failed *fedayeen* assault, Baker broke off talks with them too. Middle East peace-making had never been easy.

A changing world

Nevertheless, despite immediate problems, by the end of the First Gulf War (spring 1991) the broader circumstances for a peace deal between the Israelis and Palestinians were more favourable than they had ever been. The situation is perhaps best understood as longer-term and shorter-term factors.

Longer-term developments enhancing the prospects for peace

1 The great bulk of Palestinians accepted in reality, if not always in theory, the existence of the State of Israel. Yasser Arafat had admitted as much before the United Nations in 1988.

2 Despite the Intifada and other bloody confrontations, during the prolonged contact between Israelis and Palestinians in the Occupied Territories since 1967, many on both sides had come to realize that their so-called 'enemies' were not all the heartless monsters depicted in their media and propaganda. The bulk of Israelis and Palestinians were moderate, reasonable people who wanted to live in peace and mutual prosperity.

3 The October 1973 War and the Lebanese invasion (see pp. 117–19) had made a number of Israelis unsure about the wisdom and morality of relying on military strength for enduring security.

4 The 1978 Camp David agreement had set a precedent of a land-for-peace compromise deal.

5 The collapse of Pan-Arabism had lowered the external threat to Israel and increased the Palestinians' quest for a self-instigated settlement.

6 After exile from Lebanon, from where the last vestiges of PLO forces were finally driven in May 1991, the PLO was a homeless and impoverished organization urgently seeking to return centre stage.

Shorter-term factors hastening the peace talks

1 The disintegration of the USSR and the end of the Cold War had two effects. First, it deprived militant Palestinians of Soviet backing. Second, it enabled the US to put pressure on Israel because it was no longer a key Cold War ally.

2 In the emerging global economy Israel had to find a new economic role and fresh economic stability. Globalization was not compatible with its previous aid-dependent existence.

3 The sudden appearance of a local leadership at the beginning of the Intifada had threatened the PLO's position at the head of the Palestinian movement. It now needed to rediscover its links with the people it claimed to serve in order to fulfil their wishes.

4 As far as the White House was concerned, the Gulf War had shown Israel in a new light. For the first time, especially when Sharon was calling for retaliation against Iraq's missiles, Israel had been a dangerous liability. Consequently, for the next few years, US administrations felt an urgent need to pressure Israel into accepting peace terms.

5 At the same time, the Gulf War had gone some way to reversing the way the Israelis and Palestinians were viewed globally. By siding with Hussein – the man the world loved to hate – Arafat had undone much of the good of his previous peace initiatives. The image of Israel, on the other hand, had lost some of its militaristic tarnish: by not attacking Iraq, for the first time it had shown itself to be a nation of peace.

6 Finally, there was emergence of fundamental, radical Islam as a powerful new force in Iran, then in Lebanon and now in Palestine. Slowly, Israel and the US were starting to realize that their real enemy was no longer Arafat, with his out-dated, Soviet-style socialism, but determined Islamists who rejected many of the principles and values of the capitalist, post-Cold-War world. Against such a fundamental new threat, the West called on all who prized its values to unite.

Madrid

After the liberation of Kuwait, US President George Bush Sr proposed a combined US–Russian peace conference, or series of conferences, to tackle the entire range of Middle East issues. Secretary of State James Baker drew up a nine-point plan embracing Syria and Jordan as well as Israel and the Palestinians. It was based on the idea of bi-lateral (two-sided rather than multi-sided) talks between Israel and the various Arab teams, interim agreements and eventual final, permanent settlements.

Initially the Palestinians were offered 'less than a state' but 'more than autonomy' but without the PLO being directly involved in the negotiations. Arafat refused to participate on these terms, but was forced to back-track on account of the weakness of his position. The PLO eventually attended the opening conference as part of the Jordanian delegation, although a number of leading PLO figures had resigned rather than accept this perceived humiliation. The compromise was too much for Shamir, who for a while also refused to take part. He eventually gave way when the US threatened to withhold loan guarantees to Israel worth $10 billion.

On 30 October 1991, the conference opened in Madrid before a worldwide live TV audience of many millions. After Presidents Bush and Gorbachev had made their opening addresses, each participating nation was given 45 minutes to set out its position. Following these acerbic and often inflexible pronouncements, the conference ground to a halt in a series of procedural wranglings. Shamir had actually gone home after barely 24 hours in the Spanish capital. To find a way forward, the bilateral talks opened in Washington in December.

Background of violence

The talks dragged on throughout 1992 but the progress was painfully slow. A major handicap was what was going on elsewhere: time and again events on the ground, often violent, poisoned the atmosphere between the negotiating parties, making it impossible for even a semblance of cordiality to develop.

In February 1992, for example, an Israeli helicopter gunship killed the Hezbollah leader in Lebanon, Sheikh Abbas Mussawi, together with his wife and five-year-old son. In October, a large bloc of non-PLO Palestinian groups that included both the secular and Islamist wings of the movement (the 'Damascus 10'), united under the banner of the National Democratic and Islamic Front to oppose the peace process. November saw several shootings of Palestinian stone-throwers and others. A month later, when Hamas kidnapped an Israeli soldier, Israel deported 415 suspected Hamas militants to southern Lebanon, which refused to accept them. This provoked an Arab walk-out from the talks then taking place in Washington.

The situation was no better in 1993. *Fedayeen* slew 13 Israelis early in the new year, causing Prime Minister Rabin to seal off the West Bank. Bending to international pressure, he then said he would allow back 100 of the previous year's deportees. They refused to return without their colleagues. Eventually, they all returned. Ominously, April saw the first Hamas suicide bomb attack, killing one Israeli, while July witnessed heavy fighting between the IDF and Hezbollah in southern Lebanon.

Against such a backdrop, peace talk often sounded decidedly hollow.

Irreconcilable differences

In early 1992, the Palestinian delegates at the Washington talks had suggested the formation of a Palestinian Interim Self-Government Authority (the future Palestinian National Authority or PNA) of 180 elected officials to guide Palestinian territory towards full independence. The Israelis had not welcomed the proposal but the US thought it had some mileage. An Israeli counter-proposal, considerably watering-down Palestinian autonomy, was immediately rejected by the Palestinians.

At this point, a fortuitous accident gave Arafat's position among Palestinians a considerable boost. His plane crashed in the Tunisian desert and for some hours he and all on board were missing, believed dead. Obituaries were written. When he reappeared – as if miraculously rising from the dead – in the eyes of many his immortality had been confirmed.

The formation in Israel of a Rabin-led Labour administration at the end of July gave the peace talks a new impetus. Rabin's foreign minister, Shimon Peres, was a known 'dove'. Agreement was further helped when Democrat Bill Clinton took over as US president at the beginning of 1993. Rabin froze new settlement in the Occupied Territories and accepted Palestinians at the talks, as long as they were not PLO or PLA. Interestingly, prominent among the Palestinian delegation was Faisal al-Husseini, from the same family as the noted Palestinian leader of a previous age (pp. 41–2). At the start of 1993, the Knesset repealed the law that had made all contact with the PLO illegal.

For all these favourable signs, the formal talks remained shrouded in mistrust and progress was dreadfully slow. The PLO knew that Rabin put Israel's security before peace and even as he negotiated he was instigating a massive new road-building programme across the West Bank, for military purposes. Settlements planned before the freeze were going ahead, too. On the other hand, the Israeli premier knew that the PLO would probably return to violence if things did not turn out as it wished. Moreover, its members were under growing pressure from the Islamists to be seen as true warriors in the Palestinian–Islamic cause. Even at this stage, accord with the PLO would not automatically mean peace for Israel.

In depth: Hamas

Hamas was created in 1987, early in the First Intifada, as a Palestinian offshoot of the Sunni Muslim Brotherhood. Rumours abound about its early years, for there is evidence that it received funding from Israeli secret services hoping to set up a Palestinian movement to counter-balance the influence of the PLO and portray the uprising as an Islamist-led movement. If this was indeed Israel's policy, then it backfired disastrously. Hamas expanded steadily, boosted by fresh funding from Iran and private sources around the Middle East, and waged a devastating *Jihad* against Israel. By 2006, it had been democratically elected to govern the PNA.

Employing tactics similar to those of Hezbollah in Lebanon, Hamas gained the support of Palestinians – mainly from Gaza – by using around 90 per cent of its multi-million dollar annual budget to fund social services. These ranged from immediate relief for the impoverished to longer-term programmes such as mosques, schools, orphanages and even sports' leagues. Before its electoral triumph in 2006, Hamas was acting as virtually the surrogate government within Gaza.

Inevitably, Hamas' advance brought it into conflict with the PLO and Fatah. The two sides were opposed on a number of theoretical grounds, most obviously the position of Islam within Palestinian politics. On a more practical level, the rivalry was a power struggle for the hearts, minds and votes of the Palestinians in the Occupied Territories. By 2007 this internecine squabble had become so serious, especially in Gaza, that locals were referring to it as anarchy. Outsiders feared it might lead to open civil war.

In Israel and the West, Hamas was seen as an Islamist organization dedicated to the destruction of the Jewish state and the humbling of its allies, especially the US. The Hamas covenant, drawn up in 1988, had renounced all compromise in its holy mission. That said, the leadership had accepted ceasefires and in 2007 was prepared to share power with non-Hamas politicians so that the PNA's foreign aid could be restored. Moreover, it also suggested it might accept some form of peace with Israel if it agreed to the 2002 Saudi proposals.

Hamas began with guerrilla-style warfare against Israel, adding suicide attacks from 1993 onwards. Prepared to employ women and children on these gruesome missions, over the years it killed dozens of Israelis, civilians as well as military, and in return saw several of its leaders assassinated.

In depth: Yitzhak Rabin (1922–95)

Yitzhak Rabin is remembered as a man of both peace and war, the complex sometimes tortured Israeli minister who ordered his soldiers to break the bones of Palestinians and then, a few years later, signed Israel's first peace deal with them. His character, difficulties and career epitomized the bitter tragedy of the Israeli–Palestinian confrontation.

Born in Jerusalem to parents of Russian stock, Rabin was raised in Tel Aviv and ended his formal education at the age of 18. The next year he joined the Haganah, the first step in a long and distinguished military career. He fought in Israel's War of Independence (1948–9) and later expressed reservations about the policy of ethnic cleansing of Arab areas in which he had participated. Staying in the IDF after the war, he rose to become its Chief of Staff in 1964. He is reported to have had some sort of breakdown during the extremely stressful build up to the 1967 Six-Day War, but he quickly recovered and was bathed in glory after remarkable success in a conflict he may not actually have wanted.

Rabin served as Israeli Ambassador to the US from 1968 to 1973, before being elected to the Knesset as a member of the Labour Alignment. Within a year, he had become party leader and then prime minister. His first premiership, which featured growing accord with Egypt, ended in disillusionment and scandal and was followed by the country's first Likud-based administration.

On returning to office in 1984, Rabin found himself minister of defence in the unity governments of Shamir and Peres. He supervised the drawback in southern Lebanon and then the fierce Israeli reaction to the First Intifada (1987).

His policies were described as those of the 'iron fist', earning him a reputation as an implacable enemy of the Palestinians. Beneath the surface, though, he was beginning to accept the need for compromise – but strictly on Israel's terms. The opportunity arose when he became prime minister for a second time in 1992.

Rabin's dramatic premiership saw the PLO accept Israel's existence and renounce violence, the establishment of the PLA, and a formal treaty between Israel and Jordan. If Rabin's peace deal with the Palestinians appears to outsiders a bit one-sided, it did not look so to many Israelis. The radical nature of the Oslo Accords, for which Rabin was awarded the Nobel Peace Prize, was confirmed when a Jewish Orthodox extremist assassinated his prime minister for betraying what he saw as the Jewish people's sacred trust.

12

dashed hopes

This chapter will cover:
- the signing of the Oslo Peace Accords, 1993
- attempts to implement the Oslo agreements
- mounting violence and the slowing of the peace process.

The 1990s were a desperately tragic decade for Israeli–Palestine relations. They began with such high hopes: the two sides talking to each other for the first time and actually reaching agreement on some issues. These included very limited but nevertheless genuine Palestinian autonomy, and the promise of further steps towards permanent agreement and peace. Yet by 2000, the bright optimism had all but melted away, destroyed by the fiery hatred of the rival hard-liners, leaving the chances of a permanent and total settlement as remote as they had ever been.

Oslo

Secret meetings

By the summer of 1993, the series of formal Middle East peace talks, begun in Madrid and continued in Washington, seemed to be going nowhere. Israelis and Palestinians were sharply divided between those prepared to compromise for peace and those to whom rational agreement was an anathema. There was bitter fighting in southern Lebanon, Israeli settlements were still being built in the Occupied Territories, and Hamas had begun its campaign of suicide attacks. Beneath the surface, however, new life was stirring.

As the opening remarks of the Madrid Conference had showed, public negotiators always had more than one eye on their broader constituency. Israeli spokespeople had to demonstrate that they were not giving way to 'terrorism', while their Arab counterparts needed to remain true to the mantra of Palestine for the Palestinians. In other words, public talks were as much about rhetoric as compromise. As the Camp David talks that produced peace between Egypt and Israel had shown, true progress was generally possible only beyond the reach of the cameras and microphones of the media.

In late January 1993, a group of like-minded Palestinians and Israelis had met in Sarpsborg, Norway. For the first time, leading figures from both communities actually sat and talked peace together. Assisted by tactful and light-handed Norwegian mediation and without the full knowledge of the US, a PLO delegation that included the prominent pragmatist Mahmoud Abbas (Abu Mazen) and an Israeli delegation featuring the respected academic Yair Hirschfeld began by exploring the topics on which they could find common ground. Both realized

figure 9 Jerusalem, 2006

that at this stage, for instance, there was little point in talking about the future status of Jerusalem (see Figure 9) or Israeli settlements in the West Bank. On the other hand, an end to violence was a common desire. Gaza was another topic on which progress might be made. Given that most Israelis had little desire to retain the overpopulated strip and the Palestinians did not want them there, a solution was at least within the bounds of possibility.

This step-by-step approach produced a series of principles that was revealed to a startled world on 20 August 1993. By now the major players, including Arafat, Rabin and the new US president, Bill Clinton, were on board. Moderates everywhere welcomed the extraordinary news. The reaction of hard-liners was equally predictable. The Israeli far right denounced those who had talked with 'terrorists'; Islamist extremists, members of the old-style far left and radical representatives of Palestinian diaspora condemned negotiation with 'infidels' and 'imperialists'. Nevertheless, events moved fast. In early September, Arafat wrote to Rabin acknowledging the existence of the State of Israel, accepting UN Resolutions 242 and 338, and renouncing terrorism. Rabin replied recognizing Arafat's position and the PLO as the legitimate representative of the Palestinian people.

Remarkable though these advances were, looked at objectively they reveal that while the PLO had changed its position completely, Israel had given away very little. There was no mention of a Palestinian state, for example. The truth was, the Palestinians had been negotiating from a position of extreme weakness. After the collapse of the USSR and their disastrous support of Saddam Hussein, all they had left was an ability to make a nuisance of themselves and to evoke popular sympathy.

The Accords

The Declaration of Principles led to the Oslo Accords (Oslo I), signed by Rabin and Arafat at the White House on 13 September 1993. The two leaders' reluctant handshake to conclude the ceremony revealed just how painful the apparent reconciliation had been – and how precarious was their new amity. Nevertheless, a dramatic step towards peace had been taken.

The Accords were as much about the future as the present. They envisaged a five-year period during which the Israelis would withdraw from Gaza and Jericho, and the Palestinians would establish an elected Palestinian National Authority (PNA) to manage internal affairs, including policing, tax and health, in the areas they controlled. The agreement foresaw the Israelis gradually pulling out of further areas in the West Bank and handing them over to the PNA. Negotiations between the two sides would continue with the aim of concluding a permanent and comprehensive settlement within five years. Meanwhile, a liaison committee would help resolve practical disputes between the two sides. The Knesset ratified the Accords on 23 September and the PLO Executive Committee (minus several high-profile opponents of the deal) did the same by one vote on 11 October 1993.

The success or otherwise of the rapprochement would depend on what happened next. Even so, its critics were many, particularly in the Palestinian camp. A step-by-step approach was all very well, they pointed out, but so far the steps had been mostly side-steps. Their objections were powerful: there was no programme for the formation of a Palestinian state; Israel still controlled all security and external affairs in the Occupied Territories, where its authority had now been legitimized; the Palestinians were to be held responsible for all acts of violence against Israel while violence towards Palestinians by Israeli settlers or security forces was deemed merely retaliatory; a long list of practical issues had been left open: the distribution of water, frontiers, the right of Palestinian refugees to return to Israel, and Israeli settlements on occupied land were among the most prominent. Small wonder that, referring to the treaty imposed on Germany after World War I, a number of Palestinian opponents of the Oslo Accords referred to them as 'Palestine's Versailles'. Israel had not only won its wars with the Palestinians; it now seemed to have won the peace, too.

Accord and discord

Implementing Oslo

Whatever its critics said, the great majority of Palestinians and Israelis welcomed the Oslo agreement and sincerely hoped that it would herald a new era of peaceful coexistence between the two peoples. Therefore, despite huge opposition, violent and otherwise, the peace-making progress went forward. In April 1994, Israeli and Palestinian negotiators reached a deal on economic relations between the two peoples. A month later some Oslo principles were turned into a concrete agreement for the IDF to pull out of Gaza and Jericho and be replaced by Palestinian forces. Israel released 5,000 prisoners and detainees and cancelled a number of military orders used to govern the West Bank. Arafat, who was only too aware how Palestinian extremists were now labelling him a traitor, made his reluctance to sign the agreement patently obvious. At this stage, though, he had no choice. He was wedded to the peace process: if it collapsed, so would his credibility. All the same, he still sought to keep a foot in both camps, speaking of the Palestinian *Jihad* shortly after signing. In the end this sort of double-dealing led both Israelis and the US to lose all faith in him (see pp. 104, 212–13).

For the time being, however, Arafat was a hero. In July, when after an exile of many years he returned to Gaza, ecstatic crowds greeted him as the long-lost saviour. Further agreements followed as in 1994 the Israelis gradually handed over to the Palestinians local responsibility for education, health, tax, tourism and social welfare. Matters such as commerce, industry, agriculture, local government, post and insurance followed the following year. The process culminated in an agreement known as Oslo II, signed in September 1995.

Oslo II

The new deal, the product of months of painstaking negotiation, divided the West Bank into three zones. Zone A, comprising some seven per cent of the region's territory but containing the refugee camps and seven large cities in which the bulk of the Palestinian population lived, was to come under the direct control of the PNA. A small Jewish community remained within the largely Palestinian city of Hebron and the many thousands of Palestinian citizens of Jerusalem were still under Israeli governance. Israel and the PNA were to share responsibility for Zone B (about 23 per cent of the region), while Israel would retain its total control over Zone C (the remaining 70 per cent of the region) until final status talks had been concluded. Within Zone C came Jewish settlements and the militarily sensitive Jordan Valley.

As in Oslo I, Oslo II left aside the thorny questions of refugees, Jerusalem, water, and the settlements. Prisoners were released and optimistic noises made on both sides. In reality, though, all that had been done was implement some of the ideas of 1993 – and they had by no means pleased everyone. Prime Minister Rabin was openly called a 'traitor' and 'murderer'; furious extremists attacked his car and at a protest meeting paraded a coffin with his name painted on the side. It was ominous indeed. On 4 October 1995 Yitzhak Rabin, winner of the Nobel Peace Prize, was shot dead by a Jewish extremist. A crowd estimated at 300,000 attended his funeral.

Shimon Peres, always less hawkish than his dead colleague, took over as prime minister. As agreed, the IDF withdrew from the Palestinian towns of Nablus, Bethlehem and Ramallah, and from Taba on the border with Egypt. An international force moved into Hebron to ensure the maintenance of peace between the two communities. Meanwhile, an 88-seat Palestinian Legislative Council was elected. The turn out was high and all but ten seats went to Fatah. Yasser Arafat realized one of his lifetime ambitions when he was elected president of the PNA with 88 per cent of the vote.

Netanyahu

By now, the peace process was rapidly running out of steam. The prospects of reaching the much vaunted 'final status' agreement within the specified five-year period grew more remote by the day. Within Israel, the ceaseless waves of Islamist violence (see pp. 182–3) had turned people against the Oslo process. What was the point in talking to the PLO, they argued, if it couldn't control its own people? Gangs of youths roamed the streets of Israeli towns, condemning peace as weakness. Some Rabbis even declared that a vote for right-wing Likud would ensure a blessing. As never before, Israel was bitterly, irreconcilably divided.

The elections of May 1996 were held on a new basis: one vote for a party and another for the post of prime minister. Likud's Benjamin Netanyahu narrowly defeated Shimon Peres in the latter, while Labour won slightly more Knesset seats than Likud. However, the backing of religious and other right-wing parties (including a new Russian immigrant party) enabled Netanyahu to form a coalition. Having opposed Oslo from the outset, the new prime minister was not going to make any compromises to carry the peace process forward.

The PLO and Hamas

The peace process had divided Palestinians as sharply as it had Israelis. There were other difficulties, too. A Palestinian National Authority might have been created on paper but institution-building is a long and difficult process. Too few

Palestinians, from Yasser Arafat downwards, had the necessary experience to construct a stable and reliable bureaucracy for the new administration. Although foreign aid poured into Palestinian coffers, gross maladministration resulted in frequent chaos and massive corruption. When in 1996 the head of the Independent Commission on Citizens' Rights in Palestine publicly criticized elements of the PNA for being crooked and repressive, he was unlawfully arrested.

The formation of a Palestinian Police Authority offers a good example of the sort of thing the commissioner was complaining about. It was initially envisaged that around 9,000 police would be required to look after the areas under PNA control. As suitable men had to be found relatively quickly and Arafat had large numbers of Fatah *fedayeen* who needed rewarding for their loyalty, the obvious solution was to turn ex-freedom fighters into salaried police. However, not only did they bring their *fedayeen* attitudes with them, soon dividing into semi-autonomous bands that interpreted the law as they saw fit, but their numbers swelled alarmingly to over 45,000. This made PNA territory one of the most heavily-policed regions in the world.

In effect, the PNA police force and PNA militia became a sort of private security force for Arafat. Before long, the inevitable happened. From early 1994, under pressure to be seen upholding his pledge to prevent attacks on Israel, Arafat ordered the periodic rounding up of Hamas militants. This heightened tension between Fatah and Hamas. At the end of the year the issue suddenly escalated when PNA police shot and killed over a dozen fellow Palestinians outside a Gaza mosque. Another 200 were wounded. Shortly afterwards, up to 20,000 Gazans attended a mass Hamas rally. Tragically, instead of uniting the Palestinians, the peace process was fragmenting them, making further settlement all the harder. As we shall see, the situation got so bad that by the mid-2000s the Fatah–Hamas rivalry periodically flared into full-scale combat.

The suicide campaign

While the peace process was developing slowly and hesitantly, various groups were doing their best to make it fail. On the Arab side this included the Lebanon-based, Iran-backed Hezbollah (see p. 152). Israel responded to Hezbollah provocation with its traditional no-nonsense harshness. Rabin's self-professed policy was to pursue peace as if there were no *fedayeen* campaign and pursue the *fedayeen* as if there were no peace process.

1994 saw a number of tit-for-tat attacks and raids in Lebanon and northern Israel. Then, when Hezbollah launched 28 Soviet-designed Katyusha rockets into northern Israel in the spring of 1996, Rabin decided it was time for another major Israeli reprisal. Operation Grapes of Wrath involved a naval blockade of the Lebanese coast as well as heavy air strikes. Beirut and 147 other towns and villages were hit, almost half a million Lebanese fled their homes and around 200 lost their lives alongside several Hezbollah fighters. A UN-monitored ceasefire was eventually put in place. Katyushas may have stopped raining on Israel for a short while, but it is hard to avoid the conclusion that in the long run the assault had done nothing to further either peace or Israeli security.

Hamas and Islamic Jihad suicide attacks killed far more Israelis than did the occasional Hezbollah rocket. Within a year of Oslo I they had become a regular occurrence. In 1994, bus bombs slew 15 in April, and 22 in October. The next month a suicide cyclist killed three IDF at a checkpoint. Earlier in the year an IDF attempt to rescue a soldier kidnapped by Hamas had left five dead. The next year saw bombs on buses, in a snack bar and in other public places. As the death toll mounted, so did Israeli public disillusionment with the peace process, precisely as the Islamists intended. The violence reached a new peak in early 1996, when 58 deaths in attacks on four separate venues paved the way for Netanyahu's election victory.

It might be helpful at this point to remind Western readers just how Islamist leaders managed to find so many young Muslims prepared to sacrifice themselves in such a grizzly manner. The reason was as simple as it was abhorrent. Certain Islamic mullahs had declared the struggle with Israel to be a Holy War. Although suicide under normal circumstances was a sin, in such a cause it became the opposite: those who died while fighting the enemy had all their sins immediately forgiven and were guaranteed a direct path to heavenly life. To the idealistic young of a religious disposition, the teaching had a certain weird appeal.

Israel: peace and provocation

Accord with the PLO brought Israel benefits in several quarters. Diplomatically the pariah state came in from the cold, receiving recognition in states like Morocco and Tunisia that had hitherto sided unequivocally with the Palestinians. The Arab boycott of Israel was lifted, too, freeing major international companies to trade there. Israel also struck a valuable commercial and military deal with Turkey, and signed a long-desired peace with Jordan. Israeli–Jordanian talks had begun even before the ink was dry on the Oslo Accords. A common agenda was agreed in September 1993, an economic agreement the following January, and a full-scale peace treaty that ended 46 years of war was signed in October 1994.

Compared with the sacrifices made by the PLO, the Israeli government gave little away. It made a few gestures, such as outlawing one or two fanatically extreme Jewish religious groups and not pressing ahead with fresh settlement plans. But, as noted, there was no freeze on existing settlement plans – near Bethlehem, for example – and this fed Palestinian resentment.

Palestinian disillusionment was all too understandable. Instead of finding themselves with something approaching a state of their own as a result of the Oslo process, they were now living in ever more fragmented communities, separated by heavily patrolled Israeli roads and a constantly growing number of Israeli settlements. Some commentators compared what was happening to the policy of South Africa's apartheid governments: setting up 'Bantustans' or areas of native settlement. This concept has been labelled 'structural violence'.

Occasional acts of aggression by Israeli settlers against their Palestinian neighbours persisted. Far more terrifying was the slaughter carried out by Baruch Goldstein, a fanatical immigrant doctor from New York. Wearing an IDF uniform, at dawn prayers on 25 February 1994 he entered Hebron's Ibrahimi Mosque. The building held the tombs of Abraham and Jacob, prompting Goldstein to convince himself that it should be cleared of all Muslims. Firing an automatic rifle, he slaughtered 21 worshippers and injured a further 300 before being overpowered and killed by the incandescent mob. Some of those present claimed that Israeli guards positioned nearby deliberately chose not to hear what was happening. The massacre came close to ending the peace process there and then.

As before, the Israelis rounded up suspects en masse after *fedayeen* attacks: 370, for instance, after the suicide assaults of February–March 1996. In total, between 1967 and 2007 the Israelis imprisoned over half a million Palestinians. Nor did the peace process stop the Israelis continuing with their Palestinian-designated 'state terrorism' – singling out key leaders of opposition groups for assassination by bomb, gun or even poison. The head of Islamic Jihad was killed by a car bomb in November 1994. More noteworthy was the assassination – probably by Israeli agents, although this has not been proved – of Yihyeh Ayash. Known as the 'Engineer', Ayash was believed to have been responsible, in one way or another, for at least 60 Israeli deaths. Not surprisingly, his removal did not lead to a reduction in attacks in Israel. Quite the opposite, in fact: the pantheon of Palestinian 'martyrs' had been furnished with yet another figure to inspire would-be terrorists/freedom fighters.

Netanyahu, Arafat and Clinton

The opportunity passes

By May 1996, the date of Netanyahu's election, the high hopes of the early 1990s were fading fast. For a few years following the collapse of the Soviet Union there had been a genuine sense of global optimism in international affairs. The US, the sole remaining superpower, had been free to concentrate its massive resources and political clout on solving world problems rather than focusing on the sterile struggle of the Cold War. As far as the Middle East was concerned, now that Israel was no longer required as an ally in the fight against communism, the US had been able to bring greater pressure on it to reach an accord with the Palestinians. Without Soviet backing, the PLO and its supporters had been similarly susceptible to US arm-twisting. Yet even as the Accords were being hammered out, a new power was once again re-shaping the face of international affairs.

In 1978, militant Islam had expressed its dislike of the West when a group of fervent Iranians took hostage the entire staff of the US embassy in Tehran. Islamist hostility towards the US grew and, by the 1990s, Muslim extremists were striking at American as well as Israeli targets. In their eyes a democratic, capitalist, pro-Israeli, pro-feminist and essentially Christian America was the principal enemy of a worldwide fundamentalist Islamic revival. 1993 saw the first attack on the World Trade Center, New York. Then came assaults on US facilities in Saudi Arabia and two US embassies in Africa. In 2000, a US warship was bombed in Aden harbour. By now the CIA and other Western intelligence services were collecting an ever-growing volume of evidence relating to the extreme danger posed by fanatical Muslims.

As Israel's principal enemies – Hamas, Hezbollah and Islamic Jihad – were linked to this Islamist movement, the US reverted to its previous position of seeing Israel as key ally in a global struggle. This made it more difficult for American administrations to pressure Israel into coming to terms with the Palestinians. As ever, it was the bulk of ordinary Palestinians – in the Occupied Territories, in foreign refugee camps and even within Israel – who suffered most.

'Peace with security'

Benjamin Netanyahu was the first, and to date (May 2007), the only Israeli prime minister born since the founding of the State of Israel. His background was atypical for an Israeli political leader, too. He had lived, studied and worked in the US for many years before deciding to serve his country as a diplomat and then as a politician. His successful US-style premiership campaign had shocked many Israelis unused to such a very personal, media-savvy approach. Nonetheless, it had proved effective and he had come to power promising to 'make a safe peace'.

Peace and security were, of course, what all Israelis wanted. Ultimately the former was required in order to guarantee the latter. Netanyahu's problem was that instinctively he wanted things the other way round, putting security before peace. Moreover, his Likud-based coalition's reliance upon the support of Ultra-Orthodox Jewish parties gave him little option but to strike a hard line. In the end, he was able to provide neither peace nor security and fell from power after only three years.

Across the divide, Yasser Arafat similarly felt himself pulled in two directions. On the one hand there was the painfully slow peace process that he had helped set up and which still offered the prospect of a fully independent Palestinian state one day; on the other hand were the increasingly influential Islamist groups, hostile to a submissive compromise with Israel and determined to continue their armed struggle for a fully integrated, independent Palestine. By the end of the millennium, Arafat was clearly worried that Hamas, in particular, was undermining his PLO–Fatah, thereby weakening his control over the Palestinian movement. Ever the wily master of pragmatic scheming, it has been suggested on quite strong evidence that the Palestinian president reacted by secretly backing the Islamists in the hope of forcing Israel to make concessions. Even more duplicitous, evidence has been uncovered showing that he even allowed *fedayeen* under his direct or indirect command to conduct Hamas-style raids to show that the Islamists were not alone in their militant hostility towards Israel (see pp. 182–3).

(see pp. 182–3)

Anti-Oslo

Netanyahu had never approved of the Oslo process and his premiership was dotted with incidents that served to stoke up Israeli–Palestinian ill-feeling. Security was toughened, with the Israeli borders being closed to Palestinian workers on several occasions. Suspects were rounded up, homes searched and buildings flattened. In September 1996, the prime minister personally authorized the opening of a 2,000-year-old tunnel that passed near the Al-Aqsa Mosque. Muslims were incensed at what they believed was a threat to the foundations of the mosque and a stone-throwing mob assembled near the archaeological site. Israeli and Palestinian police arrived. Shots were fired, and by the time order had been restored, 75 people lay dead. As was invariably the case in such situations, the bulk of those killed were Palestinians.

Meanwhile, the Netanyahu coalition had further inflamed Palestinian feelings – and made a full peace deal even less likely – by lifting the freeze on Israeli settlements within the Occupied Territories. Jewish encroachment was particularly unwelcome around East Jerusalem and on land confiscated from Arabs. The Oslo Accords had specifically forbidden all such development. Other incidents played their part in souring relations. Certain court decisions did not help, for example, as when soft sentences were passed on Israelis found guilty of harming Palestinians. Other provocative acts were more violent. In 1997 an Israeli gunman opened fire on Palestinian shoppers in a Hebron market. Later in the year, Mossad – Israel's secret service organization – bungled an assassination attempt on a Hamas leader sheltering in Jordan. King Hussein made return of the Israeli agents he had captured conditional on the release of the Hamas leader Sheikh Ahmad Yassin. The Sheikh promptly went on a tour of Arab capitals to raise funds for Hamas.

The following year another Hamas leader was less fortunate when he was shot and then blown up in the Palestinian-controlled town of Ramallah. Palestinians blamed Israeli agents for the assassination; Israelis said it had been carried out by Fatah. Two weeks earlier there had been serious rioting in Hebron following the IDF's shooting dead of three Palestinians at a checkpoint.

Despite Netanyahu's security clamp down, Palestinian attacks on Israel were maintained. The targets were invariably intended to provoke maximum outrage: a restaurant in Tel Aviv, a market, a shopping centre. Such acts fostered a fresh approach to the security situation as a growing number of Israelis began taking seriously the idea of 'separation': permanently dividing themselves from the Palestinians by the erection of impenetrable walls and fences. Nonetheless, Israelis were not the only targets. In 1997 Palestinian estate agents were killed for selling land to Jewish settlers.

The Clinton initiative

For all the problems on the ground in Israel, the Occupied Territories and in the areas controlled by the Palestinian Authority, President Clinton was still pressing resolutely ahead with the peace process. Although they had to keep a wary eye on their constituencies, neither Netanyahu nor Arafat wanted to see the process collapse completely. The Israeli premier was only too aware of the economic dislocation that prolonged violence inevitably brought, while his Palestinian counterpart knew that a failure of the peace talks would be hailed as a victory for the Islamists.

Arafat's reputation among his own people was suffering, too. The frequent closure of crossing points into Israel hit Palestinian workers particularly hard. Increasingly disillusioned and desperate, they did not take kindly to the findings of a report, published in 1997, that declared two-thirds of the PNA budget to have been misspent or mismanaged. The Palestinian Assembly voted almost unanimously for all PNA personnel to be replaced.

Less than a year after coming to office, under massive US pressure, Netanyahu withdrew the IDF from Hebron. This completed the handover of territory to the PNA envisaged in the Oslo Agreements' first phase. The Israeli premier then made it clear that this was about as far as he was prepared to go. He made a number of provocative statements about Israel remaining permanently in the West Bank and about power being the only guarantee of security. Arafat responded by releasing Hamas suspects he had been holding and by refusing further cooperation on security matters.

In the fall of 1998, President Clinton broke the deadlock by holding a Camp-David-style summit at Wye Plantation, Maryland. Jordan's King Hussein, in the US for cancer treatment, was on hand to lend such assistance as he could. After long hours of talks, Arafat and Netanyahu eventually agreed to take up the peace process where it had broken off. The Wye River Memorandum, signed later in Washington, spoke of prisoner release, cooperation on security, safe passage between Gaza and the West Bank, and the PLO cutting back on anti-Israeli rhetoric. More significantly, Israel agreed to hand over to the PNA a further 13 per cent of West Bank Zones B and C in return for greater US involvement in Israel's security.

Moderates on all sides welcomed the Wye River undertaking as another important step towards a lasting settlement. The Palestinian Assembly and the Knesset both accepted it and attempts were made to start implementing some of its terms. Inevitably, though, there was fierce opposition. Islamists and the anti-Oslo 'Damascus 10' (see p. 171) condemned it outright, pointing out that there was still no mention of a Palestinian state. Ultra-orthodox Jews fulminated against handing over still more of their sacred homeland to Muslims. To mollify his supporters, Netanyahu began to renege on parts of the deal by imposing fresh conditions for Israeli withdrawal. Beset by allegations of corruption and stories about his private life, he lost a vote of confidence in the Knesset and his ill-fated administration fell.

In depth: Islamic Jihad

Islamic Jihad, also known as PIJ, had its origins among enthusiastic Palestinian students studying in Egypt. Although Sunni, the young men were inspired by the revolutionary antics of the Shia who had overthrown the Shah of Iran in 1978.

The movement took a while to crystallize and organize itself, not claiming its first Israeli victim until 1987. PIJ followers said their campaign was a Holy War (*Jihad*) against all Western and pro-Western regimes, especially Israel. Negotiation it eschewed as useless – the only way to triumph was through an armed struggle, if necessary sacrificing oneself in the holy cause. Consequently, Islamic Jihad would have nothing to do with the Oslo Accords or other peace movements, and its relations with Yasser Arafat's Fatah and the PLO were always strained. On the other hand, as their aims and tactics have converged, so relations between Islamic Jihad and Hamas gradually became more cordial.

Islamic Jihad carried out a number of attacks during the First and Second Intifadas, some of them truly ghastly. It was responsible for suicide nail bombs, for example, and for stoning to death young Israeli settlers it had captured. Needless to say, its leadership was a primary target for the Israeli security services who, in 1995, are believed to have had a hand in the shooting dead of the PIJ's commander in Malta. His Gazan replacement, the Western-educated academic Ramadan Abdullah Sallah, rapidly rose to the top of the Israeli and US most-wanted-terrorists lists and was said wisely to have taken refuge in Syria.

In depth: Ariel Sharon (1928–)

Few Israelis provoked stronger feelings than Ariel Sharon. A huge man of huge drive, he was loved and hated in almost equal measure during a long and highly controversial career as soldier and politician, warrior and peace-seeker.

Born in the Palestinian mandate to parents originally from Russia, Sharon joined the Haganah and fought with distinction during Israel's War of Independence. After serving as an intelligence officer and trying to catch up on his education, he returned to the army to lead the new anti-terrorist Unit 101. In this post he began to build a reputation as a fearless, utterly ruthless defender of Israeli interests, even at the cost of the lives of Palestinian civilians.

Sharon served in the 1956 Suez campaign and finished his university education before commanding a powerful armoured division with flair in 1967. He briefly entered politics then re-joined the IDF for the 1973 October War in which his unorthodox leadership earned him both high praise and strong criticism. Back in politics, he served as a right-wing member of the Knesset and helped form Likud. For almost all his time in government, in several offices, he used a variety of tactics to increase the number of Israeli settlements within the Occupied Territories, especially the West Bank. Many settlers came to see him almost as their patron.

Appointed minister of defence in 1981, Sharon was architect of the following year's invasion of Lebanon that led to the defeat and expulsion from that country of the PLO. He was also widely seen as responsible for the massacres within the Sabra and Shatila refugee camps, although the actual killing was done by Christian militia. As a result he was deprived of his post but remained in the government as minister without portfolio.

In the years that followed, Sharon became a more and more divisive figure. Rumours spread of personal corruption; he opposed Oslo yet participated in the Wye River talks; he put enormous energy into housing Israel's recent immigrants yet gave them sub-standard caravans. In 2000, his tactless behaviour almost single-handedly started the Second Intifada. He remained resolute through all difficulties, however, and his aura of unflinching strength won him the prime ministerial election in 2001.

Sharon saved his greatest surprises to the end. At first he toed the traditional Likud hard line in the face of *fedayeen* attacks. Then, in late 2003, he announced a unilateral Disengagement Plan. This involved pulling out of Gaza and small areas of the West Bank and relying on the Security Barrier to defend the homeland. The Knesset backed him and after Israeli settlers had left their Gaza settlements – sometimes only when forced to do so – the Strip was handed back to the Palestinians. Next, seeking support for further unilateral withdrawal from the West Bank, Sharon announced the setting up of a new political party, Kadima ('Forward'). This advance was his last, for he suffered a massive stroke that plunged him into a coma from which there was no hope of recovery.

13

impasse, 1999–2003

This chapter will cover:
- Israel and Palestine at the start of the new millennium
- the outbreak of the Second Intifada
- 9/11 and peace proposals, including the Roadmap
- the seemingly hopeless situation and the close of 2004.

The insoluble conflict

The origins of impasse

The turn of the millennium makes a useful point at which to take stock of where the Israeli–Palestinian conflict was, how it had got there and where, if anywhere, it was going.

Since almost the beginning of human history, the comparatively small parcel of land known sometimes as 'Israel' but more commonly as 'Palestine' had been regarded as especially holy. Of particular sanctity, especially to Jews, was the ancient city of Jerusalem. After classical times, for hundreds of years this special land was inhabited mainly by Muslims of Arab stock, although there was always a scattering of Jews, Christians and others. Then, starting in the later nineteenth century and continuing into the twentieth, a growing number of Jews came to live there. Some believed they were returning to a promised land, others simply wanted a new life safe among their own people.

The indigenous inhabitants of the region had never really thought of themselves as a 'nation' in the full-blown Western sense of the word. Nevertheless, largely in response to outside interference, they had developed a common identity that on occasion expressed itself as 'Palestinian'. Inevitably, tensions arose between these indigenous Arabs and the Jewish immigrants. In an act of imperial greed that it soon came to regret, after World War I Britain took over management of Palestine on behalf of the League of Nations. After failing to reconcile or even keep peace between the two communities, the British decided that the only answer to the problem was to divide their mandate in two, creating a Jewish state and a Palestinian Arab one. This idea also met with the approval of the US and, after World War II, of the newly-formed United Nations.

The Jews, whose numbers were being daily swollen by immigration, welcomed the idea, especially as the proposed state of Israel would give them far more land than they actually owned. The Arabs, on the other hand, objected strongly: the creation of a State of Israel, they said, would legitimize the theft of Arab land on a gigantic scale. Desultory fighting expanded into all-out warfare when the Jews (now Israelis) pre-emptively announced the formation of the State of Israel. Both sides received considerable outside support but it was the stronger, better-organized and better-equipped Israelis who triumphed.

On the way to victory, the Israelis carved out for themselves a much larger state than had originally been intended by Britain and the UN. They also cleared it of hundreds of thousands of native Palestinians. Furthermore, those parts of Palestine that were not in Israeli hands were now occupied by neighbouring Arab states. Palestinians who had dreamed of having a country of their own now found themselves under Israeli or Arab occupation or living in exile. Further Arab–Israeli wars, in which Israel again triumphed, only made things worse for the Palestinians as they brought still more of them under Israeli rule.

Bitter divisions

It had never been strictly accurate to speak of an Israeli–Palestinian divide. The term was too obvious, too trite to describe a highly complex situation. By the twenty-first century such a simplistic division was even less appropriate. The terms 'Israeli' and 'Palestinian' were now catch-alls that embraced vast ranges of opinion and aspiration.

By the end of the millennium, the population of Israel had grown to around 5,700,000, more than a million of whom were not Jews. Many of these, Muslim and Christian, were what the Israelis called 'Arabs' but whom some others referred to as 'Israeli Palestinians'. Most were settled but perhaps 250,000 were still considered as refugees within Israel (the oxymoronically named 'present absentees' – see p. 155). Jewish Israelis came from almost every corner of the globe, the most obvious division being between Ashkenazi and Sephardi. Their religious persuasion varied from the secular, to Reform, Orthodox and Ultra-Orthodox. In a super-representative electoral system that endorsed fragmentization, politics and religion overlapped and intertwined. As a consequence, the rational course of government policy was not always the most practicable. Minorities whose opinions might be reviled by the majority could and often did exert enormous influence. The glaring exception was the Arab minority, whose voice rarely carried far in Israeli politics or society.

If Israel resembled a complex picture put together like a jigsaw puzzle, Palestine was a similar puzzle still in pieces. To begin with, no one knew how many Palestinians there were. The last complete census of the Palestinian people had been taken by the British in 1931. By 2000, the figures for those inside Israel were relatively clear (just over 1 million) and there were believed to be another 1,850,000 in the West Bank and Gaza. Beyond that, in the refugee camps and suburbs of Syria, Lebanon and Jordan, working around the Gulf and elsewhere in the world, no one knew. Several estimates offered a figure of between 1.5 and 2 million. In 2002, over 4 million Palestinian refugees were registered with the UN. Against all the odds, the Palestinians of the new diaspora remained bound together, united by a common heritage of a lost land and a flourishing exile culture of poetry, song and stirring story.

For hundreds of years, the indigenous Palestinians had been peasant farmers, shopkeepers, merchants and landlords with little warrior tradition. It took a long time before their reaction to the disaster of 1948–9 became violent. Moreover, when it did so – in the form of *fedayeen* raids of one kind or another – it frequently seemed to make the situation worse. This was partly because the Israelis adopted a policy of disproportionate retaliation and partly because the fragmented Palestinians found it difficult to agree over ends and means. A solution might have been found by a leader of exceptional intelligence, ability and ruthless determination. Yasser Arafat had some fine qualities, but he was no George Washington or Ataturk.

There were external factors, too: Arab states mistrusted the Palestinians as trouble-makers and were prepared to use their cause only as long as it suited their own ends; the Americans, who for reasons of domestic politics and the Cold War, were prepared to go to almost any lengths to keep Israel afloat; the Soviets who sought to use the Palestinian cause to extend their influence through the Middle East; and the other states that posed, pronounced and dabbled to their own tunes and agendas.

Finally, from the 1980s onwards, there were the Islamists who sought to link a human tragedy with a religious war. To many Palestinians, tired of the stale rhetoric of nationalism, brought fresh hope and purpose. But, of course, further extremism on one side served only to foster further extremism on the other. As a result, by the end of the millennium the task of the moderates on both sides was perhaps more daunting than it had ever been.

Possible ways forward

Other than the genocide of one people or the other, there was no simple path out of the Israel–Palestine mire. Jewish extremists wanted a 'Greater Israel' extending from the sea to the Jordan River and even beyond. Palestinian extremists wanted a

Palestinian state extending over the same area, or for the same region to be part of a new, exclusively Islamic, trans-national empire.

Between these two extremes lay the suggestion of a single secular state (the original goal of first Britain and then Arafat, but now clearly impractical) or a two-state compromise. However, for a separate Israel and Palestine to come into being, three preposterously thorny questions had to be sorted out.

First, where were the boundaries to be drawn? All kinds of possibilities presented themselves: those frontiers envisaged in the original 1948 UN plan; those existing after the 1948–9 war; those pertaining after the Six-Day War of 1967; the 1949 boundaries adjusted to allow for some post-1967 Israeli settlement. There was also the split-site problem: could Gaza and the West Bank really be part of the same state, with Israeli territory between them?

Second, what was to be done with Jerusalem, the city Israel had made its capital but which the Palestinians also wanted as their capital? Could it be divided? Might it, as had often been suggested, become an international enclave?

Third, there was the problem of refugees or the 'right to return'. In 1948–9, for one reason or another, hundreds of thousands of Palestinians had left their homes and lands. Most still wanted to return. Indeed, 'the right to return' had become a kind of mantra for exiled Palestinians. In many cases, however, original houses had been knocked down, olive groves uprooted, and fields redistributed or built over. Moreover, would Israelis ever accept up to 4 million Arabs coming to live among them? It was a near-impossible dilemma.

These were the difficulties that confronted would-be peacemakers at the dawn of the new millennium. To make their task all the harder, they had to operate in an atmosphere poisoned by years of cruelty and killing, and against a background of almost daily slaughter on both sides.

We need to remember that we are now no longer in the realm of history but of current affairs, so it is impossible to say whether the struggle is any nearer its end. But it will come to an end one day, as all things must – and what follows is how it has developed over the last few years.

12 months for peace

Ehud Barak

The last year of the old millennium opened with a degree of optimism as the former IDF General Ehud Barak, the most decorated soldier in Israel's history and now leader of Israel's Labour party, campaigned on a pledge to end his people's 100-year conflict with the Palestinians within 12 months. It was a peculiarly unrealistic piece of rhetoric for one so well versed in the politics of the region, but it went down well with an electorate exhausted by countless suicide bombings, rocket attacks and the general economic and social hardship brought about by years of low-level conflict. In May, Barak won the prime ministerial election by a landslide. His new One Nation coalition party, which included Labour, also won enough seats to form the basis of a coalition administration.

Barak tried military pressure to force the Lebanese government to take firmer control over Hezbollah. At the same time, he took steps to disengage the IDF from southern Lebanon and re-opened peace talks with Syria. Further negotiations were conducted with the Clinton Administration over the Wye River Accord (p. 188) and in September Foreign Minister David Levy (ex-Likud) even held discussions with PLO leader Mahmoud Abbas about where a 'final status' agreement between Israel and the Palestinians might lead.

Talk of 'final status' was all very well, but the reality was a good deal harsher. This became clear in November, when a group of 20 leading opponents of Arafat produced a petition entitled 'The Homeland Calls Us' that in no uncertain terms damned Oslo, the PLO chairman and all compromise with Israel. In an attempt to demonstrate to the US and Israel that he was still in charge of the situation, Arafat ordered the arrest of eight of the signatories. It was not a convincing gesture. To make matters worse, Syria did not seem keen on Barak's peace proposals and even moderate Palestinians were not impressed by his failure to halt the expansion of settlements in the West Bank.

Withdrawal and negotiation

Since his administration had been formed in July, at the beginning of 2000 Barak still had seven months to fulfil his pledge of peace within a year. February saw renewed fighting in southern Lebanon as Hezbollah targeted the Israeli-backed South Lebanese Army. Israel retaliated with air strikes but after another Hezbollah offensive in May the SLA disintegrated and the IDF decided it was time to fulfil a pledge given long before and withdraw completely from Lebanese soil. Although this might have been seen as a step towards peace, the UN force posted along the frontier was unable to prevent periodic Hezbollah rocket fire into northern Israel. Nor had Barak enjoyed much success further east, where the breakdown of talks with Syria had been followed by the death of President Assad. The succession of his rather less forceful son Bashir Assad did not augur well for improved relations in that direction.

Nevertheless, things did look up as Barak's self-imposed deadline approached. He was helped by another deadline: President Clinton was in his last year as president of the United States and he wanted, if at all possible, to conclude his second term of office with a Middle East agreement that would guarantee his place in history as one of the great statesmen-peace-makers of modern times. By many accounts, he came remarkably close to achieving this.

There were three sets of talks, the first at Camp David in July 2000. The US president was clearly hoping for a repeat of Carter's 1978 triumph amid the pines and golf buggies of the luxurious but remote retreat. Barak and Arafat were there, complete with their teams of advisors. At this stage we do not know exactly what was said or offered, but it does seem as if the Israelis were prepared to concede more than ever before, even agreeing to hand over part of Jerusalem as a Palestinian capital. Clinton tried every trick he knew, flattering, hectoring and even shouting at Arafat. But all to no avail. The PNA president, only too aware of the Islamists waiting to denounce him, would not accept a proposal that amounted to a climb-down, an acceptance of a 'Bantustan' Palestine (see p. 184). In the end, the meeting broke up without a deal, although both sides agreed to carry on talking. Back home, Arafat was greeted as a hero – the man with the guts to stand up to the Americans *and* the Israelis.

Following an emergency summit in October at the Egyptian Red Sea resort of Sharm El Sheikh, in December Clinton made one last effort. We cannot be sure what proposal he put on the table at the Washington conference as Israeli–US sources differ from Palestinian ones. Nevertheless, it does seem as if Israeli concessions went even further than at Camp David. The chief US negotiator said later that the plan was for all of Gaza and 97 per cent of the West Bank to be handed over to Palestinian rule, and also for large parts of Jerusalem, including the Temple Mount, to be under Palestinian control. Palestinians present, on the other hand, say that they were offered only a fragmented Palestine that left considerable areas of the West Bank still in Israeli hands. Whatever the truth (and both sides agree that Palestinian refugees were offered no guarantee of a 'right to return'), the talks broke down. A final meeting at Taba early the following year also failed to produce a meeting of minds. By now events on the ground had reached such a dreadful pitch that further negotiations were unrealistic.

The Second Intifada

At this point, we need to try and imagine what the previous five years had been like for the Palestinians of the Occupied Territories. Hopes had been so high in the middle of the decade. Arafat, the near mythical leader, had returned from exile amid hysterical rejoicing. The IDF was going to withdraw, there would be elections, the Palestinians would govern themselves, there would be peace, foreign aid would pour in to stimulate the economy, and before long all Palestinians would enjoy a decent standard of living... And now, at the turn of the millennium, what had happened to all these golden dreams?

As so often, Palestinian hopes had been cruelly dashed. They still lived in enclaves, surrounded by Israel patrols and divided by heavily guarded Israeli highways; the Authority they had elected had been shown to be impossibly corrupt; Islamist and other attacks had led to fierce, old-style Israeli harassment, detention and targeted killings; Israeli courts seemed to turn a blind, or at least a very myopic eye on settlers who preyed on Palestinians; living standards were as low as ever, especially when the closure of border crossings deprived Palestinians of work in Israel. Surely, they asked, all the pain and suffering of the Intifada had not been for this?

In such an explosive atmosphere, a visit by an Israeli politician to the compound surrounding the Al-Aqsa mosque in Jerusalem was sure to cause controversy. When that politician was the right-wing leader of the opposition and he arrived in the company of a massive bodyguard of armed police, the situation was bound to be even more tense. And when the unwanted visitor was no less a person than Ariel Sharon, the veteran of countless bloody anti-*fedayeen* operations, the destroyer of the

PLO in Lebanon and supposed mastermind behind the Sabra and Shatila massacres (see p. 148), Palestinian reaction may easily be imagined.

Rumour abounded, fanned by inflammatory words from the mosques the following day. Stones were thrown at the Israeli police, who responded with tear gas, rubber bullets and finally with live ammunition. The rioting spread and within a week 50 Palestinians had been killed. So began the Second or Al-Aqsa Intifada. By the end of the year, the death tolls stood at 315 Palestinians and 37 Israelis. The Palestinian dead included 66 children. The shooting dead of one boy, 12-year-old Mohammed al-Durrah, as he cowered beside his father amid a hail of bullets, was captured live by a French TV camera crew. The image sped around the world, fuelling the Intifada and raising a massive groundswell of anti-Israeli feeling.

The months that followed were punctuated by further horrific shootings, bombings and lynchings. Barak's much-vaunted peace policy was in tatters and he lost the support of both left and right in the Knesset. Even the Arab members refused to back him. A vote was passed calling for early elections. In February 2001, the 72-year-old Ariel Sharon overwhelmingly defeated Barak in the nationwide prime ministerial vote and formed a new coalition administration of 'National Unity'.

Slaughter

Peace?

Ariel Sharon had been elected on the slogan 'security and true peace'. As Likud had only 19 Knesset seats, he was obliged to include Labour members in his National Unity government. His old rival Shimon Peres, for instance, became foreign minister. Given such an array of talent and a genuine wish on the part of many finally to bring years of bloodshed to an end, some sort of peace deal might have been on the cards. Instead, however, the Second Intifada continued and the year slid into a grizzly mire of tit-for-tat killings.

Sharon had established his reputation as a doughty fighter for Israel and an implacable enemy of Palestinian independence. Well into his eightieth decade, he had lost none of his bite. All the same, as the body-count mounted, his mind inevitably turned to his legacy: how fitting it would be for the man who had done so much to bring Israel victory on the battlefield also to bring triumph at the peace conference! Unfortunately, the success of his career in establishing Israel had rendered his wish to be a peace-maker all the more difficult. Over the past 50 years the Palestinians had been so pummelled and pounded, crushed, harassed, divided and fragmented that it was no longer possible to find a voice that spoke for all of them. Arafat tried desperately to be that voice, which is why he made so many contradictory statements. What in fact he was doing was simply expressing different aspects of the Palestinian spectrum.

Intifada again

With Palestinians pursuing a broad range of different aims and Israelis unable to find anyone with whom to negotiate meaningfully, the Intifada went on. Beside the traditional stone-throwing and general civil disobedience of the population at large, Palestinian groups maintained their campaigns of suicide attacks. There was also internecine strife between PNA authorities and others. To the outside world this was explained as the PNA exercising its authority over dissident terrorist groups. In reality it was Arafat attempting to maintain his power base.

The suicide attacks were too many to be listed individually. The deaths of 20 Israeli teenagers outside a Tel Aviv disco in June caught the world's headlines, as did a similar attack on a Jerusalem pizzeria two months later which left 15 dead. In December, the slaughter reached a ghastly crescendo with 26 Israelis dying in a series of coordinated attacks in Jerusalem and ten deaths when a bus carrying Orthodox settlers was attacked. Before that, Israel had seen its first Israeli–Arab suicide bomber and the killing of a government minister. During this period the attacks were nearly all the work of Islamists, mainly Hamas, although a branch of Fatah, the Al-Aqsa Martyrs Brigades, had recently been formed. Its unofficial task was to prove to the average Palestinian that Arafat's supporters could be equally destructive.

Sharon's government responded to the violence as all Israeli administrations had done, with deliberately disproportionate force. Palestinian leaders were targeted for assassination. The more notable victims were Massud Ayyad, a key figure in Arafat's bodyguard and a supposed member of Hezbollah, the

Hamas leader in Nablus, the Secretary General of the PFLP, and the Fatah leader in Bethlehem. When internment and other measures failed to curb the daily attacks, more heavy-handed tactics were used. Helicopter gunships were brought in and in May F16 jets attacked targets in the West Bank. Later, heavy armour was sent in and areas recently handed over to the PNA were re-occupied. Such ferocious tactics brought short-term lulls in the fighting, but ultimately they only added to the number of martyrs and increased Palestinian determination to maintain the Intifada. It was a truly terrible situation.

9/11

The US administration of George W. Bush was deeply concerned by the shocking scenes from Israel and Palestine that flashed almost daily across US TV screens. Former Senator George Mitchell was dispatched to the region and asked to produce a report on the causes of the latest Intifada. He duly did so and made sensible recommendations that were ignored. Sharon, Arafat and the Americans all called for ceasefires and occasionally the firing actually stopped for a day or so. At one stage Peres and Arafat met to discuss peace and President Bush attempted to mollify the Palestinians by saying that he could envisage a Palestinian state one day. Then some incident would spark off the violence again. Shouting above the roar of tanks, bombs and helicopters, the screaming of children and the weeping of women, each side blamed the other for the fresh flare up.

It was against this background that news came through of Al Qaeda's September 11 attacks on New York and Washington (2001). Throughout much of the Middle East the reaction was one of shock and horror, just as it was elsewhere in the world. Yasser Arafat and Ariel Sharon condemned the outrages without reservation. Hamas, on the other hand, refused to comment on a non-Palestinian event. This hardly endeared it to the American people. Some Muslim extremists went so far as to endorse the attacks while others claimed the whole thing had been a put-up job, a massive Jewish conspiracy to get the US to declare war on all Arabs. Quite a few Palestinian hearts had a sneaking admiration at the way so tiny a band had done such enormous damage to so powerful an enemy. They viewed their struggle against Israel in precisely the same David vs. Goliath terms. On the other side of the fence, there were Israelis who felt almost grateful to Al Qaeda for demonstrating to Americans the kind of threat Israelis had lived under for years. 9/11, they hoped, would bring the US and Israel closer still.

In the end, the Al Qaeda attacks had a double effect on the Israel–Palestine situation. In the short term they did indeed bring the US and Israel closer together, allies against Islamist extremism. Over the longer term, though, the US came to realize that the Israel–Palestine conflict lay at the very heart of much of the misunderstanding and conflict that dogged the West and the wider Middle East. Solve the Israel–Palestine problem, lance that boil, and the sickness that pervaded the rest of the body might clear up.

Arafat sidelined

Gloomy prospects

The prospects for peace were even gloomier at the end of 2002 than they had been at the beginning. The Intifada, punctuated by ineffective ceasefire announcements, continued to reap its grizzly harvest: by the end of July it had claimed the lives of almost 1,800 Palestinians and around 800 Israelis. The ratio of Israeli to Palestinian deaths was much higher than in previous violent episodes, reflecting almost daily attacks in the early part of the year. Notable Palestinian outrages were the slaughter of Israelis at a Bar Mitzvah ceremony in January, the murder by a Hamas suicide bomber of 30 elderly Jews enjoying a seaside Passover feast in March, and Islamic Jihad's killing of 12 settlers in Kiryat Arba in November.

Israeli attacks were no less vengeful. The leader of the Al-Aqsa Martyrs Brigades, which at the time were on ceasefire, was assassinated in January, and in July a Hamas leader, Salah Shahada, was blown to pieces by a huge bomb. The explosion also killed 14 others, nine of whom were children. On a far larger scale were two massive counter-Intifada actions, Operation Defensive Wall launched in the spring and Operation Determined Path in the summer. Both involved entering Palestinian areas in the West Bank with massive force, smashing homes, making hundreds of arrests, imposing curfews, shooting suspicious characters on sight and countless other forms of harsh repression. Talk of a massacre of civilians in Jenin was later disproved, although the IDF did kill dozens of militants when it entered the town. Two incidents in particular captured the attention of the world's media. One was the siege of wanted *fedayeen* inside Bethlehem's Church of the Nativity. The other was the total destruction – apart from a single office in which Arafat was virtually held prisoner – of the PNA president's compound in Ramallah. Israeli forces also risked widening the conflict by attacking Syrian positions inside Lebanon, claiming that Syria was training guerrillas for operations against Israel.

The actions by both sides could offer nothing but limited, short-term gains. In their hearts the Palestinians must have known that they would never be able to defeat Israel militarily. Even if it were technically feasible, the US would never have allowed it. For their part, the Israelis must have known that bombing and repression would not solve the problem of Palestine either. Indeed, as the experience of World War II and Vietnam had shown, civilian casualties served only to increase a determination to resist, not weaken it. The inhabitants of the Occupied Territories were indeed suffering terrible hardship – unemployment had risen to 50 per cent of the workforce and the region's GNP had more than halved since 1999 – but they were not going to react by packing their bags en masse and going somewhere else to live. To begin with, there wasn't anywhere else.

'Compromised by terror'

Amid all this mayhem, Arafat's reputation took a battering from which it never really recovered. In January, the Israelis seized a ship shown to be carrying arms from Iran. The weapons, it turned out, were supposedly destined for the Al-Aqsa Martyrs Brigades. Since the Brigades were an offshoot of Fatah, which Arafat commanded, here was pretty conclusive evidence that he had been doing precisely what he had vehemently denied doing: backing *fedayeen* attacks on Israel. So much for Arafat's much vaunted renunciation of terror, snorted Sharon. In defence of the president of the PNA it is worth pointing out, firstly, that the final destination of the captured weapons could never be guaranteed (indeed, they may even have been 'planted' by Israelis) and, secondly, that the PNA president was not the first politician to be economical with the truth. Since his primary duty was to hold together the Palestinian movement, it would have been political suicide to ignore the growing popularity within his constituency of the 'martyrs' and their tactics.

If the arms seizure was bad for Arafat, the contents of documents confiscated by the Israelis when they overran his compound were worse. Again, we cannot be certain that they were not forgeries or 'plants', although they were sufficiently realistic to convince US officials as well as Israeli. Letters, receipts, accounts and a host of other papers appeared to show not only that Arafat's regime was notoriously corrupt, even by local standards, but that he had directly funded *fedayeen* with money for weapons and bomb-belts. Henceforward Sharon declared Arafat to be 'irrelevant' to the peace process. President Bush, too, refused to have anything further to do with him, urging the Palestinians to find a new leader 'not compromised by terror'.

Glimpses of the future

Talk within some Israeli circles of a complete separation from the Palestinians took the form of plans for massive physical barriers to cut off the Occupied Territories from pre-1967 Israel. Something similar already existed around Gaza. But no sooner had the idea been mooted for the West Bank than it ran into trouble. What route should these barriers follow? Would post-1967 Israeli settlements be on the Israeli or Palestinian side? And what about legality – was the proposed division of disputed territory permissible in international law?

Disagreement over the barrier was one of many issues that caused division within Sharon's Unity government. Eventually, in November, Labour decided that it could no longer support policies that appeared to bring no hope of settlement, and it left the coalition. Undaunted, Sharon defeated Netanyahu for leadership of Likud and called for early elections to resolve the impasse.

Meanwhile, despite Arafat's fall from grace, anxious politicians on all sides were trying to suggest ways of resolving the debilitating and highly destabilizing conflict. In February 2002, Crown Prince Abdullah of Saudi Arabia – a state painfully caught up in the spate of Islamist terror that was now unsettling large swathes of the globe – proposed that in return for withdrawing to its pre-1967 frontiers, Israel might receive full and friendly recognition from the Arab world and beyond. The idea was warmly welcomed and received official endorsement from the next month's Arab summit.

Sharon rejected the Saudi proposal out of hand but, for the time being, the Bush administration kept its opinion to itself. Instead, it drew up the first tentative ideas for a 'roadmap to peace'.

Essentially, this was not very different from the earlier step-by-step approach. The main difference was that the final goal – a two-state solution – was fixed, as were precise points along the route towards that goal. The Roadmap was not published until the following year, by when it was endorsed by the 'Quartet' of the US, the EU, Russia and the UN. Together with the Saudi proposal, it gave at least a faint glimmer of hope in an otherwise depressingly dark picture.

The Roadmap

Aqaba

By now the Israelis and the Bush administration were insisting on Palestinian reform before any further progress could be made towards a peace settlement. Arafat and others interpreted this as interference in their internal affairs, and refused. Their stance was understandable when it is understood that the key specific demand was for the appointment of a Palestinian prime minister to conduct settlement talks, thereby by-passing the Palestinians' elected leader. Actually, the position of a prime minister had been planned for in the establishment of the PNA but Arafat had delayed implementing the full constitution.

In the end, a combination of both internal and external pressures forced Arafat to back down. In March 2005, Mahmoud Abbas (an old colleague of Arafat's and long-standing PLO member) was chosen as Palestinian prime minister and duly formed a cabinet. President George W. Bush produced a concrete version of the Roadmap. For talks to begin, its first phase called for the Palestinians to end all violence and confiscate illegally-held weapons. Other Arab states were to stop supporting 'terrorist' groups such as Hamas. Israel was to freeze settlement building and withdraw from those built since September 2000. Two further phases of the plan talked of a conference to establish a sovereign Palestinian state, and yet more talks to tackle unresolved issues. Once again the right of return for exiled Palestinians, the Jerusalem question and even sovereignty over the West Bank were left in the air. The chances of the more extreme Palestinian groups accepting such terms, therefore, were slight.

That is precisely how it turned out. Sharon and Abbas met at a US-brokered summit in Aqaba – the 'Quartet' was already looking decidedly lop-sided – and shook hands under the beaming gaze of George W. Bush. Sharon agreed that he would accept a sovereign Palestine, and Abbas called for the Intifada to be halted. Both men agreed to the outline principles of the Roadmap. Days later the sweet words disappeared in several puffs of acrid smoke as Islamist and Fatah *fedayeen* slew Israeli soldiers and a failed assassination attempt was made on the Hamas leader Ahmed Rantissi. More suicide attacks and targeted assassinations followed, heralding a return to the murderous atmosphere of tit-for-tat slaughter that had been a feature of the period before the Aqaba summit.

Disengagement

The broader political climate was not conducive to compromise, either. Likud dominated the Knesset after the January elections and Sharon headed a conservative coalition that included the far-right National Unity Party. To please his Likud supporters, Sharon had changed the route of the West Bank Security Barrier, also known as the 'Security Fence' and even as the 'Apartheid Wall', to include more of the Occupied Territories than had previously been the plan. This brought several Israeli settlements under its protection but had the politically embarrassing and economically ruinous effect of isolating and dividing many Palestinian communities. The Barrier was the cause of widespread protests within Israel and the West Bank and further afield. Like the occupation of conquered territories in 1967, it was condemned in the UN and also declared contrary to international law.

Perhaps the only bright point still visible as the year drew to its murky close was a proposal taken up, surprisingly, by Prime Minister Sharon. First put forward by Mitzna's Labour Party during the elections, it suggested that if talks with the Palestinians broke down, Israel should withdraw unilaterally from Gaza and parts of the West Bank, and get on with its own life as best it could behind the Security Barrier. To international astonishment and Likud's bemused fury, late in the year Sharon announced that he had come round to this way of thinking. Israeli unilateral disengagement would begin in six months' time, he declared. It was hardly a peace plan, but it did at least show that even one of Israel's most fervent patriots had begun to accept that it might not be wise to try and hold on to all the 1967 conquests forever.

In depth: the Al-Aqsa Martyrs Brigades

As their name suggests, the Al-Aqsa Martyrs Brigades emerged shortly after the Second, or Al-Aqsa, Intifada. Their provenance is somewhat obscure – and unusual. The Israelis and Americans explain the Brigades' formation as an attempt by Yasser Arafat, then president of the PNA, to prevent Islamist groups from having a perceived monopoly of militant anti-Israeli activities. Yet the president had officially renounced violence and his own neo-military organization, Fatah, was supposed to adhere to this policy. Therefore, if the Brigades were really an off-shoot of Fatah – as many claimed – then Arafat was playing a wicked double game.

Arafat himself denied all links between the Brigades and Fatah, and evidence to the contrary is all controversial. Some was provided by documents that the Israelis claimed to have uncovered when they entered the presidential compound in Ramallah. Later, Palestinian Prime Minister Mahmoud Abbas confessed that the Brigades were part of Fatah, and some Brigade leaders echoed his statement. However, such remarks may have been made for political purposes and offered only circumstantial evidence. Then there was the case of the Brigades' Chief Executive Marwhan Barghouti, whom the Israelis arrested in 2002 and sentenced to life imprisonment for multiple murders. Although Barghouti was also a Fatah member, this did not mean the two organizations necessarily worked together. Similar implications, but no proof, may be drawn from the fact that after Arafat's death the Brigades announced a change of name to the 'Brigades of Shahad Yasser Arafat'.

The Brigades were not a specifically Islamist group, but regarded Islam as a useful tool in their war with Israel. Their suicide attacks, therefore, were not religiously motivated. This secular attitude did not rule out joint operations with Muslim extremists such as Hamas and even, on occasion, Hezbollah. When President Mahmoud Ahmadinejad of Iran reportedly said he wished Israel to be 'wiped off the map' in a Holy War, the Brigades supported his Islamist outburst. Moreover, in 2006, bandits claiming to be Brigade members attacked the Gazan offices of the EU and demanded apologies from Denmark and Norway for the publication of cartoons mocking the Prophet Mohammed.

The Brigades were accused of, or claimed responsibility for, numerous *fedayeen* activities. They launched suicide attacks against Israel civilians in 2002, 2003 and 2004 and built up a feared section of female recruits. They were apparently behind many of the Qassam rocket attacks on Israel from Gaza, even turning against fellow Palestinians who objected to their activity for fear of Israeli retaliation.

In depth: Mahmoud Abbas (1935–)

Along with many other leaders of the Palestinian movement, Mahmoud Abbas came from a family that the Israelis had forced into exile in 1948. The legacy of bitterness thus created turned the young Abbas into an angry militant. Age and experience mellowed him, however, and by the twenty-first century he was regarded in Israel and the West as the acceptable face of the Palestinian leadership.

Born in the British mandate of Palestine, Abbas spent his formative years in Syria before completing his education in Egypt and Moscow. He then worked in the Gulf and became heavily involved in Palestinian politics, joining Fatah and rising to become a key member of the PLO under Yasser Arafat. Ever the pragmatic academic, he appeared always willing to try a negotiated rather than a military settlement of the Israeli–Palestinian conflict and he maintained links with left-wing Israelis during the darkest years of impasse.

Abbas kept himself in the background, perhaps deliberately, yet played an important role in the Oslo peace process and in mending fences between the PLO and the Arab states that had joined the anti-Iraqi coalition in 1990–1. He finally emerged from the shadows in 2003, when the aging and discredited President Arafat gave the post of Palestinian prime minister to his loyal lieutenant, Abbas. The appointment was a disaster as Abbas found himself in almost continual conflict with Arafat on one side and the militant Islamists of Hamas and Islamic Jihad on the other. He resigned after only seven months in the job.

Abbas' second chance came in 2006 when, following Arafat's death, he was elected president of the PNA. Again he ran up against the Islamists when trying to set up further peace negotiations with Israel. His presidency met with yet more difficulties when Hamas won a majority of seats in the Palestinian Assembly in January 2006, open fighting escalated between his PNA security forces and Muslim extremists, and Israel launched all-out attacks on Hezbollah in Lebanon. Frustrated at so many turns and constantly threatened with assassination, a careworn Abbas announced that he would not run for a second term.

14

hope and despair

This chapter will cover:
- the ongoing Intifada and the death of Yasser Arafat
- Abbas' election and Israeli withdrawal from Gaza
- the Hamas and Kadima governments and Lebanon's Summer War
- how the US, under pressure in Iraq, searched for a peace deal.

Who can tell?

Events linked to the Israel–Palestine question have moved so swiftly over the last few years that it is impossible to anticipate at close range what their significance will be. Since 2004, for example, we have seen the death of Yasser Arafat, the incapacity of Ariel Sharon, the withdrawal of Israel from Gaza, the election of a Hamas government, another war in Lebanon, numerous peace initiatives, the possibility of a Palestinian civil war, and an Israeli administration talking of leaving at least some of the West Bank. Quite what all these will mean for the conflict in the long run, only time will tell, but it seems fairly certain that the first decade of the new millennium will come to be viewed as deeply significant.

End of an era?

2004

The Palestinian National Authority's first prime minister, Mahmoud Abbas, remained in office only for a few months. His talk of a compromise peace and his Fatah background alienated him from the Islamists, some of whom tried to assassinate him. Furthermore, he found the equivocating Arafat impossible to work with. By the end of 2003, he had been replaced by the more exuberant and more Arafat-friendly Ahmed Qurei (Abu Ala). Despite attempting some corruption-tackling reforms to the PLA administration, however, Qurei found the job no easier than Abbas had done.

Israeli security forces remained in the West Bank, exacerbating the day-to-day difficulties of ordinary Palestinians. Sporadic suicide attacks continued, as did the occasional rocket attacks on Israel from Gaza and over the Lebanese border. As always, the Israelis responded with disproportionate force, this time going as far as assassinating *fedayeen* leaders sheltering within Syria. Two targeted killings in particular roused Palestinian ire. In March, helicopter gunships killed Sheikh Yassin, Hamas' founder and spiritual leader. On hearing that the wheelchair-bound paraplegic had been hit as he was leaving a Gaza mosque, a Hamas spokesperson declared that Sharon had 'opened the Gates of Hell'. Many who lived in the region had their doubts: those particular portals, they believed, had been swung back long ago. A month later, Israeli assassins took out Abdulaziz al-Rantissi, the head of Hamas in Gaza.

Shortly after al-Rantissi's death, Sharon formally announced his plan for unilateral withdrawal from Gaza and a few regions of the West Bank. Likud were thrown into disarray and Sharon was left heading a minority government. The confusion extended to the Palestinians, too. There were those who saw Sharon's announcement as a welcome concession and a reason to resume settlement talks; others regarded it as proof that the bombing campaign was producing results and, consequently, a justification for continuing it. These different opinions prompted fresh outbreaks of Palestinian inter-communal violence, especially in Gaza. It was followed by the firing of numerous home-made Qassam rockets into Israel, which in turn provoked a massive and bloody Israeli incursion into the territory it was planning to leave.

Meanwhile, Sharon's plan had suffered a technical setback. In July, the International Criminal Court declared the Security Barrier – an essential component of unilateral withdrawal – an illegal construction. The 700-kilometre (435-mile) barricade of wall and fence was not being built along the Green Line, the pre-1967 border, but twisted into the West Bank to protect Jewish settlements there. Although Israel rejected the International Court's verdict as unwarranted meddling within a sovereign state's internal affairs, the route was later altered to meet the demands of Israel's own Supreme Court.

The final months of the year were dominated by the death of Yasser Arafat. Virtually imprisoned by the Israelis within his Ramallah compound for the better part of two-and-a-half years, his health gradually declined. Finally, with her husband suffering from a mysterious blood disorder, his French wife insisted he be flown to Paris for treatment. There, on 11 November, he died of multiple organ failure following a massive stroke. For security reasons the funeral was held in Cairo. Heads of state from all over the world attended, although an official Israeli representative was notably absent.

Arafat's body was flown back to Ramallah for burial, Sharon having vetoed internment within Jerusalem's Al-Aqsa mosque. The decision probably saved a great deal of bloodshed, for the funeral was hijacked by a gun-firing mob. The hysterical screaming, shouting and wailing of the mourners temporarily obscured the dislike that many Palestinians had developed for their president during his final years, allowing the old warrior to be buried as he had lived, in passionate disorder.

Almost everything written about Arafat after his death contained a degree of truth. He was unmistakeably charismatic, remarkably brave, inspiring, devoted and determined. Furthermore, he was a good, probably great guerrilla leader, a powerful orator with a strong sense of humour and he understood his people and their cause better than anyone. Yet he was neither a diplomat nor an administrator. Rather, he was disorganized, autocratic, corrupt, tactless, unsophisticated and cursed with a furious temper. He did more than anyone to create the modern Palestinian nation and force the world to recognize it. Yet in the end it was his failings as a president that did as much as anything else to prevent his people from securing their own homeland.

2005

There were some who believed that the death of Yasser Arafat would enable Palestinians and Israelis finally to work out some form of settlement to their long-running conflict. However, despite a few optimistic signs, there was no movement on the fundamental divisions that had now separated the two peoples for nigh on two generations.

As many anticipated, Mahmoud Abbas was elected to replace Arafat as president of the Palestinian National Authority. He won almost two-thirds of the vote. The comparatively low turnout – around 60 per cent – was explained by an ominous Islamist boycott of the process and ongoing Israeli occupation of some Palestinian areas. Having made all the appropriate noises about optimism for the future, soon after taking office Abbas attended an Egyptian-hosted conference with Sharon at Sharm El Sheikh. The Intifada was declared over, ceasefires and prisoner exchanges announced, and Israel said it would leave the Palestinian towns it had re-occupied. The conference was followed by the inevitable Islamist bomb, this time in Tel Aviv, and most of the good intentions were shelved.

Nevertheless, there was some residual cause for optimism as Sharon persisted with his idea of unilateral withdrawal behind the Security Barrier. By now Likud had deserted him and he headed a unity government that had the backing of Labour. In February both the Knesset and the Israeli cabinet formally approved the plan to quit 21 settlements in Gaza and four in the West Bank. Picking up on the new mood, militant Palestinian groups meeting in Cairo agreed to suspend violent attacks on Israel for a while. Sharon and Abbas met separately with President Bush in the spring. The Palestinians were promised massive aid if the lull in violence became permanent, while the Israelis were alarmed by the US president's suggestion that a return to the 1949 frontiers (the 2002 Saudi plan – see p. 205) would be a suitable basis for negotiation about a Palestinian state. June saw a Sharon–Abbas summit that produced plenty of fine-sounding rhetoric but no new concrete peace proposals. Neither leader was strong enough to make radical suggestions that might alienate their hard-line countrymen. Sadly, like so many others, the summit was doomed to produce little but platitudes.

Not surprisingly, the ceasefire collapsed within a few weeks of the summit's closure. The Israelis resumed the targeted killing of *fedayeen* leaders and moved back into some Palestinian areas. Militant Palestinian groups, having rejected Abbas' call to join the PLA in an Israeli-style unity government, launched fresh bomb and rocket attacks on Israel. Internecine conflict among Palestinians was also renewed. This reflected the growing support for Hamas that had been evident in recent local elections within the PNA.

Nothing daunted, Sharon retained the support of the IDF and so was able to press on with the Gaza withdrawal. There was inevitable Israel opposition, some of it violent, but in general it was less aggressive than some had feared. The last Israeli soldier left Gaza on 11 September. At the time much was made of Israel forcibly closing down its own settlements and handing back land it had captured – and it certainly was an important step. But it was never more than that: one small step on a very, very long and difficult road. The Palestinians still had no state; the West Bank remained largely in Israeli hands and was being further settled and divided by the Security Barrier with every day that passed; the Palestinians had no right of return to the lands from which they had been driven in 1948–9; two peoples still demanded Jerusalem as their capital... beside all that, the Gaza issue was very small beer indeed.

More jaw, more war

2006

Many have wondered at the apparent change of tack by Ariel Sharon. For so long the man nicknamed the 'bulldog' had been hailed as the scourge of all Palestinians. Yet it was he who had insisted on the withdrawal from Gaza in 2005 and he, at the end of the year, who announced the formation of a new political party. Kadima ('Forward'), with Sharon at its head and pledged to further withdrawals, attracted widespread support from a range of moderate Israelis, including the former Labour Prime Minister Shimon Peres. Sharon's new willingness to compromise may have been prompted by advancing age and a wish to be remembered not just as a hard man of war but also as the statesman who had finally brought the Israeli–Palestinian conflict to an end. There were also other, more pragmatic reasons for his conversion. The human and material cost of the Intifada was rising all the time. By 2006, more than 4,000 lives had been lost, almost one quarter of them Israeli. Israel's unemployment rate had risen above ten per cent and it was reported that over 30 per cent of its citizens lived in relative poverty.

Israel was under increasing pressure from Washington, too. By the twenty-first century the US was propping the country up at a total annual cost – adding together aid, loan guarantees and military assistance – of around $3 billion. Moreover, as it slipped deeper and deeper into the Iraqi quagmire, the Bush administration urgently needed the moral and political support it could muster from Arab governments. The price of their assistance on the Iraq front was progress on the Palestinian front. To this end, in late 2005 the US gave Israel a massive $600 million aid package for 'joint defence projects' – but in return it wanted an improvement in its relations with the Palestinians.

At this point, as invariably happened in this tragic impasse, fate intervened to wreck the best-laid plans. First, Ariel Sharon suffered the first of two massive strokes that left him totally incapacitated. Second, Hamas gained control over the Palestinian Assembly, winning 74 seats out of 132. Democracy had spoken: the Palestinian people, tired of Fatah's corruption and failure to produce a Palestinian state, had elected a party pledged to pursue its people's cause with fresh vigour and resolve. To Fatah, surrender of one square millimetre of the West Bank was out of the question. So what now?

As Hamas refused to recognize Israel, Israel refused to recognize the new Hamas-based Palestinian government formed at the end of March. This meant serious economic hardship for the Palestinians as all kinds of funds, such as tax repayments, were not paid. Even tougher were the sanctions that followed when the US and EU also refused to recognize the Hamas government. Aid was stopped and the PLA was able to continue only with funds smuggled in from Iran and Russia. Later, some EU funds were also allowed in via NGO organizations but a lot of this money disappeared en route and the economic plight of the ordinary Palestinians remained parlous throughout 2006.

Relations between the Hamas government and President Mahmoud Abbas remained at best tense. Refusing to accept the PLO as the sole representative of the Palestinian people – the position approved by the UN and in the Oslo Accords – Hamas set up its own security militia. Abbas responded by establishing a similar organization of his own. Conflict between Fatah and the Islamists – primarily Hamas and Islamic Jihad – frequently flared into open violence marked by kidnappings, shoot-outs and assassinations. Such events became almost endemic in Gaza, where the Palestinians were now supposed to be managing their own affairs, including security. The failure of the fragmented and warring Palestinian security services to prevent the constant firing of Qassam rockets from Gaza into Israel (about 1,000 in the first half of 2006) led to harsh Israeli counter-measures. These included Operation Summer Rains, a large-scale re-occupation of parts of Gaza in the summer of 2006. There were reports that Hezbollah was paying $1,000US for each rocket fired into Israel.

Kadima

With the demise of Ariel Sharon, leadership of the new Kadima party passed to his deputy, Ehud Olmert. With an election looming, Olmert put more flesh on the bones of Sharon's plans. Kadima originally stood for unilateral Israeli withdrawal from a large part of the West Bank and establishing firm and final frontiers behind the Security Barrier. Israel would remain a Jewish state – in other words, large-scale Palestinian return would not be permitted – although parts of East Jerusalem might be handed back.

The route of the Security Barrier remained highly controversial, especially when it became clear that Kadima's proposed withdrawal from the West Bank was not quite as radical as had been expected. The Israelis would maintain a presence in Hebron, for religious reasons, and in the Jordan Valley, for security reasons. Elsewhere, the major settlements of Gush Etzion, Ariel, Kedumim and Maale Adumim (see Figure 8, p. 156) would also be part of the new, definitive Israel. 'The facts on the ground' policy had become a reality: there were now some 400,000 Israelis living in settlements in occupied West Bank.

Olmert reckoned the new frontiers would be ready by 2010. Since the total area of Gaza and the West Bank, without Israeli depredations, was only 22 per cent of the Palestinian state envisaged by the UN in 1948, the Palestinian reaction to the Kadima plan was not hard to anticipate. Nevertheless, it won favour with the Israeli electorate and after elections in March 2006 Olmert remained in power at the head of a Kadima-led coalition. The fact that Kadima won only 29 seats, Labour 19, and Likud and Shas (Ultra-orthodox Sephardi) 12 each illustrated the growing fragmentation of Israeli society and politics. The low turnout – only 63 per cent – was a worrying sign of disenchantment.

The summer war

The frontier between Lebanon and Israel had never been exactly peaceful after the IDF finally pulled out of southern Lebanon in 2000. Nevertheless, the occasional cross-border firing of artillery and rockets had been well under control – almost token warfare – when in the summer of 2006 the rules suddenly changed.

Hezbollah had been building up its forces in southern Lebanon, especially its stockpiles of rockets and anti-tank weapons, for years. In June 2006, it began to escalate its cross-border provocation. This may have been prompted by Iran, its paymaster, which wanted a mini-war to divert attention from the row it was having with the UN over its nuclear programme. Be that as it may, when Hezbollah raided Israel on 12 July, killing a few soldiers and capturing two more, the Olmert government responded precisely as the Islamists wanted. Its campaign began with air and artillery strikes against supposed Hezbollah targets deep within Lebanon. The guerrillas, clearly ready for such action and carefully hidden within areas of high-density civilian population, stepped up their rocket attacks on northern Israel.

Still without its captured comrades, the IDF launched a full-scale ground invasion of Lebanon. Hezbollah proved better equipped, prepared and organized than the Israelis had expected. For the first time, the IDF was not able to sweep all before it while suffering almost no casualties. Men were killed, tanks and other heavy armour destroyed, and pockets of resistance proved hard to subdue. Equally serious for Israel, it lost the PR war. TV coverage showing Lebanese civilian casualties and destruction of essential facilities such as roads, bridges and power-plants did not play well to audiences around the world, especially after Olmert had declared that his intention was to 'set Lebanon back 20 years'. Once again, Israel appeared the bully.

A UN ceasefire eventually came into effect in mid-August. By then 1,000 Lebanese had been killed, a proportion of whom had been Islamist guerrillas, and the Israelis had lost 120. Hundreds of thousands of Lebanese had been made homeless, the country's economic recovery had been thrown into reverse, the captured Israeli soldiers had not been returned and Hezbollah had not been destroyed. On this evidence, its leadership proudly announced that it had won a notable victory against the oppressor. Over the coming months, Hezbollah used its new-found popularity to press for the dissolution of Lebanon's moderately pro-Western government.

Within Israel the Olmert government came in for massive criticism from both left and right for its handling of the campaign. Abroad, Israel was blamed for escalating the conflict unnecessarily, for using vastly disproportionate force, for causing unwarranted civilian casualties and for using inhumane weapons such as cluster bombs. Chastened, Olmert attempted to restore his battered image by suggesting that the Saudi peace deal, first put forward in 2002 (see p. 205), might be a useful basis for Israeli–Palestinian negotiations. This represented a major change of direction. Olmert also held a summit with Abbas, as much to boost the hard-pressed president's position in Palestinian circles as to further the peace process.

2007

By the spring, the humanitarian situation in Palestinian areas had reached crisis point. Things were especially bad in Gaza. Israeli air raids – 270 in the past year – had destroyed the main power station and killed hundreds. According to the UN, enemy damage, the collapse of the economy caused by the severance of aid, and anarchy among the Palestinian security forces had driven about 80 per cent of the population into poverty. The situation in the West Bank was almost as dire. Commentators talked anxiously of the possibility of a Palestinian civil war.

In April, Prime Minister Olmert's reputation was dealt a further serious blow when a report into the Lebanese war of 2006 singled out the Kadima leader for stinging personal criticism. His alleged mishandling of the war was also condemned from within his own cabinet and mass rallies were held demanding his resignation and early elections.

In the meantime, under huge pressure, the PNA had reorganized its Hamas-based administration by taking in moderates to form a shaky unity government. This was not enough to stop the periodic internecine violence within Gaza, which in the middle of the year led to Hamas forces taking full control of the strip, driving out those loyal to Fatah and President Abbas. This development and the formation of a broader-based Palestinian government in the West Bank suggested that the US and Israel might reconsider their positions: should they help Abbas by recognizing the West Bank administration, although it was still strongly Hamas-based? Israeli Prime Minister Olmert, eager to take advantage of the Gaza-West Bank split, talked of 'major concessions' in order to get a peace deal, to which end he began a series of regular meetings with President Abbas. US Secretary of State Condoleezza Rice was also trying to forge a new initiative that incorporated the Saudi plan within the Roadmap.

Some saw these developments as hopeful, others pointed out that Israelis and Palestinians had been there before, dozens of times... Meanwhile, in the streets and markets, in their apartments and huts, at work in their offices and in their fields, it was the ordinary people who continued to suffer...

glossary

Al-Aqsa Mosque Large mosque on Jerusalem's Temple Mount.

Al-Aqsa Martyrs Brigades Extremist offshoot of Fatah (see pp. 208–9).

Al Qaeda Extremist Islamist organization dedicated to *Jihad* against Israel and the West.

Arab One who speaks Arabic.

Arab League Organization of Arab states formed to promote cultural, economic and political cooperation.

Arab Legion British-trained (Trans)Jordanian army.

Ashkenazi Jews from Eastern Europe.

Assifa Fatah battle group.

Balfour Declaration British declaration of support for the establishment of a Jewish homeland in Palestine (1917).

Byzantium Early name of the city that is now Istanbul.

Caliphate Empire comprising the entire Muslim world.

Camp David Shorthand for the peace talks and agreement between Israel and Egypt, 1978.

Crusades Wars fought by Christian warriors attempting to wrest the holy places of the Middle East from Muslim hands.

DFLP Democratic Front for the Liberation of Palestine (see p. 113).

Diaspora The dispersion of a people across the globe (see p. 5).

Druze Religious offshoot of Islam with separate leaders and emphases.

Fatah Palestinian nationalist organization with political and guerrilla wings (see pp. 87–8).

Fedayeen Palestinian guerrillas of all varieties, widely regarded in Israel and elsewhere as 'terrorists'. Similarly, the British condemned as 'terrorists' the Jews who used violence against their colonial rule. See also 'guerrilla'.

Golan Heights Disputed high ground on the Israel–Syria border (see p. 121).

Grand Mufti Authority on Muslim law and practice (see p. 34).

Greater Israel Israel extending east and west of the River Jordan.

Green Line Arab–Israeli ceasefire line of 1949.

Guerrilla Irregular warrior, usually politically or religiously motivated. Frequently denounced as a 'terrorist' by opponents.

Haganah Jewish guerrilla organization of the pre-Israel era (see pp. 42–3).

Hamas Palestinian party and guerrilla organization with Islamist links (see pp. 172–3).

Hebrew Jewish language. The word 'Jew' derives from 'Hebrew'.

Herut Israeli political party of the far right (see p. 153).

Hezbollah Lebanese political party and guerrilla organization fiercely opposed to Israel (see p. 152).

IDF Israeli Defence Force.

Intifada Palestinian uprising against Israel.

Irgun Hard-line Jewish guerrilla organization of the pre-Israel era (see pp. 42–3).

Israel An alternative name for the Old Testament figure Jacob. Technically speaking, the modern country is the State of Israel.

Islamic Jihad Anti-Israeli Islamist guerrilla organization (see pp. 189–90).

Islamist Militant Muslim accepting the need for *Jihad* against Israel, the US and their allies.

Jihad Muslim holy war.

Kadima Israeli political party of the centre-right founded in 2005.

Katyusha rockets Soviet-designed missiles of World War II.

Knesset Israeli parliament.

Lehi Extremist Jewish guerrillas of the pre-Israel era.

Likud Israeli right-wing political party (see p. 153).

Mandate Territory being prepared for statehood by an imperial power.

Mapai Israeli Labour party (see p. 57).

MIG Soviet jet fighter.

Muslim Brotherhood Long-standing Sunni Islamist organization.

National Water Carrier Israel's principal irrigation channel.

Negev Desert area in southern Israel.

OAPEC Organization of Arab Petroleum Exporting Countries.

Occupied territories Lands on the West Bank of the River Jordan, and around Jerusalem and Gaza City, conquered by Israel in 1967.

Orthodox Christianity Form of pope-less Christianity adopted by the Eastern Church.

Orthodox Judaism Fundamentalist and traditionalist form of Judaism.

Oslo Shorthand for the accords between Israelis and Palestinians, 1993–5.

Ottoman Empire Former Turkish Empire.

Pan-Arabism Movement for Arab unity.

PFLP Popular Front for the Liberation of Palestine (see pp. 135–6).

Phalange Right-wing Lebanese Christian paramilitaries.

PLA Palestine Liberation Army.

PLO Palestine Liberation Organization.

PNA (PA) Palestine National Authority (Palestinian Authority) established in 1994 as an interim government for the Palestinian people.

Qassam rockets Home-made Palestinian missiles.

Resolution 242 UN Security Council Resolution calling on Israel to exchange land for peace (1967).

Resolution 338 UN Security Council Resolution calling for a ceasefire and implementation of Resolution 338 (1973).

Revisionist Hard-line Zionist position that called for an exclusively Jewish state on both banks of the River Jordan.

Roadmap Peace process drawn up by the US in 2003.

Security Barrier Fence, wall and barrier erected by Israel in various parts of the West Bank to prevent *fedayeen* attacks.

Sephardi Oriental Jews.

Chia Minority branch of Islam centred around Iran.

Sinai Largely desert peninsular between Israel and Egypt.

SLA South Lebanese Army, a largely Christian militia backed by Israel.

Soviet Relating to the USSR.

Sunni Majority branch of Islam.

Temple Mount Holy site at the heart of East Jerusalem.

Terrorist See *fedayeen*.

Transjordan Original name for the state of Jordan.

UAR United Arab Republic, a short-lived union between Egypt and Syria.

USSR Union of Soviet Socialist Republics, the former communist empire based on Russia.

West Bank Land on the west bank of the River Jordan, inhabited mainly by Palestinians, captured by Israel in 1967.

Zionism Movement for the establishment and maintenance of a Jewish state.

taking it further

Objective history of the Israel–Palestinian conflict is rare, if not impossible to find. Readers are advised to consult as many sources as possible. Here are a few starting points:

Books

Aburish, S.K. (1999) *Arafat: From Defender to Dictator*, London: Bloomsbury.

Carter, J. (2007) *Palestine: Peace not Apartheid*, New York: Simon and Shuster.

Cohn-Sherbok, D. and El-Alami, D. (2001) *The Palestine–Israel Conflict*, Oxford: Oneworld.

Franklin, D. (2003) *A Peace to End All Peace*, London: Orion.

Gilbert, M. (1999) *Israel: A History*, London: Black Swan.

Harms, G. and Ferry, T. (2005) *Palestine–Israel Conflict: A Basic Introduction*, London: Pluto.

Kimmerling, B. and Migdal, J.S. (2003) *The Palestinian People: A History*, Cambridge: Harvard UP.

Laqueur, W. and Rubin, B. (eds) (2001) *The Israel-Arab Reader*, London: Penguin.

Pape, I. (2006) *The Ethnic Cleansing of Palestine*, Oxford: Oneworld.

Ross, D. (2004) *The Missing Peace*, Farrar, New York: Straus & Giroux.

Shlaim, A. (2001) *The Iron Wall: Israel and the Arab World*, London: Penguin.

Thomas, B. (1999) *How Israel Was Won*, Oxford: Lexington Books.

Websites

Al Jazeera:
www.aljazeera.com

Arab Gateway:
www.addameer.org/september2000/front.html

Arab world:
www.arab.net

BBC:
http://news.bbc.co.uk/1/hi/world/middle_east/default.stm

CNN:
http://search.cnn.com/cnn/search?source=cnn&invocationType
=search%2Ftop&sites=cnn&query=middle+east

Excellent chronologies, etc:
www.middleeastreference.org.uk

History in the news:
www.albany.edu/history/middle-east

Israeli government website:
www.israel.org/mfa

Modern history sourcebook:
www.fordham.edu/halsall/mod/modsbook54.html

Palestinian sources:
www.politicalresources.net/palestine.htm

UN:
www.un.org/unrwa/english.html

Disclaimer

The publisher has used its best endeavours to ensure that the URLs for external websites referred to in this book are correct and active at the time of going to press. However, the publisher has no responsibility for the websites and can make no guarantee that the site will remain live or that the content is, or will remain, appropriate. For example, in 2007 hackers broke into the Hamas website and corrupted it so that visitors were redirected to a pornographic site.

index